A man c̶ ed, but that p

Not when he f ʌadise, craning his neck to look down from that airplane window, wanting to storm the cockpit and yell, "Land here!" even though he knew there wasn't a runway.

He just couldn't imagine Mindy looking at him with anything but shock and loathing if he hit on her. Even if he was wrong, even if miraculously she turned out to feel the same way he did, how could he look at himself in the mirror knowing he had what should have been Dean's?

What *would* have been Dean's if not for a bullet.

Dear Reader,

Pregnant heroines have become very popular in romance fiction, but I find myself drawn to writing about them anyway. The nine months of pregnancy are a woman's most vulnerable time. Accustomed to being an independent adult, suddenly she needs protection and care. At the same time, her life is in flux—even a woman in a secure marriage knows that nothing will ever be the same again. If she finds herself pregnant after her husband has died, when her emotions are already in turmoil, when she has no one to turn to… How irresistible is that for any writer?

With this book I also had the chance to create a hero who believes he needs no one—until he loses the one person who *did* mean something to him. Reforming rakes has never interested me; shattering the ice around a man who believes himself incapable of love is my kind of challenge.

I hope you're as moved by these two lonely people who can't admit they need each other as I was. I'd love to hear what you think!

Best,

Janice Kay Johnson

With Child
Janice Kay Johnson

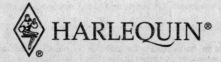

HARLEQUIN®

TORONTO • NEW YORK • LONDON
AMSTERDAM • PARIS • SYDNEY • HAMBURG
STOCKHOLM • ATHENS • TOKYO • MILAN • MADRID
PRAGUE • WARSAW • BUDAPEST • AUCKLAND

ISBN 0-373-71273-1

WITH CHILD

Copyright © 2005 by Janice Kay Johnson.

This edition published by arrangement with Harlequin Books S.A.

® and TM are trademarks of the publisher. Trademarks indicated with
® are registered in the United States Patent and Trademark Office, the
Canadian Trade Marks Office and in other countries.

www.eHarlequin.com

Printed in U.S.A.

Books by Janice Kay Johnson

HARLEQUIN SUPERROMANCE

*Patton's Daughters
**3 Good Cops
†Under One Roof

HARLEQUIN SINGLE TITLE

WRONG TURN
  "Missing Molly"

HARLEQUIN SIGNATURE SELECT

DEAD WRONG (Coming 2006)

CHAPTER ONE

BRENDAN JOSEPH QUINN was off duty when he found out his best friend was dead. Beer in hand, waiting for the microwave to beep, he'd settled in front of a Sonics game he'd taped from earlier in the evening. He was so tired his eyes kept crossing. He hadn't slept except for a snatched hour or two in days. That's what he did when a case was fresh, when every detail was vivid in his mind, when the memories of witnesses were new and relatively uncorrupted. If an arrest was ever going to happen, it was likeliest in the first two or three days. He and his partner had cleared this homicide by canvassing the neighborhood until they found a kid who'd seen someone hammering on the front door of the murdered woman's house and had been able to identify the ex-husband.

Booking and paperwork had dragged on, and it was now two in the morning. He intended to gobble the burrito heating in the microwave and then fall into bed. He might last a quarter.

When the phone rang, Quinn stared at it in disbelief. Muting the TV, he dragged himself from the recliner and snatched up the receiver.

"Quinn. This better be good."

"It's not good. It's shitty."

His sergeant could sound neutral when the streets were filled with rioters tossing cherry bombs. At the heaviness in his voice, Quinn stiffened.

"What?"

"Dean Fenton's dead."

"What?" he said again, but in disbelief this time. Denial.

"We got a call an hour ago from one of his security guards. Burglary in progress. By the time a unit got there, the perps were gone and the guard had been shot. Only, turns out it wasn't one of his employees. It was Dean. We don't know yet why he was handling a routine night shift himself. Somebody probably called in sick. Bad luck."

There had to be a mistake. Dean Fenton was his best friend, the only good to come from a bleak childhood. Quinn quelled the wave of sick fear with control he'd learned early, when his mother went out at night and didn't come back for three days.

No. Not Dean.

Dean Fenton had joined the force with Quinn. They'd gone through training together, risen in the ranks at the same pace. But Dean had a craving for the nice things that money could buy, and he'd turned in his badge to start his own security company.

"Who got the call?" Quinn asked.

"Lanzilotta and Connors. Lanzilotta was pretty shaken up when he recognized Dean."

Bernie Lanzilotta had played softball with Quinn and Dean. Bernie would know their first baseman.

Quinn shook his head hard. No. Goddamn it, no! Bernie had seen the uniform, maybe the guard was Dean's age, general build. He'd jumped to a conclusion. Dean was home in bed with his pretty nitwit of a wife right now, not knowing one of his employees had taken a bullet.

"No," Quinn said.

That same heaviness in his voice, Sergeant Dickerson said, "I asked Bernie if he was sure. He said he was."

"No."

"I'm going out there." Dickerson extended the comment like an invitation.

"Where?" Quinn flipped open his notebook.

The address was in the industrial area at the foot of West Seattle.

"I'm on my way."

The microwave beeped as he let himself out the front door.

EVEN BEFORE HE EXITED from the West Seattle bridge, he saw the flashing lights. Heading under the bridge, he drove the two blocks to the scene. Chain-link gates stood open to a storage business, the kind with four long windowless buildings containing locked units where people could stow their crap when they downsized or moved. This place also had an area where customers could park RVs or boats. It was back there that the activity centered.

Numb, his exhaustion forgotten, Quinn parked and walked past squad cars with flashing lights. Ahead was a white pickup with the Fenton Security logo painted on the doors. The driver-side one stood open.

Dickerson, a bulky, graying man, separated himself from a cluster of uniforms and came to Quinn.

"I'm sorry," he said quietly.

Fear and rage shifted inside Quinn, like Dobermans just waking.

"No," he said. "No." He kept walking, circled the back of the pickup.

The body was sprawled on the pavement. Lamps had already been set up, bathing the scene in pitiless white light.

"No," Quinn whispered, but his eyes burned and the fear swelled in his chest. His best friend, his brother in all but blood, lay with his cheek against the ground, blood drying in his mouth, his eyes sightless. Dead. A few feet from the body, Quinn dropped to his knees. A freight train of grief roared over him, the wheels clattering, metallic and deafening.

He hadn't known he could cry, but his face was wet.

Strong hands lifted him, steered him out of the harsh light into the darkness, where he slammed his fists against the brick wall of a storage building and let the sobs rack him.

THE DOORBELL BROUGHT Mindy Fenton awake with a start and an automatic flush of heart-racing apprehension. Half sitting up in bed, she turned to Dean's side before remembering that he'd worked tonight. Her wild gaze swung to the digital clock—3:09 a.m.

Had she dreamed the bell? Nobody would come calling in the middle of the night! Unless Dean had locked himself out. But he had the garage-door opener.

Sitting upright by this time, she strained to hear anything at all. Breaking glass. If an intruder had decided she wasn't home because she hadn't come to the door…

The bell rang again.

Really scared now, she turned on her bedside lamp, slipped on her bathrobe, and went downstairs, flipping on lights as she went to make it look as if several people were home.

Dean had left the porch light on. Through the stained-glass sidelight, she could make out a dark shape.

"Who's there?" she called.

The muffled reply was "Quinn."

Her heart somersaulted. Fumbling with the dead bolt, she thought, *Why? Why Quinn? Why now?*

Two men, not just one, stood on the porch. With Dean's best friend was Sergeant Rycroft Dickerson. She remembered him from her wedding. Six foot four or so and brawny, his graying hair buzz-cut, he wasn't the kind of man you forgot.

Not that you could forget Quinn, either, she thought irrelevantly. With his straight dark hair, vivid blue eyes, stark cheekbones and contained air, he would never go unnoticed.

"Is…is something wrong?" she squeaked.

Neither face softened.

Quinn asked, "Can we come in, Mindy?"

"I…of course." She swung the door open.

Quinn first, the sergeant second, they stepped in to the foyer, filling it with a threat of…something. Something she didn't want to hear.

"I could put on coffee…"

Quinn shook his head. "Mindy…"

"It's the middle of the night."

"Mindy." His voice, she realized, was scratchy, rough. "There's no easy way to say this."

She backed away, talking fast. "Uh…Dean isn't home. He will be by seven. I can tell him you need to see him. Or I can leave a note." She said the last as if it were a super idea, a solution to some dilemma that her inner self knew didn't exist. "He worked tonight."

The sergeant reached out. "We know."

She wouldn't let him touch her. Clutching the lapel of her gown, she said in a high, breathless voice, "I don't understand why you're here."

Quinn's blue eyes were almost black. "He's dead, Mindy."

"Don't be silly! He's not a cop anymore. And he drives so carefully." She laughed, convincing no one. "What could have happened to him?"

"He interrupted a burglary." A muscle jumped in Quinn's cheek. "Somebody shot him."

Dean? Shot Dean? Her Dean? The idea was ludicrous, impossible, unthinkable.

"Have you tried his cell phone? What makes you think…"

Dark and melancholy at the best of times, Quinn waited her out, his eyes bleak. When her voice hitched and died—no, not died, what an awful choice of words!—trailed off, yes, trailed off, he said in that thick voice, "I saw him. I didn't want to believe it either. But he's dead."

A keening sound seemed to come from everywhere and nowhere. Not until Quinn's face contorted and he stepped forward to draw her into his arms did she realize she was making the sound. She squeezed her eyes shut and pressed her face against Quinn's chest despite the smell of sweat that wasn't Dean's. She wrapped her arms around his waist and held on, because otherwise she wouldn't have remained upright.

She was still crying out, still muffling that dreadful, shrill, unending scream in his dark shirt. She stayed stiff, her fists filled with his shirt, and tried to smother herself against him.

Quinn muttered brokenly, "God, Mindy. God. I'm so sorry."

Perhaps shock was wrapping her in thick batting, because abruptly all strength left her, stealing the cry from her throat. She sagged, clinging. Still, Quinn held her. Strong arms, a body more solid than her lanky husband's. She hadn't known what he would feel like. He'd never hugged her, never kissed her cheek, never touched her at all. She'd always known he didn't like her. But for Dean's sake, they were polite.

Dead.

She heard the men confer, but made no effort to decipher words. Footsteps, and finally Quinn lifted her like a child and sat her on the couch in the living room. Mindy began to shiver.

"Don't you have a throw?" he said in frustration.

She squeezed her arms against her body and rocked herself, hardly aware when he disappeared and then reappeared with a comforter he must have torn from the bed in the guest room. Even inside it, she continued to shiver. Her teeth chattered.

A weight settled on the couch beside her and Quinn held a mug to her mouth. Tea. Clumsily, with his help, she drank. Hot liquid ran down her chin, joining the tears that wet her face.

After a moment she took the mug from him and gratefully wrapped cold fingers around it. She drank again, letting it scald her mouth, aware it was sweeter than she would have made it but not caring. The heat sliding down her throat felt so good. Her shivers abated.

Finally she lifted her head. The sergeant stood a few feet away, looking down at her with concern. Quinn still sat beside her, his thigh touching hers, his face so close she could see individual bristles on a chin that was normally clean-shaven.

"You're sure?" she asked. Begged.

"We're sure," Dickerson said.

Still pleading, although no longer with them, Mindy said, "What will I do?"

There was a momentary silence, and then Quinn stood. "What will *you* do?" He sounded harsh, the man who had always condemned her without knowing her at all. "I'm sure Dean left you taken care of."

"I didn't mean…" she tried to explain.

"Do you have someone we can call?" Sergeant Dickerson interrupted. "Family? A friend?"

She instinctively rejected the idea of calling her mother. Selene was her best friend, but…she was such a talker. She wouldn't know how to hold Mindy without exclaiming over and over and wanting to dissect the tragic events. And who else could Mindy phone in the middle of the night to say, "My husband is dead. Can you come hold my hand?"

Mindy shook her head. "I'll wait until morning." Until then…until then, she didn't know what she'd do. She couldn't go back to that lonely bed. Perhaps she would just huddle here and try to imagine the man she loved gone. Erased as if he hadn't existed.

"We've only been married a year." She heard her voice, high and petulant, as if Dean had broken a promise. But he hadn't. *Till death do us part.* It just wasn't supposed to be so soon!

The two men were talking again as if she wasn't here.

"I want to work this one," Quinn said. "Who pulled it? Sawyer and Asavade?"

"Dobias and Williams. And the answer is no. You're dead on your feet. And you're too involved."

"He was my best friend. I need to make this collar."

"Uh-huh. You going to do it dispassionately? Read 'em their rights? When what you really want to do is kill them?"

Quinn paced, fury and grief radiating from him like

heat from a woodstove. Mindy felt it without having to watch him.

"Goddamn it! Don't shut me out!"

"No." The sergeant didn't move. Like Quinn, he seemed to have forgotten her. "Dean radioed in a license-plate number. There may have been an arrest already."

She listened without real comprehension. Dean was dead? It made no sense. She would have worried if he'd still been a cop, but he owned his own security company. He hardly ever took a shift as a guard anymore. He met with property owners and businessmen, did payroll and billing, grumbled about how hard it was to find and keep good employees.

"They all either want to be cops or prison guards." He'd made a sound of disgust. "They like the idea of swaggering around in a uniform with a gun in a holster. They find out how boring it is patrolling warehouses and apartment complexes at night, they opt out."

Mindy came back to awareness of the present when she realized that Sergeant Dickerson had sat on the coffee table. Quinn stood to one side.

"Mindy? You with me?"

She nodded.

"Do you know why Dean worked tonight?"

She nodded again. "A new guy called in sick. Dean was really mad, because it was last minute. The dispatcher offered to go out, but Dean said he'd do it. He liked to once in a while, you know."

"Any good businessman gets down in the trenches. He'd be a fool not to."

"I wish…" Tears leaked out although she'd thought herself cried dry. "I wish somebody else had been there. But I feel guilty wishing they were dead instead."

Dickerson covered her hand with his. "It's natural, Mindy. You didn't know them."

"I do know Mick Mulligan. He's the dispatcher." She tasted the tears. "He's married, and he has two little girls."

That thought caused a lurch within her, of fear, of renewed guilt, of raw grief. Dean had really wanted to have children. She was the one to put pregnancy off.

"Let's wait a couple of years," she'd coaxed. "Let's be selfish and just have each other for a while first."

Quinn said explosively, "What if it was a setup? God-damn it, Dickerson! Let me work this one."

"Go home. Go to bed."

A vast, terrifying emptiness swelled within Mindy. They'd both leave any minute. She'd be alone in the house. It was a big house, bigger than she liked, with a cavernous three-car garage and bedrooms they didn't use, a den and a family room. She could *feel* those empty, dark rooms around her, echoing her inner fear.

She made a sound—a sniff, a gulp. Still engaged in their argument, both men turned their heads to look at her. She looked down at her hands, clutching the comforter.

"We can't leave her alone." Quinn sounded irritated. "I'll stay."

That brought her head up. "No! You don't have to." But she wanted him to stay. He made her feel safe, and tonight she was terrified of being alone.

His mouth, she'd have sworn, had a faint curl. "If you don't have a friend you can ask to come over, I do have to stay." He sounded as if he were talking to a five-year-old who had just announced that she could walk across town all by herself to Grandma's house. His gaze left her; she was dismissed. To Dickerson, he said, "You'll keep me informed?"

Mindy shrank into her comforter, wishing she had the spine to stand up, say with dignity, "No, thanks, I'd like to be alone," and walk them to the door. She'd have been grateful for Quinn's offer if it had come from anyone but him, or even if he'd made it more kindly. He'd always had a talent for making her feel small.

Her care settled, Sergeant Dickerson expressed his sympathy and regret one more time, then left. Quinn walked him to the door, and they stood out of earshot talking for several minutes, their voices a rumble.

Finally Quinn locked up behind the sergeant and came back to her. "Why don't you go back to bed?"

"No!" She shuddered. "No. I can't get in our bed."

"The guest room, then."

She didn't want to go to bed at all. Did he really imagine that she'd lay her head on the pillow and fall into blissful slumber? In the dark, all she would do was imagine a thousand times what had happened to Dean. Had the shot come from nowhere? Or had he been held at gunpoint, threatened, beaten? Did he know he might die? She both wanted and didn't want to know. *I'm a coward,* she thought. She would lie there wondering what would happen tomorrow, and the next day, and the next.

But she also saw that Quinn wanted her to go to bed, so she nodded and put her feet on the carpeted floor. When she stood, she swayed, and he was at her side instantly, his strong hand clamped on her elbow. He walked her to the downstairs bedroom, and she felt like a child being put to bed. When she climbed in, he spread the comforter over her, then stood awkwardly at the foot of the bed.

"Can I get you anything?"

Mute, she shook her head.

Quinn came around the bed, his hand out to switch off the lamp. She shook her head violently. "No! Leave it on. Please."

He frowned at her. "You're sure?"

"I don't… The dark…"

"Okay. I'll be right out there. Call if you need me."

"Thank you," she said dutifully.

Seemingly satisfied, he left, switching off the overhead light and pulling the door almost closed. His footsteps receded toward the living room.

The sheets were cold, the pillow squishy. It was like being in a hotel room. But she couldn't seem to care enough to try to bunch up the pillow or even reach for the second one. She just lay on her back and stared at the ceiling.

The house was Dean's, not hers. The life his. One she'd put on like a borrowed evening gown. She'd felt beautiful and loved and fortunate, but not quite secure. Because, she saw now, it wasn't hers.

A broken sound escaped her.

Dean. Oh, Dean.

The tears came again, so easily, as if only waiting to be released. But this time she cried silently, alone.

JUST AFTER SIX IN THE MORNING, Quinn's cell phone rang.

"We got 'em," Dickerson said without preamble. "They didn't realize Dean had had time to call in their plate."

"What were they after?"

"They're nineteen and twenty-one. They were manufacturing meth in the young one's father's trailer. He moved it to storage without them knowing. They'd come to get their stuff, or steal the trailer. Sounds like they were still arguing about that."

"And the guard that called in sick?"

"Had a hot girl over. Dobias said when he realized he'd be dead if he had gone to work, he barely made it to the toilet to puke."

"He might not be dead," Quinn said. "Maybe he'd have timed his route different. Been lazy and not gone in if the gates were closed."

"He'll figure that out eventually," Dickerson said without sympathy. "Apparently, Dobias didn't feel inclined to point that out."

Quinn sank onto the couch and bowed his head. He swore. "A couple of goddamn punks."

"Strung out."

"And that's it." He shoved his fingers into his hair, uncaring when they curled into a fist and yanked. "Dean's gone, and Daddy'll probably hire a good lawyer who'll claim they were too stoned to take responsibility for pulling the trigger."

"You know the D.A. will try to throw the book at them."

"Son of a bitch," he said clearly, and pushed End, letting the phone drop to the carpeted floor.

Two shit-faced punks who'd freaked, and Dean was dead.

Quinn didn't want to believe it. He'd dozed briefly on the couch, and in his sleep had been woken by Dean, who had punched him in the shoulder and said, "What in hell are you doing on my couch? Your own bed not good enough for you?" Quinn had met the grin with his own, and reached out for his friend's hand. He'd woken before they touched, and opened his eyes to an empty living room.

Down the hall, a bar of light still lay across the carpet. Mindy had never turned off the lamp. He wondered if she'd slept. Wasn't sure if he cared. She'd known Dean for a year and a half, not a lifetime.

Dean and Quinn had been flung together as roommates in a foster home when Quinn was thirteen and Dean twelve. Almost twenty years ago. They'd had a fistfight the first day, grudgingly agreed to a truce the second day, and by the third Quinn had lied to protect the younger boy from their foster father's wrath. Wrath, both had realized as the weeks and months went by, that was more show than reality; George Howie was a good man, as kind in a less demonstrative way as his wife. The two boys had been lucky in more ways than one. They'd been able to stay until, each in his turn, they'd graduated from high school. And they'd become close friends. Brothers.

As the night dragged on, Quinn had done his grieving, as much as he'd allow himself. His mother had taught him well that he couldn't afford to be incapacitated by fear or sadness. He didn't even know who his father was. His mother was an addict who'd progressed during his childhood from pills and pot to shooting up. She'd disappear for days at a time. He'd scrounge for food. By the time he was eight or nine he was shoplifting when the cupboards were bare. His mother got skinnier and skinnier, the tracks on her arms and legs livid, veins harder to find. He learned how to catch her at the perfect moment to get her to cash her welfare check so he could take some money before she spent it.

He remembered the last time he saw her, her eyes hectic.

"I feel like shit. I've got to score. Now, you go to school, hear? I might not be home tonight, but you can take care of yourself, right?"

She hadn't waited for an answer. She'd known he could. He'd been doing it since he was six years old.

Only, that time she hadn't come home. The police finally came knocking. She'd overdosed and was dead, they told him with faint sympathy. They'd looked at the squalor of the apartment and shaken their heads. Child Protective Services workers came to get him.

The Howies' was Quinn's fourth foster home. Either he did something wrong, or the people lost interest in fostering. One family decided to move to Virginia and didn't offer to take him. Another one got nervous when their daughter turned eleven, started to get breasts and developed a crush on the brooding boy they were collecting state money for. Each time, he shrugged and moved on.

Until he finally found somebody to care about. Dean Fenton, a skinny boy with a copper-red cowlick and freckles on his nose.

"My mom's coming back for me," he'd always said.

Quinn tried at first telling him that she was probably dead like his mother, but Dean would throw fists and scream, "She's not!" so Quinn took to shrugging and saying, "Yeah. Sure. Someday."

The adult Dean had gotten drunk one night and said, "Yeah, she's dead. I always knew. Give me hope over truth any day."

Quinn drank a toast to that—hope over truth—even though he didn't believe in fantasies. He'd have starved to death as a kid if he'd allowed himself to dream. You survived in this life by facing facts.

But Dean...Dean had softened Quinn. Made him laugh, acknowledge that sometimes faith in another person was justified.

They'd balanced each other, because Dean needed to be more of a cynic. The saving grace was that he listened to Quinn.

Had listened, Quinn corrected himself, lifting his head to look at that band of light on the carpet. Dean hadn't wanted to hear a bad word about pretty Mindy Walker. Quinn had shrugged and shut his mouth, figuring the romance would pass. He could remember his shock when Dean had come over on a Sunday afternoon to watch the Seahawks play and said, "Congratulate me. Mindy agreed to marry me."

They'd both said things they regretted then, but they'd patched up their friendship, and Quinn resigned himself to the inevitable divorce, something Dean wouldn't take well after a lifetime of instability.

Now there wouldn't be a divorce. Instead, there'd be a funeral. Quinn wouldn't be listening to drunken soliloquies and supporting a staggering friend home. Instead, he was left with the grieving widow. A flighty, shallow girl-woman with spiky blond hair and a pierced belly button who played at arts and crafts.

Quinn let out a soft oath. Dean would expect his best friend to take care of his bewildered widow, the woman whose first thought hadn't been of her husband, tragically struck down, but rather, "What will I do?"

"Damn you, Dean," Quinn said under his breath. "Why her?"

CHAPTER TWO

MINDY AWAKENED RELUCTANTLY, knowing even before she surfaced that she didn't want to face conscious knowledge of *something*.

Her eyes were glued shut and her face felt stiff. She was aware without moving that she wasn't in her own bed. A hotel?

She pried her eyes open, then squeezed them shut. The guest room. Dean.

Oh, Dean.

Grief rushed over her, wave upon wave powerful enough to knock her down if she'd been standing. She gasped for breath and turned on her side to curl into a ball as if she could resist the emotional battery by making herself compact, by covering her head with her arms.

Nausea struck with the same force, making her shudder. She scrambled from bed and ran across the hall to the guest bathroom, having the presence of mind to turn on the ceiling fan before falling to her knees in front of the toilet and retching.

Clinging to the toilet seat, she emptied her stomach. At length she sat on the floor and leaned against the wall, her bent head laid on her forearms braced on her knees. She breathed. In through her nose, out through her mouth. Ordering herself, as if a function so basic had become a challenge.

Why hadn't she told Dean? Why, oh, why keep to herself news that would have elated him? Eyes closed, she imagined his whoop of delight and huge grin.

She'd thought maybe this weekend. She just wanted to be sure. She'd always had irregular cycles. Being late this month might not have anything to do with that morning when he'd turned to her in bed and only later did they realize neither had used protection. But she'd thrown up every morning this week, and two days ago she'd bought a home pregnancy kit and watched the little strip turn pink.

She hadn't told him because… Oh, she hardly knew. Because she hadn't thought herself ready to have a baby, and she'd wanted to face what this meant to her and to her alone before she got swept up in Dean's joy. Because she hadn't totally trusted the kit and intended to repeat the results or get a proper pregnancy test in the doctor's office first. Because she'd wanted to make sharing the news a special occasion that she'd vaguely seen as including candlelight and a romantic dinner. He'd been busy all week, distracted, exasperated at being shorthanded at work and unable to find qualified applicants for the position he had open. She'd waited for a better moment, a better mood.

All week, Mindy had hugged the secret to herself, not stirring from bed until he left the house because the instant she moved the nausea hit. She'd always been an early riser, and he had teased her about becoming a sloth, to which she'd wrinkled her nose and laughed because he hadn't guessed.

Sitting on the cold bathroom floor, Mindy cried until exhaustion made her blessedly numb. Then she dragged herself up, peered without interest through swollen eyes at the mirror, and splashed cold water over her blotchy face. Her hair poked out every which way, but she didn't care.

The house was quiet, one lamp on in the living room. Was Quinn gone? She didn't care about his presence or absence any more than she did about anything else. She put on her robe and shuffled out to the kitchen simply because going through the motions of living was all she knew how to do.

The smell of coffee brewing and bacon frying filled her nostrils before she'd taken a step into the kitchen. If she hadn't already emptied her stomach, she wouldn't have been able to bear either. As it was, after a brief hesitation she continued into the kitchen, made bright by a skylight and a double set of French doors opening onto the back patio. Although she could hardly have made a sound, Quinn turned from the stove and gave her an appraising look.

"How are you?"

He couldn't tell? She only shook her head and sat down at the table set for two in front of the French doors. She and Dean had loved eating here rather than in the more formal dining room. The table was just as she'd left it last night, set with woven place mats from Guatemala and a vase of daffodils.

"Coffee?" Quinn asked.

"No, thank you."

"Juice?"

She almost said no, but she had to eat and drink for the baby's sake.

"Thank you."

He brought her cranberry juice and a plate of scrambled eggs—not fried, thank heavens—and bacon. Mindy tried not to look at the bacon.

Quinn added a plate of buttered toast to the middle of the table and jam still in its jar. He sat down across from her with his own breakfast.

When she didn't immediately pick up her fork, he ordered, "Eat."

She complied because she'd already decided she had to eat and because she didn't care one way or the other. Neither spoke. She managed to finish the eggs and most of one piece of toast before she pushed her plate away. Quinn's appetite didn't seem much better, despite the spread he'd cooked.

"Dickerson called this morning. They've already made an arrest."

From a great distance, she stared at him. "What?"

"Two punks. Nineteen and twenty-one." He talked about a meth lab and two strung-out young men who had in an instant snuffed out Dean's life.

"How…"

"You mean, how did they make the arrest so fast? Dean. The minute he saw a burglary in progress, he called it in. We had the license-plate number."

She did remember them talking about that last night. It just hadn't sunk in.

"Do you think he *knew*…"

A nerve jumped beside Quinn's eye. "Things like that happen fast. He probably saw that they were young, got out of his pickup to confront them, and one of them pulled a gun."

She nodded, wanting to believe he was right, that it had happened so quickly Dean hadn't had time for fear. She hoped he'd died instantly.

"His body…" Again, Mindy hardly knew what she was asking. Where his body was, she supposed, and what she was supposed to do to plan a funeral.

Quinn understood. "They're doing an autopsy today, and then I imagine his body will be released." He suggested a funeral home and they talked about when and where to hold the funeral. It was as if they were planning a bake sale, concentrating on details so they didn't have to think about what the occasion was really for: lowering Dean's body into a grave.

"Do you have people you need to call?" he finally asked.

"Yes, I suppose… His friends…"

He raised his brows. "I'll let them know."

Mindy felt a twinge of resentment at his sense of entitlement but then felt guilty. Quinn was surely grieving as much as she was.

She nodded and stood, picking up her plate. "I think I might lie down again."

Was she imagining the disdain in his eyes?

"It's ten-thirty."

She stopped in the middle of the kitchen. "So?"

"There are arrangements to be made."

"Dean…" She swallowed. "Dean hasn't been dead twelve hours. Arrangements can wait." She continued to the sink, set her plate down hard enough it clunked and kept walking. Out of the kitchen, to the bathroom—barely pregnant, and already she had to pee incessantly—and then back to the guest bedroom, where she climbed in and curled into a fetal position on her side.

The pillow was almost flat where her head had been when she'd awakened this morning. The sheets felt cold again and smelled faintly of fabric softener. She'd washed them just a couple of weeks ago, after Quinn had stayed over. As she'd always done when Quinn was around, that evening Mindy had tried hard to be friendly but finally made excuses and went upstairs to watch a video and then read in bed, leaving the men to their beer and basketball. She would hear shouts of laughter once she left them, and an easiness to their voices they didn't have when she was present. Had Dean been aware how strained the relationship was between his best friend and his wife? He had to have noticed something, but he'd never said a word to her beyond, a few times, trying to explain Quinn.

"He had a rough childhood."

"Any rougher than yours?" she remembered asking, a hint of tartness in her tone. "You grew up in a foster home, too."

"Yes, but before that I knew my mother loved me."

Dean had frowned, his usually laughing face serious. "I trusted her. Quinn never had anyone he could trust."

He hadn't wanted to tell her too much, and Mindy did understand. Quinn was a very private man, and would probably hate to find out Dean had said even as much as he had.

"Get Quinn to tell you someday," Dean suggested.

He couldn't have realized the disdain Quinn felt for her, or he wouldn't say something so ludicrous. But he had felt the tension; she'd sensed he was working extra hard to keep conversation light and flowing when Quinn was over.

She really should make some calls, Mindy thought drearily. Quinn must hate feeling obligated to stay even this long. If she had a friend coming over, he could leave in good conscience.

But it wasn't as if she'd *asked* him to stay. He could go home any time he wanted. She wished he would go.

Mindy felt a pang of guilt, because the truth was she'd been grateful last night that he was staying. She'd even been grateful that he had come with Sergeant Dickerson to give her the news. It had been possible to cry on him because she knew that, in his own way, he loved Dean, too.

Perhaps he would just leave, now that he'd realized she was done weeping on his shoulder. If she closed her eyes, and shut out the world, perhaps when she awakened the next time, he'd be gone. And she could cry again, and drift through the empty house, and try to imagine life in it without Dean.

WHY WAS HE SURPRISED that she left the dirty work to him?

Quinn drove home that afternoon to collect some clean clothes and toiletries, phoned in to clear a couple of days from work, then went back to Dean's house to do jobs that should have belonged to Dean's widow.

Sitting at the breakfast bar in the kitchen, he called the funeral home, then flipped open Dean's address book. Starting with the As, he methodically worked his way through, leaving messages some of the time, speaking to a few people.

Yes, it was a terrible tragedy. Dean's wife was prostrate. The funeral would probably be Saturday; they would notify everybody once they knew for sure.

Quinn hesitated when he flipped the page to the names that began with G and H. He'd have to call the Howies. Dean had stayed in closer touch with them than he had. They'd been at Dean's wedding, of course, but otherwise it had been...oh, hell, two or three years since Quinn had called them. They always sounded so damn grateful, his guilt would rev up another gear.

He almost skipped them now, put off contacting them until later, but wouldn't let himself. He had plenty of flaws, but cowardice wasn't one of them.

"Nancy?" he said, when a woman answered the phone.

"Yes?" His foster mother's voice had acquired a fine tremor. She must be—he had to calculate—in her seventies.

"It's Quinn. Brendan Quinn."

"Oh, my goodness! Brendan?" Her voice became

muffled. "George, it's Brendan on the phone!" She came back. "How nice to hear from you. My goodness, it's been a while."

"I know it has. I'm sorry. Time seems to race by." He despised himself for the weak excuse.

She'd always let him off the hook too easily. "Oh, it's just nice to hear your voice now."

"Nancy, I'm afraid the reason for my call isn't good." He drew a deep breath. "Dean's dead."

The silence was achingly long.

"Dead?"

"He was shot last night. On the job." As if to quiet her moan of grief, he kept talking, told her about the circumstances, the arrest, that he was at Dean's house right now.

"Oh, his poor wife!"

Even as he said the right things—Mindy was resting, in shock—Quinn felt anger again. She and Dean hadn't known each other that long. Dean had had girlfriends who'd lasted longer than he'd known Mindy. In fact, Quinn was going to have to call one of them, who had stayed friends with Dean. But Mindy was the wife, and therefore assumed to be the person who would be most devastated by his death.

Knowing damn well he was being petty, Quinn still couldn't stamp down that spark of something that was a hell of a lot closer to jealousy than he liked to admit.

Nancy handed off the phone to George, who asked for the details again. Quinn told him when the funeral was tentatively set for and promised to call again when plans were firm.

"Now, you take care of Mindy," George ordered.

After hanging up, Quinn stood to pour himself another cup of coffee. The Howies had sounded as if they'd lost a son. Had they really cared that much? Dean, of course, had been easier to love; despite his often expressed faith that his mother would be coming for him any day, he had craved closeness in a way Quinn hadn't. Quinn had never known whether he was just a paycheck from the state, an obligation they punctiliously fulfilled, or something more. They'd respected his reserve, his pride, and saved the hugs for Dean.

Shaking his head, Quinn took a long swallow of coffee and reached for the address book again.

He was hoarse by the time he reached Smith and Smithers. Dean had had a lot of friends.

Unlike Quinn, who had never had that talent. Didn't even want it. He didn't much like crowds and therefore avoided parties. He hated small talk and polite insincerity. Sometimes realized he just didn't know *how* to make friends.

God. Pain rose in a shattering wave, like the agony when a bullet had splintered his shoulder blade. He'd just dialed a number but had to hit End and put the phone down.

Twice now in not much over a year he'd had to face how badly he needed his one close friend. The only person who knew his secrets, his weaknesses, his history. Having to watch Dean marry someone who was so wrong for him had been bad enough.

But Quinn hadn't felt this swirling void of loneliness since he'd answered the door to find policemen on the doorstep, there to tell him his mother was dead. Maybe it had been there inside him the whole time, but he'd closed it off. Built a floor, firmly nailed down, to seal off a dank, dark basement that seemed to be occupied with rats that scurried out of sight when he looked but watched with blood-red eyes and the glint of sharp teeth when he half turned away.

He let out a rough, humorless laugh. What an idiotic image! Okay, damn it, he didn't let himself dwell on his occasional loneliness, sometimes wished he had Dean's gift for closeness with other people. But rats! *Poor me,* he mocked himself.

What he was feeling was the grief of losing family. For most people, there must be a moment when they realized that the last person who'd known them when they were young was gone. When parents died, or a sister or brother. For Quinn, Dean was that person. Like anyone else, he'd deal with the loss.

Mindy reappeared at five o'clock. She looked like hell, he thought critically, seeing her hover in the kitchen door, her vague gaze touching on microwave, refrigerator, table, as if she'd never seen any of them before.

She was pretty, he'd give Dean that. She always had had an air of fragility, accentuated now. Maybe five feet four or five inches tall, Mindy was incredibly fine-boned. She kept her golden blond hair chopped short in a sort of unkempt Meg Ryan style that somehow suited the long oval of her face and her huge gray-green eyes.

The first time Quinn saw her, she'd worn tight jeans cut so low, he'd raised his eyebrows. A smooth, pale stomach had been decorated with a gold belly-button ring. Her baby T had been tight enough for him to see that she wasn't wearing a bra, and that her breasts were small, high and nicely formed. Dean had leaned close to say something that made her giggle. Not laugh, like a grown woman, but giggle.

According to Dean, she was twenty-five. Twenty-six now; Quinn had had no choice but to attend the party Dean had thrown for her birthday, during which she'd clapped her hands with delight, danced with such abandon she'd kept whacking people, and almost cried when she'd failed to blow out all the candles.

"Oh!" she'd cried. "I won't get my wish!"

Dean had blown out the last two, then wrapped a comforting arm around her slender shoulders. "Sometimes you need help to get a wish."

Her absurdly long lashes had fluttered quickly, as if she had to blink away tears, and then she'd flung herself against him and kissed him passionately. The crowd whistled and applauded.

Except for the passionate part, Quinn had felt as if he were at a birthday party for a friend's sixteen-year-old daughter. He'd wondered what she and Dean had to talk about. She was an artist, Dean had always said proudly, but the only product of her artistry Quinn had ever seen was the hand-painted Welcome sign that hung over their front door. It was pretty. Michelangelo, she wasn't.

He hadn't thought much of it when Dean had first started dating her. She'd seemed young and flighty, but she was legal and willing. Some people enjoyed having yappy miniature poodles, too. Not his choice, though.

But marriage? He was still shaking his head.

At the moment, half her hair was spiky, the other half flattened from the pillow. Her face was puffy, her eyes bloodshot, her slender figure hidden inside a thick terry-cloth robe that was bright turquoise decorated with red and gold stars. Barefoot, she shuffled toward the refrigerator as if she were an old lady.

"Hungry?" he asked.

Her gaze swung toward him as if she hadn't noticed he was there. It registered his presence without interest.

"Um," she mumbled.

"I can cook or order something. Pizza?"

She shuddered.

"How about Chinese?"

Her response was slow, as if neural synapses weren't firing at normal speed. "Okay," she finally agreed.

She did manage to pour herself some juice while he called. When she carried it to the table and sat down, she said, "You're still here."

"I didn't want to leave you alone. Since you never got around to calling your mother or a friend." Quinn shrugged.

"I don't want anybody right now."

He tried to hide his exasperation. "Then you're stuck with me."

She was quiet for several minutes. Then, like a puzzled child, she asked, "Why don't you like me?"

Because you're silly, not too bright and self-centered. Because sooner or later, you were going to get tired of Dean and break his heart.

Quinn didn't say a word of what he thought. Instead, he snorted. "What makes you think I don't like you?"

Okay, maybe the not-too-bright part wasn't true. She looked at him with knowing, sad eyes.

He found himself amending. "It's not that I don't like you."

She kept waiting. Or maybe she had lost interest in any answer and was just staring into space he happened to occupy.

"I didn't think you and Dean were a good match."

Anger flared in her voice. "And you were the expert…why?"

"I knew Dean a hell of a lot better than you did!"

"And me not at all."

His jaws knotted. "That might be because you were too busy giggling and flirting with Dean to hold a rational conversation."

"I didn't know I was required to present my credentials to you."

They glared at each other.

Then, as quickly as their petty argument began, it ended. Her face crumpled. Her voice drifted. "Oh, what difference does it make?"

After a moment of struggle, she regained control, sipped juice and went back to glancing vaguely around the kitchen. Eventually, her gaze reached the address book and phone at his elbow.

"Have you already called some of Dean's friends?"

"I called everybody."

"Everybody?" Her gaze lifted to his face. "Shouldn't I have done that?"

"You didn't seem up to it."

She was starting to look mad again. "You mean, I wasn't willing to do it today, before Dean's body is even cold."

"Did you want his friends to find out he was dead from the six o'clock news?"

"No." Emotions waged war on her face. "Will it be…"

"On the news? Damn straight. He was a cop."

"Not anymore."

"As far as we're concerned, he was one of us. Reporters will see it the same."

"You could have said…"

Sharper than he had meant to be, Quinn said, "Murder makes the news. I didn't know I had to tell you that."

Resentment smoldered in her eyes and made her lips pouty. She even *looked* childish.

"I read *The Times*. I don't watch much TV. And following local murders is not my hobby."

Which part of *The Seattle Times* did she read? he wondered uncharitably. The comics?

"Dean's murder will be in the morning papers, too. I thought the news would better come from one of us."

"So you just took over."

A headache began to bore into his skull. "I took over when you decided to spend the day napping."

She rose to her feet, looking anguished, furious and completely grown-up. "When I spent the day grieving! Instead of worrying about whether somebody Dean played golf with once in a while found out in the first twenty-four hours that he was dead!"

The doorbell rang.

Quinn shook his head and went to answer it. He half expected that by the time he got back to the kitchen, she'd have retreated to the bedroom. Instead, she stood at one of the French doors looking out, her back to Quinn.

Quinn wondered, though, how much she could see through her own reflection in the glass. Maybe nothing; maybe she was studying her own haunted face.

"Dinner," he said, lifting the sacks.

"I did love him, you know."

Pain squeezed his chest, roughened his voice. "I know."

He hadn't been sure, not when Dean was alive. Now, he was beginning to believe she did.

"Just so you believe that much." Sounding incredibly weary, she turned from the view of the garden and came to the table.

He got plates and silverware and dished up. She waited docilely, her head bent as if she found the weave of the place mat fascinating. He wondered if even the slight effort of spooning moo goo gai pan and kung pao beef onto her plate would have stopped her from eating.

But once he put food in front of her, she picked up her fork and took a bite.

Like this morning, neither of them ate much. But they tried. When she pushed her half-empty plate away, he did the same.

"Why," he said, trying to understand, "won't you call your mother?"

She gave a seemingly indifferent shrug. "We're not that close."

"Doesn't she live around here?"

"Issaquah."

Fifteen, twenty minutes away.

Mindy stood. "Excuse me. I have to…" She fled.

Staring after her, Quinn wondered what he'd said wrong. Or did she just hate Issaquah, the mecca of up-scale shopping with the chic shops that made up Gilman Village? Mama, he concluded, must have money to live in Issaquah. Somehow that didn't surprise him. He added *spoiled* to Mindy's list of sins.

He turned on KOMO news and watched as the camera panned "the storage business where in the early hours of this morning a former Seattle Police detective was struck down, allegedly by two young men trying to steal this travel trailer." The camera focused on the white pickup truck with Fenton Security emblazoned on the door, then zoomed in on the Fleetwood. When Quinn was gravely told that "a source informs us that the young men may have been manufacturing methamphetamine in this trailer," he used the remote to turn the damn TV off.

Quinn's stomach roiled. Too vividly he saw Dean's

body sprawled on the pavement, the blood in his mouth, the glazed eyes. Why had Dean decided to confront the two punks? Why in hell hadn't he waited for the cops?

Quinn's fist hit the table so hard the dishes jumped and a shockwave of pain ran up his arm.

He heard a small sound and looked up through the blur of tears to see Mindy staring at him from the doorway. He knew what he must look like, his lips drawn back from his teeth in an agony of anger and grief.

After a moment, she turned and left him to mourn alone.

Quinn let out a harsh sound. The two people who Dean had loved most couldn't stand each other. Pretty goddamn sad.

CHAPTER THREE

ON A SUNNY MAY DAY, hundreds watched Dean Fenton be laid to rest at the cemetery. Endless tears rolled down Mindy's face. Struggling with grief that balled in his throat like a jawbreaker that was trying to choke him, Quinn remained rigidly conscious of his dignity. Mindy, apparently, didn't care.

She looked inappropriate for her role as grieving widow to begin with. With a suspicion she'd have nothing to wear, Quinn had suggested a couple of times over the week that she go shopping or order something online. She'd ignored him, of course, and now wore—well, he guessed it was a business suit for a twenty-something, which meant the skirt hugged her butt and left a long expanse of leg bare while the jacket was form-fitting over what seemed to be a camisole, the lace showing at the V. It wasn't even black, but rather white. Call him old-fashioned, but in his opinion a widow shouldn't go to her husband's graveside wearing clothes that advertised her body.

Naturally, she hadn't thought ahead enough to bring tissues, and had turned to him with wide-eyed desperation earlier at the church when tears and snot had begun to run down her face. Wasn't that a mother's job? he'd wondered, but he could already see that she was right: she and her mother weren't clòse.

Mom had shown up today, he had to give her that, but had seemed annoyed at the necessity of missing a luncheon for some club she belonged to. From the minute she'd arrived, Mindy looked sulky and even younger than usual.

The Howies were here, too, of course, Nancy looking much as she had at the wedding except for the sadness on her sweet, soft face, and for the tremor that affected not just her voice but her hands. Every time Quinn looked at her, she held them clasped together, as if one could control the other. Parkinson's?

George, in contrast, seemed to have aged ten years in one. A thick head of graying hair had turned white and fine, a dandelion puff instead of strong sod. His shoulders stooped, and his knuckles had become gnarled. Quinn had felt the difference, when they'd gripped hands in greeting and grief.

Now the first clod of dirt was flung atop the casket. Quinn shuddered and felt Mindy do the same beside him. A cry escaped her lips. He laid a hand on her back and she gave him one wild look before turning back to the raw earth and shining cobalt-blue casket. Her mother had somehow managed to be standing on the other side of Sergeant Dickerson, who had been heavily paternal in response to her dabbing a tissue at the corner of her eye.

As the crowd broke up, she turned immediately and

took in her daughter's ravaged face. Her own froze. Laying a hand on Dickerson's massive arm, she turned toward the parking lot without waiting for Mindy. The Howies hesitated, then started on their own toward the cars.

Quinn had no objection to hanging back, although he frowned at the few scattered rhododendrons rather than letting himself look again into the hole.

Finally Mindy let out a deep sigh and turned in a confused way as if unsure where to go. He took her elbow, pointed her in the right direction, and they followed the stream of mourners returning to their cars. Unfortunately, they still had to face the reception to be held in a hall at the church, where everyone would want to say a few words.

She lurched and almost went down. Quinn's grip saved her. He hoisted her upright.

"I'm sorry! My ankle turned."

He looked down at her spiky white heels.

"You could have worn flat shoes."

"These are the only white ones I have," she said, as if that was any kind of answer.

"Black is traditional, you know."

"But Dean hated black. Didn't you know that?"

In fact Quinn, who wore black much of the time, hadn't known that. The minute she pointed it out, though, he realized Dean had tended to wear bright colors and chinos rather than dark slacks.

"He…" Her voice faltered. "He'd have rather seen me in white than black."

All right. So she meant well. Her appearance still

wouldn't play well with the older cops and much of the viewing public, who—thanks to the ever-present news cameras—would see a sprite who appeared to dress out of the Victoria's Secret catalog weeping at graveside and flashing a hell of a lot of leg on tonight's local news.

But he forbore to tell her that.

"You want to go by the house so you can, uh, touch up your makeup before we go back to the church?"

"I don't know. I don't care." She paused. "I suppose."

While he waited in the living room, she disappeared for about two minutes. When she came back, her face was still puffy but clean, and she'd renewed her mascara.

"I'm ready."

He nodded and they let themselves out the front door. She sat in silence beside him as he drove. Not until they pulled into the parking lot did she let out a broken sigh.

"Dean would have liked an Irish wake. A celebration, not…"

She didn't have to finish. He knew what she meant. Not a lament, a ceremony to share regrets.

"Yeah," he agreed. "Maybe when we're ready."

They exchanged a rare glance of accord before getting out of the car, standing side by side looking at the open door to the hall, and—in his case, at least—gathering composure.

Her ankle turned in those damn silly shoes on the steps leading down to the daylight basement reception rooms. Once again, he grabbed her in the nick of time. Shaking his head, he led her in a meandering route among the mourners so she could accept their condolences. Her tears returned within minutes and the mascara began to run again.

Half the Seattle police force was here, of course, but also plenty of people Quinn either didn't know or had a feeling he'd met once or twice. Dean had had a lot of friends. Maybe some of them *were* casual golf buddies, but they'd cared enough to show up at his funeral, decked in dark suits and ties, on a sunny Saturday perfect for golfing.

"You're Quinn?" some of them said, shaking his hand. "He talked about you. Said he hoped you'd end up his partner in the security business someday."

Despite the spasm of pain he felt every time he thought of Dean, Quinn managed a crooked smile. "He knew I'd never quit the force, but he was too stubborn to take no for an answer."

One of them grinned. "Yeah, hell, he made us play thirty-six holes one day last September even though it was eighty-six degrees, because he couldn't get a handle on his slice and he was too damn stubborn to quit." The grin faded as the friend remembered he'd never watch Dean Fenton take a swing with his three wood again. "He bought us a round afterward."

Quinn made time to talk to the Howies, who reminded him about some of Dean's more outlandish exploits when he was their foster son, then hugged Mindy, asked Quinn not to be a stranger and left. Frowning, he watched them go, George stooped like an old man and Nancy with the shakes she'd told him with one stern glance not to mention. Not today.

Mindy, Quinn realized reluctantly, wasn't the only obligation he'd just inherited. Dean had been, for all practical purposes, the Howies' son, the one who remembered their fiftieth wedding anniversary and sent them for a weekend to the Empress in Victoria, the one who called unexpectedly, who made sure they were all right. He hadn't mentioned Nancy's tremors, maybe because he hadn't thought Quinn would care.

But, damn it, he did care, whether he wanted to or not. The thought made him uncomfortable. An obligation. That's all he had to think of them as. Dean would expect him to step in.

With no booze being served, the crowd trickled away fairly fast. Mindy, Quinn saw, looked skim-milk pale and on the verge of collapse as she thanked people for coming. He looked around for her mother but didn't spot her.

At Mindy's side, he said, "I think we can leave now."

"Really?" Her gaze went past him and she gave a shaky smile at someone behind him. "Thank you so much for coming today."

The couple, who looked vaguely familiar to Quinn, said a few kind words about Dean and left.

"Where's your mother?"

"Gone." Again she looked past him, and her eyes filled with tears. "Selene! Oh, I'm so glad you're here."

Selene wore a sleeveless white sweater and a flowery skirt that swirled to her calves. Her wild dark curls were barely subdued by a barrette. He made a private bet that she was a college student.

After the two women hugged, Mindy turned to him. "Quinn, this is my best friend, Selene Thomas. She's a grad student at the UW."

He nodded and said by rote, "Thanks for coming today."

Big dark eyes filled with tears. "Dean was such a sweetie."

The two hugged and commiserated some more while Quinn shifted from foot to foot. He just wanted to get the hell out of here. Maybe take a run, or go to the gym. He wanted to work himself into mindless exhaustion. Maybe then he'd sleep tonight.

"Selene is going to stay with me tonight," Mindy told him. "So you're off duty."

He felt a lurch of profound relief.

"We can talk all night," her friend promised.

Personally, Quinn thought what Mindy needed was to sleep. She was looking frailer by the day, to the point where he'd had to set aside his cynicism. She wasn't eating enough to keep a bird alive, and judging from the dark circles under her eyes wasn't sleeping either. She seemed unable to think about practicalities.

Dean's will had left everything to her except a few mementos to Quinn. She'd wept and refused to worry about where a safe-deposit key might be or whether bills might be coming due. Quinn had made himself keep his mouth shut. So far. It had only been a week. She hadn't buried her husband yet. Even a nitwit like she was would start thinking about money and groceries and hiring a lawn service soon.

He hoped.

"Off duty?" Selene echoed, blinking at him.

"Quinn's been making me eat and mowing the lawn and returning phone calls." Mindy's huge, smudged eyes met his. "He doesn't think I'm capable of taking care of myself."

He *knew* she wasn't capable of taking care of herself. He was hoping like hell that the state was temporary. Being the long-term guardian of a twenty-six-year-old adolescent wasn't his idea of a good time. *Damn it, Dean,* he asked for the thousandth time, *why her?*

"You want to prove you can," Quinn suggested, "why don't you start eating more than a few bites at a time?"

"Because…" Color touched her cheeks and her gaze slid from his. "Because I can't eat when I'm upset."

Quinn's eyes narrowed. That wasn't what she'd intended to say. He'd have liked to know what she'd been unwarily about to admit. But he only nodded and asked Selene if she had a car.

Well, no; she'd ridden the bus.

"I'll drive you two home. If," he added with courtesy to Mindy, "you're ready?"

She sniffed and nodded.

Selene chattered during the drive. What a nice ceremony. Everybody really liked Dean, didn't they? The house must seem so big without him!

At the last, tears began to roll down Mindy's face. Again. Quinn glared at the rearview mirror, but her friend was oblivious.

"What are you going to *do?*" she asked.

Mindy swallowed hard. In a watery voice, she said, "I don't know. I haven't thought... Not yet..."

Quinn pulled into the driveway. "Shall I come in?" *Please, no,* he begged.

Mindy shook her head and gave him a shaky smile. "We'll be fine. Thank you, Quinn." To his surprise, she reached out and squeezed his hand. "I mean it." Then she got out to join her friend on the sidewalk.

"Nice to meet you!" Selene called, as he waved and put the car into reverse.

He flexed his fingers. Mindy didn't touch him if she could help it. He didn't touch her, except recently when it was obvious somebody had to steer her to where she was supposed to be. They'd never been comfortable with each other. He'd seen that she was physically demonstrative with everyone else—with her youthful gaiety, she hugged, kissed, danced and even sat on laps without the slightest inhibition. He guessed he'd killed her spontaneity toward him the first time they met. Except for falling into his arms to sob the night he came to deliver the news, this was the first time she'd voluntarily touched him.

His mouth twisted into a sour smile. He must have looked good in comparison with her charming mother.

Quinn grabbed his gym bag and went to the health club. After changing into his usual gray T-shirt and old sweatpants, he snagged a basketball and went into the gym. Late afternoon on a Saturday, it was completely empty. He dribbled the ball, each bounce echoing sharply. Instead of the sound annoying him, he liked it. It seemed to accentuate his solitude.

He warmed up with a few easy layups, then free throws, finally challenging himself with tougher and tougher shots, driving to the basket, spinning, shooting backward, shooting from damn near halfway down the court, from the corners. When he'd worked up a sweat, he dropped the basketball back in the bin and went to the weight room. He wasn't quite alone here, but the few men who'd claimed a machine or a bench were preoccupied with their own rhythms.

When Quinn's muscles began to groan, he moved on to a treadmill, setting the timer for half an hour. By fifteen minutes, he was wearing down. He'd been too inactive this week, spent too much time holding the pitiful widow's hand, figuratively rather than literally, of course.

His shirt was soaked by the time he finished, his legs as shaky as a newborn colt's. He wiped his face on a towel and went back to the gym to shoot some more baskets anyway, testing his control, his discipline, satisfied only when the ball dropped neatly through the hoop without ruffling the net.

Finally, he showered, changed into swim trunks and dived into the pool. The cool water closed over him, sliding across his skin, insulating him for a few brief moments from the world. By the time he showered again, got dressed and slung his gym bag over his shoulder, he felt almost like himself.

FOR THE ONE DAY, Mindy had actually *liked* Quinn. He'd been her rock. A silent chauffeur, a hand when she needed one, a steady gaze to help her ground herself. For all his composure, she'd felt the magma beneath, the hot, unsettling grief that matched her own, and she was grateful for that as well. Dean had been liked by many, but loved, she suspected, by only a few. The Howies, Quinn and her.

Her gratitude and warmth of feeling didn't last through the next day, never mind the next week.

He wanted her to call people, to do whatever it was the attorney needed to start probate. He wanted her to make decisions.

"What are you going to do about the business? Mindy, Mulligan says he's left several messages and you haven't called him back."

She'd spent the morning puking her guts up and had barely had time to force down a piece of dry toast and some juice. "I'll call him."

"When?"

"What are you, my conscience?" Didn't he *ever* go to work anymore?

"When people start coming to me because they can't get answers from you, I figure a little prodding is due."

Anger flared, along with renewed nausea. "I said I'll call!"

He didn't budge, just stood in front of her with his arms crossed and his expression unyielding. "And what will you say?"

"I don't know!" she all but shouted. "Why do I have to decide now?"

"Because Fenton Security employs fourteen people

and has a couple of hundred clients. The employees are waiting to find out whether they still have jobs. Without Dean, the clients are going to start dropping away. A business doesn't run itself."

"Mick..."

"Is a fine dispatcher. He can't charm businessmen or handle billing. He might hire, but he'll never fire anyone. Besides," Quinn continued inexorably, "Dean didn't work sixty-, seventy-hour weeks for fun. He did it because shit happened if he wasn't around, because there are things he couldn't delegate. And," he paused, waiting until she defiantly met his eyes, "the business can't afford to pay someone to do what Dean did. Mindy, you've got to look at the books. If you hire someone to replace Dean, you're not going to be making a damn thing. And you'll be trusting a stranger."

She felt as if he were trying to stuff her into a small closet. Dark, claustrophobic, the air thick and musty. She was grabbing for the door to prevent him closing it those last inches.

"So what are you suggesting?" She heard the rasp of her breathing, as if she were asthmatic. "That *I* run it?"

Worse than that idea was the slight curl of his lip and the pity in his eyes. *Don't be ridiculous,* he might as well have said.

"No. I'm suggesting you sell it."

She moved restlessly. "I don't even know how..."

"So you're going to take another nap and refuse to think about it?" he asked with raw contempt.

"No!" Her eyes filled with tears. *Yes.* He was stripping her bare, finding out how utterly incapable she was and holding up a mirror so she could be sure not to miss her own inadequacies. Clasping her arms around herself, she said, "Why won't you leave me alone?"

"Because I owe it to Dean to make sure you don't lose everything he worked so hard for. He'd expect me to be sure you're all right."

"I'm not all right!"

His voice softened. "I know. But you still have to make decisions. That's the way it is."

So, despite her nausea and the tears that kept flooding her eyes, Mindy sat down and pored over computer printouts. What salaries and taxes and benefits cost, the expense of keeping a fleet of Fenton Security pickups prowling dark corners of the city at night. She looked at income and outgo and Labor and Industry statistics, discovered how much Dean had been involuntarily contributing to build Safeco Field and the Seahawks Stadium. She saw personnel records and realized with dismay that the average security guard didn't stay with the company more than eight or ten months. Dean had been hiring constantly, wasting money on training, then regularly having to let shirkers go.

"How," she whispered at last, "did he make any money?"

"By cultivating clients and by making damn sure his guards were doing their job, not spending the night sipping coffee at a diner."

"Oh." Exhausted, she sat back. "Will anybody want to buy the business?"

"Sure. He's in the black. Not many small businesses are."

"Do I advertise it?"

Quinn frowned. "No. You might scare the clients." He paused. Hesitated, she might have said, if it had been anyone but him. "Do you want me to ask around? There are plenty of cops with the same dream Dean had."

"Please," she said, but without the gratitude she would have felt two hours ago. Why couldn't he just have made this offer then?

"All right." He squared the pile of papers. "Now, the bills—"

"No!" Despite her tiredness, Mindy shot to her feet. "Not now. Maybe tomorrow."

With scant sympathy, he said, "They're piling up."

The attorney had left half a dozen messages, too, and she didn't want to talk to him, either.

"I did what you wanted. Now, will you just go?"

"All right." He nodded. "We've made a start."

A start, she thought hysterically.

After he left, she took a nap. Then she made herself listen to phone messages. Mick had questions, the attorney had questions, several people had left condolences. A reporter from the *P.I.* was still hoping for comments. After deleting them all, she carried to the table the basket into which she'd been throwing correspondence. Quinn was right; the bills were piling up.

The attorney had said she could continue to write checks to pay bills and daily expenses. Okay, she thought, she could do this. She'd paid her own until she'd married Dean, so it wasn't like she didn't know how to write out a check for the phone bill. And it would give her enormous pleasure the next time Quinn showed up to say, *Oh, I've already done that.*

She opened a tablet of paper and decided to list what she owed first. She didn't even know what Dean paid for.

Mindy found a bank statement first and discovered that the mortgage was an automatic deduction. An enormous one. She stared at the amount with dismay. A neighbor had sold recently, and if this house was worth about the same… There must not be very much equity, or Dean wouldn't have been making such big payments.

After a moment she shrugged. It wasn't as if she had a choice.

A few lines down she spotted two more deductions, both car payments. His and hers. She'd driven a beater when she'd met Dean, and he'd insisted on buying her a new car. He'd worry about her, he'd said when she'd protested. And Dean had loved the Camaro he drove, but he still owed an awful lot on it. Thinking about the car, fire-truck red, sitting in the garage made her falter and blink back more tears.

Swallowing, she made herself go on, reaching for the next envelope and neatly slitting it open with the letter opener she'd found on Dean's desk.

This one was a MasterCard. He owed $4,569. Mindy had never even had that big a credit limit before. She wrote the amount of the debt, the creditor and the payment on the second line, after the mortgage.

The gas bill was way higher than she'd expected, too,

as was the water and sewer and the Nordstrom bill and bills for two different Visa cards. He owed a whole lot of money on the boat that occupied a third of the garage. He'd loved that boat, too, a white cabin cruiser he'd re-named *The Mindy* after he'd met her. He loved to take friends out on the Sound. Mindy, who didn't swim very well, hadn't actually enjoyed going out. She'd pretended she got queasy, but the truth was that panic had flooded her from the moment water opened between the dock and the hull.

The boat, at least, was easy—she'd sell it as soon as she could.

There was enough in the checking account to pay all the bills, but not much would be left over. Especially since some of these payments were already late, and the next month's bills would be arriving soon. Dismayed, she recalculated a couple of times. She guessed she would have to call the attorney. Dean had had invest-ments, hadn't he? Maybe they could sell some stock, or cash in a CD, or something.

She debated whether to write a little note on each bill saying something to the effect that Dean Fenton had died unexpectedly, that the will was in probate and she, his wife—no, widow—would be the one now paying. But wasn't that something the executor should do? Dean's executor, of course, was Quinn, who in that ca-pacity had every right to nag her and maybe even over-ride her decisions. She didn't know.

She opened the checkbook, but didn't write anything for a long time. Dean L. and Mindy A. Fenton, the checks all said. Only, now it would just be Mindy A. *She* was responsible for all those debts. Debts she hadn't even known they owed.

With shame she realized she *should* have known. Would have, if she'd ever asked or expressed any interest. But she hadn't. Dean had acted as though he loved to take care of her and give her anything she wanted, and with this house and the boat and the Camaro and his own business, he'd looked as if he could afford to. She knew he'd been a cop until not that long ago, but it just hadn't occurred to her that he'd borrowed heavily on future success that wasn't going to happen.

With a sinking feeling, she admitted if only to herself that some of Quinn's contempt was justified. She'd been some kind of...*trophy* wife, something fun and pretty like the Camaro or the boat. Not really the partner she'd imagined, or she would have known.

The panic she felt as she wrote checks, one after another, wasn't much different than the panic that bounced in her when the expanse of water opened between the boat that began to feel oh so tiny and the shore, shrinking to a faint smudge like a mirage.

Dean was dead, and she was pregnant, and unless— please God!—he had lots of investments, she wasn't going to have enough money to keep up with these bills.

She had to start selling things, and soon. Quinn, she thought with a small coal of anger, suspected how things stood, or he wouldn't have been nagging the way he had. How dared he not say anything and make it sound like it was *she* who'd been lax!

And Dean… How dared *he* keep buying and buying, throwing parties and playing golf and insisting she had to have the little BMW in the driveway, and never tell her he didn't really have the money!

After she'd put stamps on the bills, she would mount a search for the safe-deposit key the attorney kept asking about.

She had to know where she and the small flutter of life inside her stood.

CHAPTER FOUR

ONCE HE'D GOTTEN HER to thinking about money, by God that's all she seemed able to think about. When could he find a buyer for the security business? How did she go about selling the boat? Now the Camaro. The cherry-red Camaro Dean had coveted all his life and loved with a passion.

"What?" Quinn stared across the paper-strewn kitchen table at Dean's widow. "You're already planning to sell his car?" When he wasn't even cold in his grave?

She heard the unspoken part. Her face took on that closed, stubborn look he was coming to detest even more than the frail, woe-is-me expression she'd worn for the first few weeks.

"I don't want to drive it, and I can't afford the payments."

"How much are they?"

She pushed the bill across the table.

Quinn picked it up and frowned. She was right. Dean owed a whopping amount, and she really couldn't keep up the payments.

Quinn had been spending most of his off hours either making decisions in Dean's place for Fenton Security, mowing the lawn and doing upkeep on the house, or helping Mindy untangle her husband's financial affairs.

Secretly, Quinn was appalled by how recklessly Dean had borrowed. Maybe he shouldn't be—Dean always had wanted the nice things in life, and had been a bigger risk-taker than Quinn. But damn it! He'd been living on the financial edge, Quinn was discovering. Balancing fine, because his business was successful and expanding, but without a hell of a lot in the way of reserves. He'd have been in deep doo-doo if the economy had taken a downturn, for example, and a good share of his clients had gone out of business or decided they could do without security.

But Quinn wouldn't have criticized Dean aloud to anyone, much less to the cute little blonde who'd enjoyed all of Dean's toys as long as someone else was paying the bills.

"I'll buy the Camaro," he heard himself say.

"And paint it black?"

That stung. "Thanks."

She flushed. "Are you serious?"

"Yeah, I'm serious. Dean loved that car."

"Then…if you'll take over the payments, it's yours."

He was blown away by the offer even though there was no way in hell he could take it. He'd started to think of her as greedy, but, okay, maybe she had some conscience.

"I'll pay you." He hesitated, then forced himself to say, "But thanks."

Her eyes were wide and luminous. "I meant it. Dean would love to know you'd kept his car."

"And I can afford to buy it." He held up a hand. "No argument."

The momentary glow on her face was extinguished, and Quinn felt like a crud.

"Okay," she said, voice dull. "Do I really have to wait for probate to finish before I sell stuff?"

"We'll talk to Armstrong," Quinn promised. Surely the attorney would be reasonable. "If the bills can't be paid, something has to go."

Mindy nodded and said like a child, "Are we done?"

He pictured her, a tiny, scrawny kid, asking politely, "May I be excused now?"

"Bored?"

As she stood, anger flashed on her face, erasing the childlike impression. "Frustrated. I might as well go watch TV. I can't do anything about any of that." She waved at the piles of bills and bank statements.

With strained patience, he said, "Solutions don't always happen instantly, just because we want them to."

"Have I ever mentioned that you're a jerk?" she snapped, and shoved the chair in.

He rubbed the heel of his hand against his chest, where his heartburn was acting up. "Your opinion was obvious enough, thank you." And rich, he thought, coming from the drama queen. No, not queen—princess. Little Miss I'm Entitled.

She stomped out. Suppressing his own frustration, Quinn put away the papers in a plastic file box and left it on the table. He was almost glad when his beeper went off. A dead body would be a welcome diversion.

HE BEGAN TO WONDER if she was throwing parties every night, or maybe just attending them. Far as he could tell, she was never up before ten or eleven in the morning, and then she would look puffy-eyed, wan and repelled by any suggestion that she should make decisions. Quinn didn't remember Dean ever commenting that she was a night owl, but then he and Dean had hardly ever talked about Mindy at all. It had been safer that way.

As far as Quinn could tell, she wasn't job hunting, so he guessed she was planning to live on her inheritance as long as it lasted. Thus her panic about unnecessary drains on the final total.

Quinn had originally figured she'd be left a wealthy young woman, but clearly that wasn't going to happen. Too many bills had come to light, too few investments. Still, when it all shook out, he thought she'd have a decent amount left. If she was careful, enough to get by for a couple of years without working. Pretty good deal considering she hadn't been married that long and hadn't had a damn thing when she'd met Dean.

Quinn recalled she'd worked as a barista at a Tully's downtown, which was where Dean had met her. She'd apparently been making a little on the side with her "art." She'd probably sold a few painted wood signs to friends. The talent Dean raved about hadn't been discovered by the wider world. She'd lived with a houseful of minimum-wage friends and students near the university.

Given her background, what right did she have to be unhappy to find out she *wouldn't* be wealthy? But clearly she was. She got more petulant by the day, more determined that everybody hurry, hurry, hurry so she could sell whatever wasn't nailed down.

He'd stopped by this morning to tell her he thought he had a buyer for Fenton Security. A pair of buyers, more accurately.

Quinn was beat, after a hard night. A body had fallen from the Olive Street overpass, landing on the windshield of a semi and shattering the glass. The semi had jackknifed, resulting in one hell of a traffic snarl that had closed I-5 south for three hours. The poor schmuck who'd hit the windshield was grizzled, dirty and wearing three layers of clothes and boots with soles that must have flapped when he walked. Staggered, more likely, from the powerful odor of cheap wine that had wafted from him along with the sickly tang of blood. Turned out he was well known in the missions around the Pioneer Square area. Nobody knew his name. Said he went by Crow. Just Crow.

A witness out walking his dog late had spotted a souped-up Toyota pause on the overpass just before she was distracted by the sound of splintering glass, the squeal of brakes and the scream of metal striking concrete abutments. Weirdly, she had even remembered half the license-plate number.

"Because it's identical to mine," she had said. "ALN. I call my car Alan because of the license plate." She'd looked a little embarrassed at the admission. "But the numbers were different." Her eyes had gone unfocused, and then she'd said in triumph, "Seven hundred. It was seven hundred something. I don't remember the rest."

"Ms. Abbott, you're amazing," Quinn's current partner had told her with a generosity that didn't come so easily to Quinn.

Ellis Carter was bumping against retirement, which meant he could be a little slow in the rare event of a chase, but his warmth and ease with witnesses more than atoned for the potbelly and arthritic knee.

They had run the plates and—bingo!—had come up with only one blue Toyota Supra carrying license number 7—ALN. It was registered to a twenty-something scumbag who, when he'd answered his doorbell, smirked at the idea that he might have tossed a drunk from the freeway overpass just for fun. The smirk had faded when he'd heard there was a witness. The friend hovering in the background had broken and run. Getting him to babble had taken less time than cleaning up the mess on the freeway.

All Quinn wanted to do was go home and crash, but he figured he should share the good news first.

He rang the doorbell, and after a long delay, Mindy appeared, still in her bathrobe.

"Quinn." She didn't sound thrilled to see him on her doorstep at ten in the morning.

Face it—she probably wasn't thrilled to see him no matter what time of day it was.

He studied her puffy, tired eyes and the dark circles beneath them. "Still not sleeping?"

Mindy let out a puff of air that was half laugh, half exasperation. "So I look like crap. Tell me something I don't know."

"I didn't mean…"

"It doesn't matter." She could go from animation to lifeless quicker than most of the residents of Seattle who actually died. "Did you need to talk to me about something?"

"Can I come in?"

"I suppose." Still in zombie mode, she stepped back. Looking at the floor, she waited, seemingly unaware that her robe gaped open exposing…

God. Was that one of Dean's T-shirts? Yeah, Quinn decided, it was. She'd taken to sleeping in her dead husband's shirts. And boxer shorts that he hoped like hell weren't Dean's. He caught a glimpse of those long, long legs and of her bare feet. Those he'd seen before, as she went barefoot most of the time at home and conceded to necessity by wearing flip-flops when she went out except in the direst weather. She used to paint her toenails, though. Not just pink or red. He'd made a habit of glancing at her feet just to see what she'd done now. Sometimes her nails were turquoise, or silver glitter, or had tiny flowers or eyes of Osiris or peace signs painted on crayon-bright backgrounds.

Now, he saw a chip or two of red clinging to the cuticles, but she must not have touched them since… He stopped there. Since before.

Still in the entryway, he faced her. "I might have found someone to buy the business."

"Really?" Accentuated by the smudges beneath them, her eyes looked more gray than green when she lifted her gaze to his face.

"You know Lance Worden? Scarecrow?"

Her face cleared at the nickname and she nodded.

"He and a buddy of his were looking to start a security company in south King County. Didn't want to compete with Dean, and Scarecrow—Worden—thought with Federal Way and that area growing it would be good territory. But depending on price he'd be interested in Fenton Security instead."

"Would he keep the name?"

"We didn't get that far," Quinn said with scant patience. He'd expected her to be pleased, maybe even excited, and instead she was worrying about something meaningless.

Maybe *he* should share her regret at the loss of one more piece of Dean's identity, but honest to God he was getting tired of answering the phone five times a day to answer questions for Mulligan, who in the absence of Dean had lost any ability he'd ever had to be decisive.

"Oh." Mindy's mouth twisted. "It's just…Dean was so proud of the company. Sometimes he'd wash one of the trucks here, in the driveway, you know, and I'd see him stop when he was drying it and give a few extra rubs to the logo. Sort of *polishing* it."

Oh, damn. Quinn had seen Dean do that, too.

More harshly than he'd intended, he said, "There's no more Fenton."

Her chin came up. "*I'm* a Fenton."

The idea was jarring. "You're going to keep the name?"

She was pissed off now. "Of course I'm going to keep the name! Dean and I didn't get a divorce!"

"I didn't mean…"

"What *did* you mean?"

He had no idea. "Just…you haven't been Mindy Fenton that long. The name must still feel strange to you. I thought…"

Her eyes narrowed. "I'd want to ditch any memory of Dean as quickly as possible."

As so often happened around her, a band of pain began to tighten around his skull. "Can we not argue?"

"Fine." She turned her back on him and stalked toward the kitchen.

Quinn followed.

Mindy poured herself some juice and didn't offer him anything. She carried it to the table and sat without inviting him to join her, either.

"So I just need to come up with a price?"

Leaning against the breakfast bar, Quinn reminded her, "Probate…"

"Oh, God."

"We might be able to come up with an agreement that makes it a done deal except for the formality of the sale closing," he suggested. "So Scarecrow and his partner could take over the business as soon as possible, even if we can't tie the bow until Armstrong says it's okay."

"But I wouldn't get the money until then?"

"Maybe not." He frowned. "Probably not."

Her eyes got misty. God almighty. She was going to cry over a check being delayed for a few months.

"You're not that broke, are you?" he asked.

"No. No, I… No." She sniffed, wiped at her eyes, and said, "Everything makes me cry. I'm sorry." One more sniff and she squared her shoulders. "How do I set a price?"

"I've already done that."

She set down her juice glass. "You've…what?"

"I found out there are formulas. Assets and income minus debts and costs."

Voice tight, she said, "I don't get any input?"

His jaw muscles spasmed. "What input would you have given?"

He apparently had a gift for infuriating her. "You don't know any more about Fenton Security than I do! What makes you…"

"Who the hell do you think has been running it for the last month? Or didn't you wonder why Mulligan gave up calling you?"

"Even Dean took a few days off! I thought the company could run itself for a week or two. I never gave you permi—"

"I'm the executor," he interrupted her. "That gives me the right to put a value on assets, and to make damn sure they don't *lose* value."

She didn't like that, but couldn't argue. Finally she said sulkily, "Do I get to know what your *formulas* say Fenton Security is worth?"

He told her.

She blinked, sat in silence for a long moment, gave her head a little shake, and then said, just above a whisper, "That's less than I thought it would be. Um…quite a lot less."

Quinn didn't want to be doing this. He wanted to be home, the window blinds drawn, stretched out on his bed in his shorts. A couple of aspirin would be dulling his headache and sleep would be dragging him deep.

But something like pity made him go over and pull out the chair across from Mindy.

"Yeah. It's less than I thought it would be, too. But Dean borrowed a lot on the business. There are some big debts."

"Oh." She sounded and looked forlorn. "I wish…"

"What?"

"He'd told me."

Quinn wished the same. Hadn't Dean known how shaky the footing was, how far the plunge to the ground would be? Why hadn't he taken success a little slower? Waited to get a boat, to expand the business, to drive the dream car?

But Quinn knew the answer. Despite the fact that his mother never did come back for him, Dean had been the eternal optimist. Hell, the eternal adolescent. "Nah," he'd have said. "That won't happen to me."

But death had happened, and he hadn't expected that, either.

Quinn tried to smile. "He enjoyed the damn boat and the car and…" His pretty wife.

Her eyes filled with tears again, even as she gave him

a smile as wry as his. "He did, didn't he?" She sniffed again. "Will you, um, negotiate for me?"

He'd already begun, but he was smart enough not to tell her that. He only nodded.

"I guess I should shower," she said, starting to stand.

It struck him suddenly that she'd lost weight. Her pixie face had acquired some hollows that hadn't been there before. The robe hung off one shoulder, exposing a bony protuberance on her shoulder and the most pronounced collarbone he'd ever seen.

"You're not eating enough."

She yanked the robe around herself. "And you know this how?"

"I haven't seen you eat more than a few mouthfuls in…" He couldn't remember. "You look skinnier."

"You know, Quinn, Dean always said you didn't have a girlfriend because you had trouble trusting anyone. I'm starting to think it's because you're a heck of a lot better at insults than you are at compliments."

He'd gone rigid halfway through this speech, hating the idea of her and Dean talking about him, of Dean telling her things about him that were supposed to stay between the two of them.

Her face changed. "I shouldn't have said that. I'm sorry."

Quinn just walked out. He was hardly aware of her staring after him.

Goddamn you, Dean, he thought, and didn't even

know if he was angriest at his best friend for psychoanalyzing him for the benefit of anyone who'd listen, or for dying.

TWO WEEKS LATER, Mindy stood naked looking at herself in the full-length mirror on the closet door. She was pretty sure she was three-and-a-half months pregnant, and she could already see changes in her body.

She *was* skinnier, thanks in part to grief but mainly to the never-ending nausea. Morning sickness, ha! When she first got out of bed in the morning was her worst time, sure, but her stomach stayed queasy most of the day. If she actually threw up, she'd feel better for a little while—long enough to realize she was starved and to stuff her face—but then she'd just get sick again. So she barely managed crackers and celery and carrots—the clean sharp taste of raw vegetables tasted especially good—and clear soup. Juice and crackers for breakfast, chicken noodle soup for lunch, and vegetables and more crackers at intervals the rest of the day.

She'd lost almost ten pounds, which she knew couldn't be good. But she was trying. And the morning sickness would go away soon. Please God.

Despite the weight loss, she was starting to have a little pooch below her belly button. If not for the missing ten pounds, her jeans might have been getting tight around the waist. And her breasts, too, looked fuller.

She made a face at herself. Or maybe they just looked bigger because the rest of her was so skeletal.

Brendan Quinn sure knew how to make a girl feel good.

Dean had been dead six weeks now, and she was starting to dread the very sight of Quinn. That made her feel petty, because he was doing so much for her. Most of it unasked.

Sighing, she glanced once more at her skinny, pregnant body and turned away, picking out underwear, T-shirt and jeans from the dresser.

A couple of weeks ago, she'd started sleeping up here again, in the bed she'd shared with Dean. She felt less lonely here. Sometimes she'd even pretend to herself that he was just working late, that he'd wake her when he got home and...

She gave a sad laugh. *Everything* nauseated her right now. Making love would not have been in the cards.

But that wouldn't have mattered, because she'd have long since told Dean about the baby. As excited as he'd have been, patience would have come easily.

And morning sickness *did* pass. Or so the books assured her.

Except for the obstetrician she'd seen for the first time a couple of weeks ago, Mindy hadn't told a soul yet about the pregnancy. Not her mother. Not even Selene. And not Quinn. Especially not Quinn.

Her jeans on, the T-shirt in her hand, she frowned into space. Quinn already treated her as if she were fragile, and not in a good way. Not as if he wanted to take care of her, but rather as if he thought she was completely incapable of taking care of herself. He did things without asking whether she wanted him to, then managed to look irritated because he had to do them. If she admitted she could hardly go out to the grocery store because she was so sick to her stomach, he'd be unbearable.

She let out an exasperated puff of air. *Be* unbearable? He *was* unbearable. Ten times in every conversation she had to remind herself that he meant well. And he was incredibly capable. Apparently he'd been fielding calls night and day from Mick Mulligan, who really did need his hand held, Dean had said. Quinn dealt with the lawyer, he'd negotiated the sale of Fenton Security, he'd arranged for the boat to be trailered to a marina and put up for sale, he mowed the lawn, for Pete's sake!

And he judged her. She saw it in his eyes. He thought she was selfish, silly, lazy. At first he hadn't believed she really loved Dean; now he seemed to think she should get over it and whip her life into shape. Except he obviously didn't think she could.

In fairness, he was doing his best to see that she walked away with as much money as possible. Presumably because he didn't believe she was able to make a living, and he felt he owed it to Dean to be sure she was okay.

That was what rankled: the fact that he despised her and was helping only out of a sense of obligation to Dean. At first she'd been grateful no matter what. The truth was, she didn't have anyone to step in, and at first she *hadn't* been in any shape to make decisions. But now she could make her own, only Quinn persisted in treating her as if she were a developmentally disabled adult who needed a new guardian.

And, oh boy, if he found out she was pregnant he'd

become ten times worse. Instead of being the proverbial thorn in her side that *could* be plucked out, he'd become something painful but permanent. Arthritis that sent white-hot jolts through her knees every time she stood up. Because Quinn would feel an obligation to be sure Dean's child was okay. And given his attitude toward her, he'd be positive she was incapable of being an adequate parent. Everything she did, he'd criticize, if only silently, with a lift of a dark eyebrow or condemnation in his eyes.

Mindy sank onto the edge of the bed.

She wasn't sure she wanted him to ever find out about the baby.

There. She'd thought it. Maybe that did make her selfish, because it was possible that a relationship with Dean's son or daughter would mean something to Quinn. He and Dean had been friends for a very long time.

But maybe…maybe later she could deal with him. Once she'd had the baby, and gotten her life together. Maybe then she'd call Quinn and say, "Hey. You want to meet Dean Jr.?"

And then, if he glanced around and said something like, "Shouldn't his crib be in *his* bedroom, not yours? He's got to learn to be independent," she would be able to stand up to him. Right now, that was really hard for her to do. She owed him too much.

So right now, she didn't want him to know she was pregnant. And that was a problem, because pretty soon he was going to notice. He wouldn't be able to *help* noticing.

Only, there was a way to make sure he didn't notice. That was not to let him see her.

Not to see Brendan Quinn—maybe never to see him again—would be an enormous relief.

CHAPTER FIVE

QUINN COULDN'T BELIEVE how fast the fight blew up.

He came over to mow the lawn only to find it had been done. He could tell whoever had done it had used a mulching mower, which was supposed to be good for the grass. He'd have raked anyway, but he supposed it looked okay.

Mindy answered the door in a sacky T-shirt and shorts, her legs long and tan. She must have seen him stop on the way up the walk, because she said, "I hired a lawn service. I shouldn't have let you do it as long as you did. I'm sorry."

So as he followed her in, he asked who she'd hired. After she told him, he merely asked whether she'd shopped around, and suddenly she was mad.

"You know, I'm not quite as stupid as you seem to think I am. I made it on my own for a lot of years before I met Dean."

Uh-huh. Two or three years, maybe.

"Did you ever have a lawn?" he asked.

Eyes glittering with anger way out of proportion to the argument, she snapped, "Gosh, did I miss something? Is shopping for the best price to have your lawn mowed any different than shopping for someone to replace your garbage disposal?"

"I just asked."

"No, you assumed!"

He swore. "As far as I could tell, Dean took care of you."

She stiffened. "So you felt obligated to continue the job? Isn't that a little above and beyond the call, Quinn? It's not like you signed on to the job like Dean did."

His grip on his temper slipped. "And I have to ask myself a dozen times a day whether he had the slightest goddamn idea what he was doing when he signed on."

"You know, somehow I could tell. You never gave me any slack, Quinn. Not even for Dean's sake."

He hadn't seen that knife coming before it slipped between his ribs. But he wouldn't let himself wonder if she was right, if he should have tried harder for Dean's sake. What did she know about the kind of friendship that saved two lost kids, that gave each the bedrock to build a life on? She didn't even have a friend close enough to call when her husband was murdered!

Quinn gave her a scathing look. Funny time to notice she'd painted her toenails again. Pale pink. Nothing vivid, but a sign of recovery.

"Maybe that's because I was too good a friend to shrug and say, 'Hey, guy. Learn from your mistakes. Divorce. Broken heart. What the hell. You'll get over it.'"

Voice crackling with anger, she said, "And you were so sure I was going to break his heart *because...*" Then she shook her head and made a disgusted sound. "You know what, Quinn? I don't care why you don't like me. Unlike you, for Dean's sake I tried to be friends. But I don't have to try anymore. I'm grateful for what you've done, even though I know it was done out of love for Dean, not out of any sympathy for me. But I can manage on my own now." She marched to the front door and held it open. "You're a free man, Quinn. Consider your obligation canceled. Go back to your life."

He laughed in disbelief. "With pleasure!" Three strides and he was out the front door into the warmth of the June day, the scent of newly mown grass filling his nostrils. Hearing the quiet sound of the door shutting behind him, he only wished this was it, that he'd never see her again.

But he knew better. Unfortunately for him, she'd be calling. She wasn't stupid, he didn't believe that, but her real-life skills were not what he'd call impressive. She'd get the paperwork for the sale of Fenton Security and not be able to make heads or tails out of it. Or her cute little BMW would break down some day, and who would she call? A scary sound in the night, and his phone would be ringing. Lucky him.

He was just grateful that she *would* have enough cushion of money to let her go back to school—or take some time to find another husband. If Fenton Security had been in trouble and even the house had had to be liquidated to pay debts… Getting into his car and slamming the door, he shook his head. Thank God for small favors.

Right now, he'd just enjoy a brief vacation, so to speak. He'd hope for a week before she got over her snit and realized she needed him more than she resented him.

A WEEK TURNED INTO TWO before Quinn knew it. High-profile murders tended to suck up time in a big way, and this week's was a doozy.

A hot young rock star was in town to play the Key Arena. In fact, he had played to a sold-out crowd at the Key Arena. Then he partied with his band members and some groupies before heading for his room at the waterfront Edgewater Hotel with a cute blonde tucked against his side.

Come two o'clock the next afternoon, the band members gathered in the lobby and the limo showed up to take them to the airport for their flight to Portland, where their next concert was scheduled. Only the rock star didn't appear, and he didn't answer the knock on his door. The concierge let one of the band members into the room, where he found their headliner dead on the king-size bed, a bullet through his temple.

What was meant to look like a suicide wasn't. Wrong angle for the path of the bullet, and wrong temple for a lefty. Murderers made stupid damn mistakes, lucky for the cops.

Turned out the rock star was married to *another* rock star with an ego bigger than his. She'd been heard to say, "If I ever catch him with his dick out for another woman, he's dead."

Turned out also that he had a restraining order on a

stalker, who happened—gee whiz—to be in Seattle. For entirely innocent reasons, of course.

The cute blonde who'd gone to his room with him had completely vanished. No one at the party knew her; they all thought she'd come with someone else.

The case had all the makings of a thriller. Within days, Quinn had a camera in his face every time he turned around. His photo was in *People* magazine the following week. Mindy Fenton was far from his mind.

Week two, the cute blonde's corpse floated in with the tide. At least, a young blond woman, whose body had been in the Sound the right length of time, bumped up against a moored sailboat and scared the crap out of the rich forty-year-old couple who had taken it out for a sail and were just tying up.

The stalker, also young and blond, admitted to stalking, but claimed that in the wee hours she'd seen a *second* woman knock and enter the hotel room. She insisted that she'd then returned to her own hotel and gone to bed. A night clerk confirmed he'd seen her cross the lobby and get in the elevator. Apparently even stalkers needed sleep.

The woman was undeniably crazy as well as grief-stricken. "I would never have hurt him!" she kept crying. "I love him." When she realized her verb was wrong, that the obsession of her life was now past tense, a sob escaped her. "He loved me, too! I know he did! He needed to get out of being married to *her*." Loathing was easy to read. "The other women was so he'd divorce her. And then we could be together."

The restraining order?

She made him get it.

Right.

But Quinn believed she hadn't hurt the love of her life. Her faith in their future was still too solid. Stalkers didn't kill until they were disillusioned and had to face the reality that the loved one would never be theirs.

Quinn flew to San Francisco, where the rock-star wife had supposedly been the night her husband had been murdered. Funny thing was, no one could confirm her whereabouts. In fact, a maid at her hotel swore no one had slept in the bed on the night in question.

Interestingly, the stalker had apparently bought *two* airline tickets to Seattle—one from Southwest Airlines on the same day the band had flown in to Seattle, and another on Alaska Airlines the day of the concert. That one had been bought at the counter just before the flight, too late for the purchaser to have checked baggage. The ticket seller remembered her because she'd cut it so close and because she looked vaguely familiar.

"I assumed I'd waited on her when she flew Alaska in the past."

When Quinn showed her a photo of the stalker, she shook her head decisively. "No. That wasn't her." Cute blonde dredged out of the water brought an equally certain, "No." When he produced a paparazzi photo of the wife trying to slip out to the grocery store or the gym without makeup, her hair back in a ponytail, she said, "Yes! Yes, that's her." Then her eyes widened. "Wait. Isn't that…"

He tucked the photo away. "I'm going to ask you to keep what you know to yourself for a few days."

"Oh!" Eyes still wide and glassy, she nodded and kept nodding. "I can do that. Sure. Wow."

Back in Seattle, Quinn and Ellis Carter flashed the wife's photo around some more and found a taxi driver willing to swear he'd picked her up at the airport—"Yo! That woman is a bitch!" he declared—and a desk clerk at the Alexis Hotel who had registered her for a room.

"I knew who she was," he said with composure. "We often have guests who choose to register under an alias to avoid the public eye. I thought nothing of it."

All suggestive enough to earn a search warrant, executed by San Francisco P.D. They called within a few hours.

"Here's a bizarre one," the San Francisco detective told Quinn. "Get this. We found a lock of blond hair in a little crystal candy dish with a lid. The hair had been dipped in blood. Dried now, but you could tell what it was. The lab's got it. If the DNA matches…"

If the blood had just been the rock star's, his wife might have dreamed up an excuse for treasuring the two-inch chunk of blood-soaked hair. They weren't exactly a normal couple with all-American habits. Unfortunately for her, some of the blood came from the blonde whose body had been fished from the Sound.

The arrest brought huge headlines and ensured that the faces of the dead musician and his wife dominated the covers of the tabloids. Quinn got damn tired of the endless requests for interviews and was grateful to have a couple of quiet days off.

His own lawn had gotten shaggy and the milk in his refrigerator was sour when he poured it on his cereal.

"Damn," he growled, and dumped the rest down the sink. The bread was growing mold, too. He cut it off and toasted a couple of pieces for breakfast. Grocery shopping needed to come ahead of mowing.

In the produce section at the store, he saw a pair of long legs that turned out to belong to a teenager with short tousled hair like Mindy's, but also a nose ring. Still, he stood in the checkout line wondering how she was doing. She hadn't left a phone message. Maybe she'd seen him on the news and realized he wouldn't have had time for her anyway. Or maybe she was more stubborn than he'd expected.

He wouldn't make her beg, but by God she was going to have to ask for help. All he was doing was honoring her declaration of independence, not holding a grudge. In that spirit, he sure as hell wasn't going to drive by as if by chance just to see what the house looked like, even though the thought crossed his mind as he turned out of the grocery store parking lot.

Another week passed, and then another, and he began to wonder if she would call. Dean's attorney phoned at last to let him know that probate was coming along.

"With the boat and the BMW sold as well as the business…"

Quinn interrupted. "She sold her car?"

"Mrs. Fenton is a levelheaded young woman," Armstrong said with apparent approval. "Without a substantial income of her own, she could see that continuing to make such steep payments doesn't make sense."

So the little bright blue car was gone. Quinn frowned, wondering what she'd chosen to drive instead.

"I was going to buy the Camaro," he said.

"Yes, in fact I have it here. That's really why I called. She's already signed the papers so we can transfer the title." He went on, but Quinn didn't listen.

She didn't want him at the house even to pick up the car. Maybe he was just dense not to have realized she disliked him so much.

Stupid to be shocked, but he was. He was also suddenly conscious of a hollow feeling under his breastbone. He shouldn't have had that Philly sandwich for lunch. The damn onions.

"Yeah. Okay. Sure," he said, only belatedly noticing that Armstrong was still talking. Into the silence that followed his interruption, Quinn said, "I'll, uh, pick up the car at your office. This afternoon? Good. Sure."

By the time he slid behind the wheel of the Camaro late that afternoon, anger had taken the place of the shock. Mindy might dislike him, but she sure hadn't hesitated to use him. Funny thing, but she hadn't told him to get lost until Dean's affairs were pretty well wrapped up and she knew she'd have enough money to get by.

Well, he'd done as much as he had for Dean's sake, not hers; she was right about that.

"I tried," he said aloud, figuring he was as close to

Dean here in the car he'd loved as he'd get anywhere.
When Quinn turned the key in the ignition, the engine
started with a throaty purr. Accelerating out of the parking lot in the candy-apple-red Camaro, he remembered
how much Dean had enjoyed the way heads turned
when he drove this car. Quinn did like the power, the
sense that he had only to ask and the car would surge
forward like a thoroughbred out of the gate at Emerald
Downs. The bright red, though, made him feel conspic-
uous. But the car would stay red. He wouldn't give
Mindy the satisfaction of finding out she was right.

His jaw flexed. No, damn it! The Camaro would stay
red because Dean had liked it that way. The car was a
memento, a reminder of Dean's boyish delight in expensive toys, starting with the mountain bike the Howies
had bought him that first Christmas in their home. He'd
grinned and cried at the same time.

"You mean, it's mine?" the gawky kid had asked in
wonder. "I can take it, even if my mom comes for me?"

Quinn had considered his matching bike a loaner.
The only gifts he'd ever had were from men sniffing
after his mother back before she got so strung out. Those
hadn't really been for him; even as a little kid, he'd
known that. Gifts came with strings attached. He'd
hated the knowledge he'd seen in his mother's eyes.

He hadn't known what the Howies thought he'd give
in return for that bike or the other Christmas and birthday gifts that followed, and they never had explicitly
asked for anything. Even so, he'd continued for his own
self-defense to think of everything they'd given him as

borrowed, like the bedroom and his place at the dinner table. When he'd graduated from high school and left the Howies', he hadn't taken much: a few clothes, the clunker of a car he'd bought with his meager income from bagging groceries, and that was about it.

Dean had thought he was an idiot. He reveled in owning nice stuff.

"I miss my mom," he'd confided once. "But she never had any money. Sometimes she bought me clothes at the thrift store, but mostly they came from school. You know how they have that room where you can pick out what you need?"

Quinn, to his eternal shame, had known. He'd been ashamed of taking clothes from the Howies, too, but that was a different kind of humiliation. At least now he didn't have to walk down the hall at school wondering if some other kid was going to recognize his discarded shirt.

"When Mom comes to get me, I won't mind being poor again," Dean had added hastily. "And the Howies said I could take everything."

His attitude was probably more natural than Quinn's. Having grown up without giant piles of presents under the Christmas tree, Dean had apparently saved up all that wanting. Quinn had always watched him indulgently, even when he'd become a man who could fulfill his own wishes. He hadn't been surprised when Dean had gone into business for himself so he could have more than a basic paycheck. Quinn was satisfied with a house and car, bought and paid for with his own money. Dean had seemed to have an empty place inside he never could fill. He'd developed cravings: for a bigger, fancier house, a flashy car, then a boat. His excitement had always been high when he first bought the new thing, whatever that was. But pretty soon, he'd start dreaming about something else.

Quinn had been surprised when he'd married Mindy. Dean had tended to follow the same pattern where women were concerned. He'd develop a huge crush, then court a woman with single-minded, romantic intensity. When she succumbed and became "his," he'd seem happy. For a while. Then his interest would start to wane. Next thing Quinn would know, Dean had the hots for someone else.

Mindy was the first and only one to last. Quinn hadn't understood why. He'd guessed that she had held out for marriage, but even then Dean's interest hadn't strayed. Maybe she'd filled that empty place in him. Maybe that hunger for something more, for someone who would never leave him, had been satisfied. Quinn hoped so.

He'd watched her, waiting for her to lose interest instead. As young and shallow as she was, he knew it had to happen.

Maybe, he thought now, he hadn't been fair to her. Maybe she really had loved Dean.

Now he guessed he'd never know for sure.

MINDY DIDN'T CALL.

Quinn went days without thinking about her. When he did, it was in passing, part of his mourning. Irritatingly often, when he remembered something about Dean, she was in the picture.

Funny thing was, he missed Dean more now than he had in the weeks after the funeral. Maybe the absence was just starting to seem real. But maybe the huge hole in his life hadn't been so apparent when he had something he could do for Dean. He's been so busy as executor, dealing with Fenton Security and taking care of Mindy he hadn't had time to miss talking to his best friend. He'd *wanted* to stay too busy to think about Dean's death. But now the hole gaped at his feet, as raw and shocking as if a building he passed every day had been blasted from its foundations. Some days he could walk by and avert his face. Other times…hell, other times, he couldn't look at anything but.

He could focus at work. There, nothing had changed; he didn't have to pass the damn hole. But the minute he walked out to his car, he was faced with a life that felt empty even when he managed to occupy himself.

His track record with women wasn't any better than Dean's had been before he'd met Mindy. Before Dean's murder, Quinn had been seeing a redheaded dispatcher with a great laugh.

By the time he remembered to call her weeks after the funeral, she said, "Quinn? Yeah, seems like I used to know a guy named Quinn. Bart? Ben? Brian?"

"Funny."

"I was sorry to hear about Dean."

"Yeah. Thanks."

"I left a couple of messages."

He rubbed his neck. "I should have called you."

"Yeah, you should have," she said frankly. "See, I had this illusion that we were friends. But maybe I should be glad that you kind of set me straight."

Crap. "It wasn't you. I've just…been having a hard time dealing."

"Uh-huh," she said without sympathy. "Quinn, it's been five weeks. I'm dating someone else now. And here's the weirdest thing—his kid just got diagnosed with leukemia, and you know what? I was one of the first people he called."

She didn't slam the phone down. She set it down gently, which gave greater punch to her message.

Quinn hadn't asked a woman out since. He supposed he should give some thought to dating again, but nobody had crossed his path recently who interested him. Going out looking seemed like too much effort.

He realized he hadn't called the Howies in a long time, put it off for another day, then phoned them in the evening.

George answered.

He sounded surprised. "No more bad news, I hope."

"No. Just…trying to stay in better touch," Quinn said awkwardly.

"You mean, checking up on us now."

"You've been taking care of yourself for a long time." Quinn prowled his living room. "But since I don't have Dean to keep me updated on how you two are doing…" His throat closed.

"You're missing him."

"Yeah." He swallowed. "Yeah, I am."

"We do, too." George Howie's voice sounded thick. "Dean was a nice boy who turned into a good man."

Quinn nodded but couldn't seem to speak.

"We were proud of both of you. Dean was the easy one. You were always more complicated."

"I've been remembering," he admitted. "Dean loved getting presents. That first Christmas…"

George laughed. "If Schwinn could have filmed him, they'd have had the ad of the century. Boy lit up like the Fourth of July sky." He was silent for a moment. "Now, you… I could see your struggle. You wanted that bike real bad, but you didn't like taking anything from anybody. Or maybe you just didn't like feeling hungry for something. I was never sure."

They'd known him better than he'd ever guessed.

"A little of both," Quinn admitted. "I told myself the bike was just a loaner. I was already taking food from you, so why not wheels?"

"You know, we still have things you left packed away in the attic. Couldn't get rid of them. You ever want your football or skateboard, you just let us know."

"You really still have them?" he asked, incredulous.

"Sure." George sounded reproving. "Your kid leaves home at eighteen, you don't strip the house of everything that was his. He might need to come home."

Your kid. Had they really thought of him that way? He rubbed his breastbone, conscious of that ache beneath it.

"Have you talked to Mindy?"

"She's called a few times." George paused. "She hasn't wanted to say how she stands financially."

"Dean had one hell of a lot of debts," Quinn said bluntly. "Now that she's sold the business, she's also had to sell the boat and the cars to cut down on payments. I bought Dean's Camaro."

"She did mention that." He grunted. "I'm not surprised that Dean got in over his head."

"I didn't say that." Long habit had Quinn defending his friend. "He was managing the payments fine. He didn't plan to die."

"In other words, no life insurance."

"Unfortunately, no. You know, until this last year, he didn't have anybody to worry about. No reason for it."

"Too bad he didn't buy some when he got married."

"She's okay, George. Just not as well off as she'd probably imagined she'd be."

Acid must have crept into his tone, because his foster father said, "You don't like her."

Denial came as instinctively. "She's nice enough." He rubbed his forehead. "We've never gotten to be close. I didn't think she'd last."

"Didn't want her to last?" George asked quietly.

The implication was there: He'd been jealous. God. *Had* he been?

"I didn't think she was right for Dean," Quinn said. "If she has any depths, I never found them."

"Except for some grief over his mother, I'm not sure Dean went deep, either," George suggested. "He didn't spring surprises on you with time."

Quinn wanted to deny that analysis, too, but found his protest died in his throat. Maybe that description wasn't even an insult. Dean was a nice guy. Smart, but not a thinker. Not someone who brooded. He pretty much closed the book on each day, looked forward to the next. He'd never been much of a reader and had been an adequate student but no valedictorian. He wasn't interested in going to college, while Quinn would have liked to go but hadn't wanted to owe anyone another nickel.

Only Dean knew that Quinn had spent the past ten years working his way toward a B.A. He'd started at Central Community College on Capitol Hill, just a class a quarter. Just a year ago, he'd finished his bachelor's degree in history at the University of Washington. Didn't mean a thing to anybody but him, but he was glad he'd done it.

Long after he'd hung up the phone, he thought about whether George was right about Dean. As far as Quinn was concerned, their friendship *had* gone deep. Their very ease together came from what they'd shared, what they knew about each other, what they had in common that separated them from people who took family for granted. But they tended to talk about the job, about cases, about Fenton Security, about women or sports or occasionally politics. They played golf, shot hoops, shared a six-pack during a Seahawks game on the boob tube. Quinn couldn't remember the last time they'd had a discussion he might not have had with anyone else he knew.

Dean, he thought, had kept that childish pleasure in

the moment. It was something Quinn had always envied. He'd been robbed of that pleasure before he'd started eating solid foods. He didn't remember ever letting himself totally relax and trust that something good would last.

All roads led to Rome, and he found himself thinking about Mindy again, too. Maybe he hadn't so much misjudged her as misjudged Dean, and what Dean wanted and needed in a woman. Quinn had assumed because she wouldn't fascinate him forever that she wouldn't keep Dean enthralled, either, and maybe that just wasn't true.

His reflections roiled inside him like a meal that didn't settle. He was left wondering if he'd known Dean as well as he thought he did, or whether he'd pretended there was more to Dean than showed on the surface because if there wasn't, he might have had to admit he'd sometimes been bored sipping beer on the boat or in front of the TV, talking about the same things they'd talked about the week before and the one before that.

Maybe what he'd been uncomfortable with about Mindy was that she *was* too much like Dean in her interests and fun-loving personality. Quinn's head ached by the time he admitted to himself that he'd wanted her to be more because he'd wanted Dean to be more.

And maybe he was overanalyzing. Because, damn it, Dean was his brother in all but blood, and he still missed him in a way he'd never missed anybody, even his mother. He might get so he didn't very often notice that yawning pit where the building had once stood, but it would always be there if he turned the wrong corner or let himself remember.

He wasn't a man to rebuild, even if that were possible.

CHAPTER SIX

MINDY WALKED THROUGH the house one last time, even
though doing so was like worrying an aching tooth with
her tongue. Except for small mementos, everything was
gone—the furniture, the artwork that had hung on the
wall, even the power tools and the lawn mower. What
little she'd kept was packed into boxes that filled the
aging Saab she'd bought to replace the BMW. Her
woodworking tools, of course; they took up most of the
trunk. A few pans, dishes, utensils, the toaster and
blender, blankets and two sets of sheets, a couple of
photo albums, her clothes and little else.

Even Dean's clothes she'd donated to the Volunteers
of America. She'd once asked Quinn if he wanted any
of them, and he'd shuddered. They weren't really the
same size, anyway. Dean had been a couple of inches
taller, rangier, while Quinn was more…solid. Dean's
shirts would be too long in the sleeves for Quinn, too
small around the neck. Besides, Dean loved bright colors. He almost always wore red or school-bus yellow or
purple or even pink. Gaudy Hawaiian shirts were his favorite. He'd had Hawaiian-print shorts, too, and some-

times wore clashing prints on top and bottom. No, she couldn't see Quinn in any of them.

That had been the worst part—packing up Dean's clothes, remembering a day when he'd been wearing this jacket, the sight of him grinning at her from behind the wheel of the Camaro wearing *that* shirt. Their first date, their first kiss, his proposal, she could track in his wardrobe.

At first, she set aside some garments to keep. But the pile grew, and finally she chose not to keep any. Tears had dripped onto the cardboard as she'd taped shut the boxes.

Her back ached and she gently rubbed her belly as she walked through the kitchen and paused at the French doors looking out on the patio. The baby somersaulted in an unusual display of daytime acrobatics. Usually he or she rested quietly during the day. Bedtime was playtime. But perhaps her distress had flowed with her bloodstream into her unborn baby, agitating him. Her, she amended, as always reminding herself. Which would Dean have preferred? A boy or a girl? Or would he have cared at all?

Her eyes were wet again when she turned away from the patio and the roses that now, in August, were looking parched.

She laid her house keys on the kitchen counter beside the appliance manuals she'd found neatly filed away and had set out for the new owners. Then, almost steadily, she walked straight out, locking the front door behind her.

Even the act of walking down the driveway and getting into her car was different than it used to be. Already, at five and a half months pregnant, she felt unbalanced by her protruding belly. Awkward.

Dean would have thought she was beautiful. She blinked away the moisture in her eyes and gave an unladylike snuffle. She fumbled for a tissue and blew her nose and mopped her cheeks. She wasn't beautiful at her best, and she sure as heck wasn't anything approaching it right now. Her face looked puffy and any semblance of a waist had disappeared. Her belly button had popped out! Just that morning she'd taken out the tiny gold ring she wore in it. Why a belly-button ring still looked cute on Kate Hudson when she was pregnant but not on her, Mindy couldn't guess. But it didn't. She'd wondered if she would ever put it back in. Did mothers wear belly-button rings?

"Okay," she told herself. "Time to go." She turned the semi-functional air-conditioning up, because she was already sweating, and backed out of the driveway.

She had rented an apartment on Beacon Hill a few blocks above Rainier. It wasn't the best part of Seattle, but the small houses in the neighborhood looked cared for, and rents were cheaper than around the university or in West Seattle or any other part of the city she'd lived before. And she wanted to save as much money as she could. She'd have to draw on what she had to get started—even for the small basement apartment she was moving into, she'd had to write a hefty check for first and last months' rent. She didn't know if she'd earn enough from the job she'd found as a barista to pay for rent and utilities and food. She hoped she would, because she didn't have health insurance and would be facing doctor and hospital bills for the birth. Plus, she wanted desperately to take two or three months off work after her baby was born. Just to get to know her.

That was as far as Mindy's plans had gone. Paying child care out of minimum wage was going to be impossible. So she'd have to keep drawing on the money Dean had left. Someday there would be ballet lessons or Little League sign-ups and a bike would have to be under the tree some Christmas morning. And college. She gave a small laugh. Already she was worrying about tuition!

She hoped that somehow she could go back to woodworking once the baby was born. Right before she got pregnant, she'd had what she thought was a good idea… But then she didn't have the energy, and now she'd decided that she shouldn't be inhaling either sawdust or paint and polyurethane fumes. And even if her idea *was* good, she wouldn't be able to make any kind of living, not at first. Since she'd rather live in a mission than beg for help from her mother, she had to take a job.

She'd decided that, after the baby was born, she would have to tell Quinn. Maybe she'd softened a little, after a peaceful two months without him. As annoying as he was, he *had* loved Dean. The two men had considered themselves brothers. Maybe playing godfather or uncle or whatever would give him comfort.

She left West Seattle, crossed I-5 on Columbia Way and circled the steep side of Beacon Hill. After almost two months of drought, the neighborhood looked more run-down than she'd last seen it, the small yard of the house where she was to live brown and weedy. Half-hysterically, she wondered what Quinn would think of this lawn, left to wander into abandoned flower beds and tangle with the trunks of lilacs and leafless trees before, unwatered, it had died.

Her landlords, an older Hispanic couple, didn't seem to be home. She wished they were. A cheerful greeting might have made the tiny basement apartment more welcoming. She backed as close to the cement steps as she could get, then went down and unlocked.

Even now, in August, sunlight barely came through the narrow high windows. Most were painted shut, so she couldn't open them to let in fresh air. With the shrubbery overgrown, pressing against the windows, the basement felt claustrophobic. It also had a distinctly musty smell despite the hot, dry weather.

This apartment was cheap, she reminded herself, and felt safe, with the nice landlords up above. There was room in the driveway for her car, so she wouldn't have to hunt for a spot every day, and Mrs. Sanchez had even hinted that she might be interested in babysitting when the time came.

Mindy carried in a fan and plugged it in before she went back out to her car to begin unloading. The sooner she'd made up the bed and had her own towels in the bathroom, the sooner she'd feel at home.

A bleak thought crept in. Really, what choice did she have?

TWO MONTHS LATER, she was coping. Barely.

This was one of the moments that fell in the "barely" category. It was eleven-thirty at night, she was alone closing the business, her back ached, her head swam, and she wanted to cry.

Damn. She was forty-five cents off. Mindy stared down at the rolls of nickels and dimes and quarters. She should count them again.

If only she wasn't so tired! Nobody had ever told her that pregnancy was exhausting. Maybe it wouldn't be if… She put a brake on her wistful thought. If Dean hadn't been killed. If she weren't working forty-hour weeks and sometimes more, mostly on her feet. If she were pampered and loved and able to be lazy.

Mindy squared her shoulders. Well, she wasn't, and she couldn't be. *Don't even think about it,* she ordered herself. She'd made it this far. She was seven and a half months along now. With a flutter of anxiety, she turned the timetable around: she had only six weeks to go.

Tonight, she was too weary to count the wretched change again. Without hesitation, she scooped a quarter, a nickel and a dime out of the cup that held her tips for the evening and added them to the take that she was bagging to put in the safe.

She didn't really like closing. Although she'd locked

the front door at eleven, she kept stealing uneasy glances at the glass door and front windows. A group of young men had been hanging out on the sidewalk for the past hour, rap music from a boom box seeming to thud through the floorboards into her bones. Occasionally they laughed or shouted or a car would pull up to the curb so that friends could exchange a few words.

She wasn't exactly afraid of this particular crowd; they were often around, and had never paid her much attention. As pregnant as she was now, she didn't even merit a flirtation. She was more nervous about going out the back door to the alley, where she'd parked her car. There, sometimes shadows moved behind a Dumpster or she'd hear a murmur of voices. She always stuck her head out the door like a turtle peering out of its shell, checked to be sure that she was alone, then slammed the metal door and rushed to her car with her key already in her hand. She'd timed herself; she could make it in twenty seconds. But maybe she should start parking in front instead, even if it was a block or two away.

Every day she debated, and every day she ended up parking in back. She didn't like the idea of going out the front, obviously locking up, then having to walk two blocks so late at night.

This evening's tips were meager. She counted: $24.75. Three dollars an hour, on top of her minimum wage. She'd done lots better than that when she'd started two months ago. She guessed she'd been prettier then, maybe more animated and likely to chat and tease and laugh. Now she was too tired to do more than prepare a double mocha latte and say, "Six-fifty, please." And then, to the next customer, "What can I get you?"

Tonight, she'd just closed the back door and checked to be sure it was locked when she heard a clang and then a shout so close by, her heart bounded and she ran to her car. Her hand was shaking, and it took her extra seconds to get the key in the lock. She fell in and hit the lock, her heart drumming and her vision blurred. She started the car, turned on the headlights and rocketed forward without even fastening her seat belt.

She didn't see a soul in the alley. Somebody had probably been yelling at a dog beyond the fence. She sometimes heard a deep, snarling bark there.

Somehow she drove safely the half mile to her apartment. There, she parked, went in, and sank down on the couch as if her legs couldn't hold her for another second.

Her ankles were so swollen, she saw in dismay. She was due to see the doctor this week. She'd have to ask about the swelling. She'd gained an awful lot of weight this month, too, if the scale in the bathroom was anywhere close to accurate. And she didn't eat that much! She didn't. She'd already given up drinking soda at all, since she'd read that could make your ankles swell. She didn't have anything with caffeine, and she tried to eat lots of fruits and vegetables and whole grains and all the things she'd never thought about before. All she wanted was for her baby to be healthy.

Thank goodness she had tomorrow and Monday off. Then she had her doctor appointment Tuesday morning before she went to work at two-thirty. She'd feel more rested by then.

Usually Mindy did her housecleaning on Sunday afternoon. This Sunday, she had breakfast, read the newspaper that she shared with the Sanchezes, then felt so tired she went back to bed for a nap. A knock on her door woke her.

Her dazed eyes found the clock. Oh, no! It was almost three. She'd wasted the day. Thank goodness she'd gotten dressed this morning, at least. She heaved herself off the bed, finger-combed her hair and went to see who was knocking.

On the doorstep was her mother, wearing a sweater that had to be cashmere with a deep V-neck that showed cleavage. She gave an exaggerated shiver. "Aren't you going to let me in?"

"Yes, I…" Mindy gave her head a shake. "Of course. But…what on earth are you doing here?"

"Visiting, what else?" Passing her, Cheri Walker peeked into the tiny kitchen and wrinkled her nose. "This place is nasty! How can you bear it?"

Feeling huge and sullen, Mindy gestured at the couch. "Would you like to sit down?"

Her mother studied it as if a cockroach might be lurking in the crack between the cushions. Finally, she perched on the very edge, without leaning back.

Mindy flopped into the easy chair.

"You hardly return my phone calls," her mother said. Knowing she sounded sulky, Mindy couldn't help herself. "I most often work nights. And you're at work in the mornings when I'm free."

"You must have days off," her mother pointed out, unanswerably. When Mindy didn't respond, she swept her with a gaze. "Honey, you look awful."

Mindy gritted her teeth. "Gee, thanks."

"You shouldn't be working."

"I can't afford not to be." Her mother didn't want to hear unpalatable reality. "Dean's money won't go that far. I know I'll need to take time off after the baby is born."

"You're planning to bring a baby to live *here?*" Cheri Walker made it sound as if the apartment was a cell at the state penitentiary.

"I can't afford…"

"Oh, for gracious sakes!" Her mother stood. "You're just being a martyr! What do you want me to say? You can come home to live with me?"

Mindy would rather stand at a freeway exit with a sign begging for money than go live with her mother.

"I know you're far too busy to want me home again." Oh, how civil she could be! "Are you seeing anyone right now, Mom?"

A smug smile curved her mother's mouth. "Yes, and he's such a doll! Mark is manager at QFC…"

Or maybe it was Safeway. Or Albertsons. Mindy quit listening. Her mother always had some fabulous man around. The strange men wandering into the kitchen first thing in the morning had been one of the reasons Mindy had left home the day after she'd graduated from high school.

Her mother was nearly fifty, but she had kept a slim figure. Although she hadn't admitted to a face-lift, Mindy suspected she'd gotten one a couple of years ago. Now, no more than the tiniest lines beside her eyes hinted that she was over thirty-five. Her golden hair had more life and shine than her pregnant daughter's, and she had a delighted, warm smile that gave men two left feet and a sudden desire to treasure her for all eternity.

Of course, her relationships all petered out. Mindy thought that usually her mother was the one to lose interest. She'd never figured out why her mother had married her father, or stayed with him for fifteen years until his shocking death of a heart attack when he was barely over forty. If she'd been deeply in love with him, she wouldn't have had a new man in his bed within weeks.

Mindy tuned in to hear, "Now, if he were as good-looking as that friend of Dean's…"

She did *not* want to hear what a hottie Quinn was. "Would you like a cup of coffee?" Mindy interrupted.

Her mother glanced toward the kitchen. Her nostrils quivered. "Thank you, but no. I don't dare stay that long."

Or imbibe anything that came out of that kitchen, apparently.

"I should have spent today housecleaning," Mindy admitted. "But I'm so tired. When you were pregnant, were you…"

Her mother made a moue. "Pregnancy is horrible. Why do you think you don't have a younger brother or sister?"

Maybe because you discovered you hated being a mother?

"Of course I was tired! I made your father get me housecleaning help."

Not an option for Mindy.

"You are seeing the doctor?" her mother asked.

"Yes, of course. I'm not stupid." Even to Mindy, that sounded childish. She sighed. "Actually, I have an appointment Tuesday."

"Oh, good." Her mother surveyed her once again. "Because you really do look…"

She rolled her eyes. "Like hell. I know."

"I wasn't going to say that. It's just…" Tiny lines furrowed her brow. Genuine concern—could it be?—battling Botox. "You're too pale. And puffy. I'd hoped to see you blooming."

"I'm sure I'm fine." Did anybody *bloom* at seven and a half months pregnant? "It's been a long week, and I just got up from a nap."

Her mother glanced at her watch and stood. "Oh, dear! I didn't mean to stay so long. I just wanted to see where you're living, since you've been so evasive."

"I haven't been evasive." Mindy began levering herself forward so that she could rise, too.

"Oh, you just haven't invited me over?" The tiny snap in her voice silenced Mindy. She gave one last, disdainful glance around. "Spend his money, Mindy. Don't keep feeling as if you have to keep it in some sort of trust for the baby. You're entitled."

She swept out, leaving Mindy still struggling to stand.

At the sound of the door closing, Mindy gave up the battle and sank back into the chair.

Entitled! Her mother made marriage sound like legal prostitution! She'd given him sex, and therefore now had the right to run through his money as fast as she could? Mindy fumed.

And people wondered why she wasn't closer to her mother! Mindy had seen it in Quinn's eyes. He just couldn't imagine why she hadn't wanted to call her mother to come comfort her.

Gee, could it be because after her own husband had died, Cheri Walker had been so busy screwing other men she hadn't noticed how her fourteen-year-old daughter grieved?

Mindy had never forgiven her mother, and she never intended to. Her father had loved her mother, and she'd apparently been desperate to be single and giddy again. If she'd just waited a few months…!

Mindy squeezed her eyes shut and took a deep breath, trying to will away the familiar resentment. She couldn't change the past, and fortunately she didn't need to depend on her mother.

She just wished…oh, that she had someone who would go with her to the doctor on Tuesday, someone to give her back rubs and make her cups of herbal tea and maybe pamper her just a little bit. Someone she *could* depend on.

QUINN HAD GIVEN UP the battle one day in late September and driven by the house. Not in the Camaro, of course; he'd have jumped from the observation deck on the Space Needle before he took a chance of Mindy seeing him hovering.

He felt like an idiot. What would a quick glance at the house tell him? But he told himself he still owed it to Dean to keep an eye on her. He wasn't absolved of responsibility just because she'd become petulant.

He'd barely turned the corner when he saw the real-estate sign planted out front. Then he spotted the Sold sign.

Despite himself, his foot lifted from the gas. She'd sold the house already? Then, stunned, he saw the bike lying on the lawn and the shiny green Toyota SUV parked in the driveway. A planter, filled with rust and orange mums, had been added to the front porch.

His car eased to the curb as his gaze searched for other changes and found them.

The front blinds had been replaced by drapes. Wind chimes hung from a corner of the front porch. Through an upstairs bedroom window he could see that posters covered the wall.

Mindy had not only sold the house, she'd already moved. She was gone. He didn't even know why he was blindsided, but he was. Clearly, her intention was to walk away and never look back.

He shouldn't have even minded, but he did. Dean had connected them in a way Quinn had considered indelible. It would appear she didn't feel the same.

Familiar anger curled in his stomach. Hell, why should she? She hadn't known Dean that long. Easy come, easy go. She'd made a nice profit on an eighteen-month commitment. She'd enjoy it more without any anchors to drag her down.

He drove away with barely a glance back himself.

Once he got over being pissed, he made a halfhearted effort to find out where she'd gone. Not because he was going to contact her, just to be easy in his own mind. But her name, married or maiden, didn't pop up anywhere. No telephone, which wasn't uncommon these days. She was probably using a cell phone. She hadn't changed her address with the DMV.

Pride kept him from checking with the lawyer or her mother. Chances were, neither knew where she was anyway. Once the will had been filed and the money was hers, why would she have kept Armstrong informed? And she and her mother didn't have a real warm, fuzzy relationship. Besides…the choice was hers, he admitted. She knew how to find him.

That night and plenty of other nights, he escaped churning emotions he didn't want to identify in his usual way—by going to the gym. A police-department basketball league had started up, and he joined that. But all too many evenings, he went home, tried to read or watch TV and finally, swearing, grabbed his gym bag yet again and went out the door. Loneliness, grief, anger, regret, could all be sweated out like toxins. He lifted weights, hammered down three pointers, swam laps, or ran miles on a treadmill until he was too exhausted to mourn or feel sorry for himself.

He despised self-pity, and hardly recognized it when it first crept up on him. He'd be shaving in the morning and stop and stare at himself, and he'd think, *There's not a single person in the world who gives a good goddamn about me.* The idiotic thing was, he knew it wasn't true; he had friends. Not as close as Dean, but friends.

Then he found himself dreading going home. He'd tell Carter to cut loose, then he'd sit back down to do paperwork in the past he'd have put off. If anybody suggested stopping by the tavern, he'd go along even though he wasn't much of a drinker. He'd watch Seahawks games there on the big screen instead of at home, which he'd once have preferred. Anything but solitude and the inescapable realization that he was living a lonely, loveless life.

The one thing he didn't do was ask any women out. He just couldn't seem to summon any interest. Given his bleak mood, the idea of having sex with a woman he didn't give a damn about seemed lonelier than jacking off alone under the beat of water in his shower would be.

In mid-October, he took the ferry across the Sound to Bremerton to have lunch with the Howies. He hadn't been back in three or four years, and then it had felt like a duty. Beyond a few observations about changes in the neighborhood—new houses, a widened street and sidewalks where they hadn't been before—he hadn't connected himself with the house or felt any sense of homecoming.

This time, he did. He drove the Camaro to please them or himself, he wasn't sure. After driving off the ferry, he had this sense that it knew the way, like a horse heading for the barn. Every turn was familiar, and felt ingrained in a way the drive home to his existing house never would. And every landscape reminded him of escapades and girls and trouble he and Dean had wriggled out of. He was smiling by the time he pulled up in front of the small house on the quiet street above an inlet of the Sound.

The Howies had bought this house back in the early fifties; nowadays, they wouldn't have been able to afford it. All the houses on the street had been modest, although several, he saw, had recently undergone dramatic remodeling with additions that looked out of place. Given the setting and the value of these lots now, every house on this street would be razed or remodeled within a few years.

Nancy and George both came out to meet him. George walked around the Camaro, stroking its gleaming flanks, pretending to admire the car when Quinn could see that his eyes were damp.

"Dean was so proud of that car when he bought it!" Nancy's smile was a little tremulous. "But come in, Brendan! Oh, it's so good to see you here. Are you sure you can't stay?"

He hadn't been ready to do that, to sleep in his boyhood room and think back to who he'd been. "I work tomorrow. But I wanted to see how you two are doing." He paused on the doorstep. "It's been a while."

"Too long," she said, quietly.

They hadn't changed a thing inside. Maybe that's why he *didn't* come. It was like time traveling. Except for finding Dean, there wasn't much about his youth that he wanted to remember. Here, remembering was unavoidable.

The living room was a little dim, the oak floors mostly covered with dark Oriental rugs. The furniture was mahogany or upholstered in deep forest green, the paintings on the wall landscapes in oils. As a teenager, he'd felt…stifled in this room. Now, for the first time, he realized it was restful.

But then, he'd felt stifled by the Howies and this house from the minute the social worker had dropped him off. They'd been old to have young teenage boys in the house, and maybe had been old-fashioned even for their age. The jump from squalor and terrified self-sufficiency to a Norman Rockwell perfect slice of Americana had been too jarring for Quinn. The movie *The Truman Show* had jolted him. Living here had felt like that to him, as if this house and neighborhood and the kind older couple who'd taken him in were unreal. Scripted.

He'd reacted like the Jim Carrey character, poking and prodding and trying to find the rip in the fabric. When he could, he'd escaped.

Even though police work wasn't the best way to see how normal people lived, he'd gotten an idea since that the Howies weren't that abnormal. They were just nice people who'd held middle-of-the-road jobs and were content with themselves, with unchanging traditions, even with an annual vacation to the same resort on the Oregon coast, taken the same two weeks every summer.

Then, he'd have said they were oblivious to anything

but the surface he let them see. Now, he noticed a sharpness in George's fading blue eyes that had probably always been there, a perception in Nancy's memories of him and Dean.

In the middle of lunch, he said, "You always knew how uncomfortable I felt here, didn't you?"

Their smiles were sad. "We kept hoping," Nancy said. "But you never let yourself trust us."

George nodded. "But you did trust Dean. That let us have confidence that you still could care about someone and even have faith in them."

"But you've never married," Nancy added.

Quinn picked up his fork again. "Would you believe I just haven't met the right woman?"

His foster mother patted his hand. "If Dean did, you can. Keep looking, Brendan."

She'd made his favorite casserole and, to follow it up, blueberry pie, which he'd loved. Eating here with them, at the maple table set in the dining alcove with small-paned windows that looked out on the rocky inlet, the wooded backyards that ran down to it and the docks and small boats—he and Dean had had a twelve-foot skiff with a small, noisy outboard motor—he kept having to shake off disorientation.

Deliberately, he dragged his gaze from the inlet and settled it purposefully on Nancy's hand, shaking as she reached to pick up her coffee cup. Seeing his expression, she withdrew her hand quickly.

"Parkinson's?" he asked.

Her face set in stubborn lines. After a moment she

surrendered enough to nod. "But I'm fine. Just fine. They've got me on all kinds of medications. You should see me lining up my pills at night to be sure I don't forget one of them!"

He'd have been proud and unwilling to admit vulnerability, too, so he only nodded. "You'll let me know if there's anything I can do for you?"

She gave a watery smile. "Thank you, Brendan. You were always a good boy. It's nice to have you home."

He asked casually whether they'd stayed in touch with Mindy.

"She's called several times, but not since she moved." Nancy's wrinkles deepened. "She said she'd let us know when she was settled, but we haven't heard from her. I do hope she's all right."

Annoyed afresh that she had worried these nice old people, he didn't like realizing that a thread of tension underlay his dark mood these last months. Yeah, damn it, he was worried, too. Couldn't she just drop them all a note that said, "Hey, went to Hollywood to make it as an actress, having fun spending Dean's money."

But he didn't let her presence hover. She didn't belong here, wasn't part of this homecoming. He went down to the bedroom in the basement that he and Dean had shared, and felt a pang when he saw it unchanged, too. He and George walked down the wooden steps to the dock and sat there talking about nothing much.

George climbed the steps slowly, with a few pauses and apologies for being an old man. Quinn felt like a shit for not being here to see them age, and for not realizing sooner that they were already getting so they needed help.

He accepted when they invited him to Thanksgiving and was already thinking ahead to Christmas, something he hadn't done since he'd lived here and felt some of the same anticipation other kids did, even if he would have let someone yank his fingernails out before he would have admitted it.

When he drove away, Quinn was glad that he'd come. Maybe, after all, his roots weren't so tangled with Dean's that they'd died this summer, too.

CHAPTER SEVEN

"WAIT." MINDY SHOOK her head. Hard. "What did you say?"

The doctor, a woman in her forties with a kind face and a brisk manner, repeated, "I'm prescribing bed rest. I don't think it's necessary to hospitalize you, but…"

Panic swelled in Mindy's chest. "I don't have health insurance."

"I know. And I truly think we can keep you and the baby healthy without a lengthy hospital stay. *If*—" she held up a hand "—and this is a big *if*, you follow my instructions."

"What," Mindy asked carefully, "do you mean by bed rest?"

"You won't have to stay in bed twenty-four hours a day, but I want you there most of the time." Dr. Gibbs talked about Mindy resting on her left side to prevent compression of a major blood vessel and therefore improving blood flow, about a medication that would lower her blood pressure, about eliminating as much salt from her diet as she could.

Mindy felt as if she were underwater, seeing someone above the surface moving her mouth, but unable to hear the words. When the doctor's mouth quit moving, Mindy said, "I don't understand. I've never had high blood pressure. I'm young!"

"I'm afraid we don't really know the causes of pre-eclampsia. There may be genetic influences, or there could be a nutritional or hormonal connection. It is most common in a first pregnancy or in a woman who has had multiple pregnancies."

"You're sure?"

Her smile was gentle. "Yes. You've noticed some of the symptoms yourself. You've put on weight suddenly, your ankles are swelling, you've been conscious a few times of your vision blurring. What I'm seeing is protein in your urine and blood pressure higher than I like. Your blood pressure should return to normal after delivery. If the baby was more mature, I'd consider inducing labor, but I really think we need to wait a few weeks at least. Now," her tone became bracing, "I'm referring you for an ultrasound. Here—" she ripped a sheet off a tablet "—is the prescription, which I'd like you to fill immediately."

Mindy was still struggling to understand things the doctor had said five minutes ago. "This means I can't work."

Dr. Gibbs's voice softened. "I'm afraid not. And, while you can certainly get up to go to the bathroom or shower, you shouldn't be grocery shopping or doing housework. You're going to need someone to help you. Do you have family?"

Whatever she said—something about her mother,

Mindy thought—seemed to satisfy the doctor, because she was ushered out and found herself standing in the parking lot looking around as if she had no idea what her car looked like.

She had to go home. No. She had to fill the prescription first. The women's clinic didn't have a pharmacy.

Mindy looked down at the keys in her hand, wondered how they'd gotten there, then wandered down the row of cars until she saw a bumper sticker that had been affixed to her Saab when she'd bought it. Peas on Earth, it said, and showed a small Earth covered with green peas. The bumper sticker had sold her on the car.

She got in, started it, backed out and then turned onto Rainier as if she knew what she was doing. The grocery store, she decided, with that still logical, collected part of her mind. She could fill the prescription and load up on groceries both. While she could.

Beneath, hysteria welled. She was in a tiny, windowless room, trapped. She searched for a door, but the walls were seamless.

No way out.

Bed rest. How could she just lie in bed for weeks? Her apartment was dank, with mold appearing in corners of the bathroom and in the shower if she didn't scrub almost daily. She had to houseclean! And grocery shop.

And if she quit her job now, so suddenly, Bud wouldn't hire her back after the baby was born. The medical costs were already going to be high. If she had to be hospitalized… And even if she didn't, she had to eat and pay rent and utilities—she'd go insane without cable TV.

She pulled into a slot in front of the grocery store,

put the gear shift into park, set the emergency brake and felt a sob shake her.

"Oh, God," she whispered. What would she *do?*

Prescription. Groceries. *Stick to the plan,* Mindy told herself. She could cry when she got home.

Somehow she managed to smile at the pharmacy technician, then push her cart through the store loading up on double, triple the amounts of everything she usually bought. Halfway through her shopping, she stopped. Salt. Dr. Gibbs had said she had to cut her salt intake. Dismayed, Mindy looked at the pile in her cart.

Discarding most of the ready-made food took longer than picking it out had. It also scared her even more. If she wasn't supposed to cook, but most of the ready-made stuff was high in sodium, what was she supposed to do?

The doctor had said she would need to have someone to help her. Panic flapped great wings in Mindy's chest again. She squeezed her eyes shut. No. Finish shopping. She couldn't break down until she got home.

By the time she carried the groceries down the concrete steps into her basement apartment, her panic had shifted focus. Dr. Gibbs had sounded confident that the baby was fine, but maybe she wasn't really. She wouldn't have ordered an ultrasound unless she had doubts, would she?

Mindy put away the groceries, then lay down on her bed, on her left side. And cried.

"Wow, I'm sorry," Selene said. "If Carrie hadn't already moved in, I'd tell her you needed the room, but I can't kick her out. She's already paid the rent for this month and everything."

"Of course you can't." Mindy held the phone to her right ear and stared at the cement block wall. In the living room, it had been drywalled. Here in the bedroom, it was just painted. If she touched it, she would feel the cold and moisture. "I just remembered Deb was moving out, and I thought if you hadn't found a new roommate—" She stopped. "Really. That's okay."

"But…what will you *do?*"

"I don't know. Um…call my mom, I guess."

"I could sleep on the couch," Selene offered. "You could have my room."

"Aren't you still seeing Ty?"

"Sure, but he'd understand," Selene lied.

Mindy knew he wouldn't understand at all. She thought Selene's boyfriend was a jerk. No, more than a jerk: a little creepy. He tried to keep Selene from spending time with her friends. He'd get mad if she wasn't home when he thought she would be. And, although he still shared a house with some other guys, he was at Selene's most of the time. If Mindy could have had her own room, one where she could shut the door, maybe she could have lived there. But she couldn't take Selene's bed and then live with Ty's sulking.

"No." She gave a shaky smile her friend couldn't see. "I love you, Selene. You're a good friend. But no. I'll figure something out. I promise."

With an almost steady hand, she dialed her mother's number next.

"Bed rest?" her mother said a minute later. "Are they kidding?"

Mindy told her mother what she remembered about preeclampsia. The fact that her blood pressure was high and that she had to get it down, reduce the swelling in her hands and feet. "I'm really scared," she admitted, "for the baby's sake."

"The doctor wouldn't have let you go home if she wasn't sure the baby was fine. You know she's probably overreacting. And it's a bit unrealistic to expect you to lie in bed for weeks, isn't it?"

"I can't ignore her!"

"I didn't say you should. You can take naps, can't you? And lie down while you're watching TV."

Mindy closed her eyes. "She told me I shouldn't even grocery shop. I can't clean house or cook. Or work."

There was silence for a moment. "I suppose I could do your grocery shopping once a week. And if you need money…"

Mindy took a deep breath and said words she'd sworn would never even enter her mind, never mind be spoken aloud. "Mom, I think I need to come home to stay. Just for a month or two."

"Honey, Mark has moved in with me."

Who was Mark? Then Mindy remembered—the grocery store manager. Her mother's latest.

"You're serious about him?"

"Oh, I don't know," her mother said breezily. "But

his apartment was being turned into a condo, and he didn't want to buy it. He's been spending a lot of nights over anyway, so it made sense for him just to move in for now."

"Do you think he'd mind…"

"I'm afraid I don't even have a spare bedroom any-more," her mother continued, as if she hadn't heard Mindy. "Mark's using it as his office. I got rid of the bed ages ago. I never liked having houseguests any-way."

Except the men who shared her bed, Mindy thought with the remembered bitterness of the teenager who had seen her beloved father replaced in her mother's bed within weeks of his funeral.

"Why don't you just hire your landlady?" her mother suggested, with the pleased tone of someone who'd come up with a perfect idea. "You mentioned that she might babysit for you."

"That's because she already takes care of her grand-children. At their house."

"Well, why couldn't she have them come to her house instead? And then she could pop in on you several times a day. I'll bet if you ask her, she'd consider it."

Mindy thought of her landlady's living room, tiny and cluttered with porcelain collectibles. They sat atop the doilies on every table and even marched along the top of the television set, which looked like an anachro-nism in what might have been a Victorian parlor. Three preschoolers in that living room evoked images of King Kong marauding through Manhattan.

"Or Selene!" her mother added. "Why don't you suggest that she get a place with you?"

"She has two roommates. And a boyfriend."

"Or what about Isabel? You two used to giggle in high school about how someday you'd get an apartment together."

Tears oozed from beneath Mindy's lashes. "Mom, she doesn't even live around here anymore."

"There are all kinds of possibilities you haven't considered," her mother scolded. "You know if you get absolutely frantic, I'll figure something out, but honestly, right now isn't very convenient. It's not like you're eighteen and I *expected* you to bounce home again."

A huge lump in her throat kept Mindy from whispering, *I am frantic. I wouldn't have called you if I weren't.* But instead she said, "Yeah, okay, Mom."

"Let me know if you want me to grocery shop for you."

Mindy pressed End and let the phone drop onto the bed beside her.

She was alone. Completely, utterly, alone.

No, not alone, she thought in panic—responsible for another life. For Dean's child. And she couldn't even take care of herself.

QUINN COULD JUST BARELY SEE the woman's face through the grey haze of the closed screen door. The latch had stayed hooked.

"When is the last time you heard from your son?" he asked.

"That boy knows I don't like the stuff he's gotten

into," she declared. "He calls sometimes and I say, 'Are you clean, boy?' Until he say yes, he's not welcome in my door and he knows it."

"Do you remember when you spoke to him last?"

"It was back a while. Three, four weeks. Why you looking for my boy?"

"Right now, just to ask him some questions," Quinn said. "His fingerprints were on a gun."

"A gun!" The screen door rattled, and he saw that she'd grasped the frame. "My Marvin?"

"I'm afraid so." He paused. "Will you let me know if you hear from him? We'll find him sooner or later. It would look better for him if he came in voluntarily for questioning." He held out his card. "Here's my phone number."

After a long silence, a hand lifted the latch and the screen cracked open just long enough for her to snatch the business card from him.

"I'll tell him what you said," she promised, then stepped back and shut the door.

He was inclined to believe she didn't know where her son was and disapproved of his behavior. He also doubted she'd actually turn him in. A judge might okay a wiretap, but Quinn thought he'd pursue other possibilities first.

Back in his car, he yawned and decided to get a cup of coffee. He'd passed an espresso place half a mile back.

There was a spot open at the curb right in front of the place. He swung in, nodded at a trio of young men loitering one business down, then went in.

Three small tables were crammed into the tiny space. The only other customer, a young guy with a mohawk and an eyebrow ring, briefly lowered *The Stranger,* a counterculture weekly, to see who'd come in. Behind the counter, the barista hadn't even glanced up. Her tousled blond hair gave Quinn a pang.

Just as he reached the counter, she lifted her head. Shocked, he found himself staring at Mindy. A Mindy who looked very different.

His gaze traveled from her blue eyes and a face that looked puffy down the front of the red apron. It…swelled.

"You're pregnant," he said stupidly.

She bit her lip. "Quinn. What are you doing here?"

He let out a ragged sound. "Why didn't you tell me?"

"I…" Her eyes welled with tears. "I don't know."

"You don't know." God almighty, she'd kept from him the knowledge that Dean would have a son or daughter, and *she didn't know why?*

"That's a lie." She clasped her hands together over her belly, the fingers writhing. "You're so bossy! So…disapproving."

Quinn shook his head in disbelief. He remembered why he'd been relieved when she'd told him to get lost. He'd forgotten how exasperating she could be. But…she was pregnant. Very pregnant. He calculated quickly.

"Did Dean know?"

Now the tears sparkled on her lashes and she shook her head. Her whisper was thick with those tears. "I hadn't told him yet. Oh, Quinn! I wish I'd told him. I wish I could go back and do it over again."

Quinn heard the scrape of chair legs on the tile floor and he turned his head to see the punk with the mohawk tuck *The Stranger* under his arm and saunter out. The bell on the door rang.

"Is anybody else here?"

Mindy sniffed. "No."

Quinn stalked to the front door, locked it and flipped the Open sign to Closed.

"I can't close in the middle of the day!"

"You just did." He turned to face her. "Will you come out from behind there and sit down?"

After a minute she nodded. "I'll get in trouble."

He swore. "You don't need a crappy job like this! Damn it, if Dean could see you…"

Just emerging through the waist-high swinging door, she winced. "I do need the job." She took a deep breath. "I did need it. This is my last day."

She needed a minimum-wage job? Had she blown Dean's money already? You could do it fast at a casino.

He waited until she'd lowered herself into one of the small wrought-iron chairs. Then he pulled out the one across the round table from her and sat, too. Seeing the apprehension and misery on her face, he said as gently as he could, "Will you tell me what's happened to you?"

She wiped angrily, he thought, at her tears. "Even after I sold everything, there wasn't that much money left, Quinn. You know that. If I wasn't pregnant, I could have used it to go back to grad school or to live on while I tried to make it as an artist. But there isn't just me anymore. I don't have health insurance, so I have to use some to pay the doctor and hospital and to live on for a couple of months after the baby is born. And then kids are expensive. I mean, they need toys and bikes and piano lessons and soccer shoes."

He nodded.

She sniffed. "And I wanted to put some away for college. Not for me. For…him." Her hand fluttered toward her belly. "Or her. So I got a job right away. And I have an apartment."

"But you've been doing okay?"

"I thought I was. I mean—" she rubbed her belly "—I really was. Until, I don't know, the last month. I've gotten so big and so tired."

God. He hated the idea of her standing all day. And alone here in a neighborhood that wasn't the best.

"You're not on by yourself at night, are you?"

She shrugged. "Sometimes." A shadow seemed to cross her face. "I don't like closing."

She closed by herself. Counted money from the cash register while anybody could be looking in the front window. Then she walked out, locked the door and had to get to her car. His teeth ground together.

Her eyes widened at his expression. "Nobody's bothered me," she said hastily.

Okay. Today was her last day. He made himself relax, muscle by muscle.

"So now what?" he asked. "Will you be staying with your mother?"

Mindy bowed her head. After a moment, she shook it.

"You're staying in your apartment?"

"I don't know what I'm going to do!" she burst out, lifting her head to show him eyes again swimming with tears. "I hate not even being able to take care of myself!"

What in hell? "Are you out of money?" he asked carefully.

She grabbed a napkin and gave her nose a defiant blow. "No. It's not that. It's…" This look was wild, her eyes shying from his.

There was something she didn't want to tell him. Something that scared the crap out of her.

"What?" he asked.

When the defiance left her, she seemed to crumple. Hands splayed on her belly, she rocked, her head bent and her voice muffled.

"The doctor wants me to stay in bed until the baby comes. I just don't know how I can do that. If I can't even grocery shop—"

"In bed?" he interrupted. "Why?"

This small sniff sounded forlorn. She still didn't look up. He focused on the top of her head and on the graceful, somehow vulnerable line of her slender neck.

"I have a condition called preeclampsia. My blood pressure is elevated and I have protein in my urine. If I was another few weeks along, the doctor would induce labor, but it's too soon. So I started on medication for the blood pressure and she wants me lying down most of the time. But I can't! I just can't!"

Voice brutal, he asked, "Will you hurt the baby if you don't?"

"I…" She pressed her fingers to her mouth. Nodded hard.

In that same hard voice, he said, "Risk your life?"

Barely audible, she whispered, "I… Maybe."

"Then what in hell are you doing here?"

"I told you!" she cried. "It's my last day!"

Still angry, he asked, "How long have you been working since the doctor prescribed bed rest?"

"Only two days. I saw her yesterday morning. I had to give my boss a day to find someone else. Or rearrange the schedule."

He felt as if he'd wandered into Wonderland. He wouldn't have been surprised if the queen had ordered his head off.

"Let me get this straight. You won't be working, but you're refusing to commit to resting in bed?"

"It's hard when you live alone," she mumbled. "Okay?"

"I know you hate the idea of going home, but damn it, Mindy! Isn't this the time to take your mother's help?"

She didn't move. Just sat there with her head bent and her hands over her face. "She…doesn't want me to come home. She doesn't even have an extra bed."

The desolation in her voice pierced him. He knew what it must have cost her to admit her own mother couldn't be bothered to help her.

Shoving his chair back, he circled the table and squatted beside her. He wrapped a hand around the fragile nape of her neck and gently squeezed. "I'm sorry, Mindy. God. I'm so sorry."

After a moment she turned, just the smallest amount, but he wrapped his arms around her and she leaned into him. Without drama, she cried against his shoulder, wetting his shirt. One hand gripped his shirtfront, as if she were afraid he'd run if she let go.

Quinn ran his hands over her back, kneaded her neck, murmured God knew what. At last, she went still, resting against him as if she weren't strong enough to sit up.

"When I was a little kid, my mother would disappear for days on end," he said. "She just…left me to take care of myself, even when I was only five or six. I got good at it. I didn't know any different. I could see her addiction driving her. But, you know, when you *need* a person, it hurts when you realize you can't count on her."

Her head bobbed against his shoulder.

He patted her again, a little awkwardly. "I guess I don't have the world's best people skills."

She gave a watery laugh.

A smile tugged at the corner of his mouth, despite himself. "Okay. I suck at any kind of long-term relationship. I drive people away." Except Dean. Dean was the only one who'd ever been in it for the long haul for Quinn.

Except, he realized, the Howies. He just hadn't let himself notice that they still cared.

He cleared his throat. "The thing is, if you don't let me help now, I'll worry. About you and the baby."

She stirred and started to push away from him. He found he didn't want to let her go, but he made himself.

Mindy's eyes were puffy and red, and her lashes stuck together. Her hair poked every which way and she needed to blow her nose again. But she said, "I don't need any money, Quinn. Really. Mom did offer financial help, but that's not…"

As if she hadn't spoken, he said, "I have a big house. Well," his shoulders moved, "not like Dean's. But three bedrooms. I can't take much time off work, but if you'd be okay by yourself during the day…"

She gaped. "You're inviting me to…to *live* with you?"

"Uh…yeah. For now. As long as you need to."

She made a funny sound. Half sob, half laugh. "You'd drive me crazy. *I'd* drive *you* crazy."

"Probably," he admitted. But he wanted her to agree anyway. No, damn it! He wouldn't let her say no. He'd abduct her. He'd…

Her eyes narrowed. "You're offering because you think I can't take care of Dean's baby. Right?"

He stood, perhaps to give himself a chance to avoid her gaze. "No. It's you I'm worried about. Dean was the closest thing I had to family. I guess that makes you family, too."

"You mean, we had a sort of sibling squabble?"

He had never thought of her as a sister. Never would. Maybe that was part of the problem.

"Could be," he lied.

"Oh." Her shoulders relaxed. She sat in silence for a moment, her forehead puckered. At last she looked searchingly at him. "Do you mean it, Quinn?"

"I mean it."

Mindy groped for the paper napkin on the table and blew her nose. Wadding it in her hand, she said in a small voice, "All right. If you really…"

"God damn it, I said I meant it!"

"Don't yell at me!" she yelled back.

He pinched the bridge of his nose. She would drive him crazy.

Knowing she had nobody to help her would drive him even crazier.

"Okay. I'm sorry." He paused. "How late are you supposed to stay here?"

"Um…" She glanced instinctively toward the clock. "Until five. This guy, Diego, is coming in for the evening."

"All right. I've got a couple more people I have to talk to. How about if I come back at five?" He didn't like knowing she'd be on her feet even that long, but didn't see an alternative. "We'll go by your apartment and pick up the necessities, then you'll come home with me."

She hesitated, but finally nodded. "Okay. I hope…" She gave her head a quick shake. "Never mind. Thank you, Quinn."

He walked to the door, flipped the sign back to Open, then paused with his hand on the knob. "Why didn't you call me?"

"I…" She was quiet behind him. "I think I would have. Soon. But after I told you I didn't need you anymore, calling to ask for help… Um, the idea wasn't very appealing. I know you've never thought very much about me, but I do have some pride."

He didn't dispute her belief that he hadn't thought

much of her, because it was true. On the surface. Beneath the surface, down where it was dark and quiet and hard to see, he didn't know what he felt for her.

Without turning around, he said, "I'm sorrier than I can tell you that I made you feel that way. If it's any consolation, right now I feel like scum." He hesitated, didn't know what else he should say, and finally made himself open the door. He walked out, tossing over his shoulder, "I'll see you at five."

Quinn got in his car, shoved the key in the ignition, and thought, *I found her.*

He hadn't lied: he did feel like a real son of a bitch. She was in danger of losing the baby and she hadn't been able to turn to him because he'd treated her with such contempt before.

But self-loathing wasn't as powerful as the relief that swelled in his chest, and something that might have been happiness.

She was coming home with him. She was going to let him take care of her.

And she was having a baby. Dean's baby.

As Quinn started the car, he thought, *Wait'll George and Nancy hear they're going to be grandparents.*

CHAPTER EIGHT

HIS HOUSE WAS PERFECT. Darn it. Mindy didn't want to like Quinn too much, or else she'd have to admit she'd been wrong about him. She'd half hoped his house would be okay to visit but not appealing—all chrome and black leather, or maybe heaped with magazines featuring naked women in come-hither poses and decorated with pyramids of beer bottles and posters of professional wrestlers.

No such luck.

Way back when, she'd dreamed up all kinds of hideous possibilities once she realized that Quinn was never going to invite her to his place, even if she was his best friend's wife. No, when he felt obligated to reciprocate their hospitality, he paid for a dinner out. She'd known perfectly well that Dean went over to Quinn's sometimes; she was the one who wasn't welcome.

Which made his offer to take her in even more extraordinary. She must seem really pathetic to him. Like a pregnant stray cat.

The house was probably an old one—most homes in West Seattle were. It had been dramatically remodeled at some point, preserving the brick exterior but opening the interior into large airy spaces. The kitchen was separated from the dining room only by a breakfast bar, and a low wall of bookshelves was all that divided the living room from dining room. Open beams above were stained the color of honey, the walls were white, the floors gleaming wood she thought wasn't oak. Pecan, maybe? Or maple?

The furniture was scaled for a man and upholstered in leather and sturdy brocades, the colors browns and russets and licks of scarlet. Like a typical man, he'd left the walls too bare, tabletops empty, concentrating instead on shelves for books, an impressive audio system and one of those flat plasma TVs that she'd seen only in stores. Even so, she liked the warm feel of his house.

Laden with her suitcase and a box packed with her framed photos and albums and a few favorite books and mementos, Quinn watched her turn and survey his house.

"The bedroom is in here," he said, after a moment. Three doors opened off a short hall. He turned into the first and set down the carton on a dresser.

Her eyes filled with tears. All she seemed able to do lately was cry.

"This is so nice," she whispered.

A puffy denim-covered duvet made a bed with a bookcase headboard look comfy. A rug that had apparently been woven of scraps ripped from worn jeans warmed the floorboards. A pair of sash windows looked out on a backyard dominated by a huge, gnarled tree, the kind children loved to climb and hang a tire swing from. The room was plain but…inviting.

"I know it's not much, but…"

"It's wonderful." She gave him a wavery smile.

"The living room couch is a sleeper, too. We can pull it out during the day so you can watch TV if you want. Or you could stay out there all the time…"

"No." She sniffed. "You don't want to be tripping over me all the time. And I like the view in here."

He grunted. "At least there's no mold growing under the bathroom sink."

He hadn't been impressed with her apartment. He'd insisted on packing most of her things while she lounged like a lady of leisure on the bed. After he'd found the mold, he'd kept muttering things about the place not being habitable, and the baby's health, and cockroaches, which the apartment *didn't* have.

She rolled her eyes. "It wasn't that bad!"

"Yeah, it was. You're not going back there."

"Quinn! As much as I appreciate your help, I make my own decisions. Remember?"

He scowled at her. "We'll argue about it later. Right now, I want you to lie down while I bring the rest of your stuff in."

Okay. He was definitely going to get on her nerves. At the moment, though, she was so pathetically relieved to have found a refuge that she was actually touched that he cared enough to be bossy, instead of mad that he thought he had the right to tell her when to stand, sit and brush her hair.

On the way out the bedroom door, he said, "The bathroom is the next door down. There's only one downstairs, so we'll be sharing it."

A staircase had risen from the front entry. "What's upstairs?" she asked, curious.

"Another bathroom and a bedroom I use as an office. It seemed too small even to be a guest bedroom, and the bathroom doesn't have a shower or tub."

"A house built for one."

His brows lifted. "Or two." Then he disappeared from the doorway, leaving her just a little breathless.

She didn't want to be too obedient, but maybe lying down was a good idea. Mindy slipped off her shoes, hung her jacket in the otherwise empty closet and pulled back the duvet to find navy-blue flannel sheets. How like Quinn. Maybe he couldn't find black sheets. Or maybe he had, but used them on his bed.

Smothering a giggle, she climbed into bed, lay on her left side, nudged the pillow into shape, and gazed at the dark, gaunt branches of the old tree. In spring, she thought dreamily, she'd feel as if she were lying right under the leafy canopy. Really the tree was too big for the small yard, but she could see why he didn't take it out.

This bed was an awful lot more comfortable than the slightly lumpy one in her apartment. It yielded just enough to make lying on her side bearable.

"I'll get you a body pillow," Quinn said behind her, making her start.

"Oh! I didn't hear you coming!"

He stepped to the foot where she could see him without looking over her shoulder. "We could turn the bed so you face the door when you're on your left side."

"No, the view out the window is more interesting." She smiled at him. "A body pillow might be nice. I could sort of drape myself around it."

He went very still and his eyes seemed to darken. Or perhaps she'd imagined it, because after that curious pause he only nodded. "I've got a small stereo upstairs with a remote control. I'll bring that down here."

"I have some CDs in my car." She'd driven here, following Quinn's car. She'd need it to get to her Lamaze classes.

"I'll get them later. I'm going to put on dinner right now. Take a nap if you'd like."

Was that a thinly disguised order? Again, she tried to muster some irritation and managed only to feel her eyes getting heavy. She was so tired all the time! Despite her exhaustion, worry—okay, fear—had kept her awake the night before. Just a little nap *would* feel good.

She woke to delicious smells and the murmur of voices from the television set. Mindy got up, opened her suitcase and found her flip-flops, and went to the bathroom.

The floor and the walls to waist-high were tiled in a black-and-white checkerboard pattern. An enormous claw-footed bathtub was surrounded by a white curtain, and the thick towels were black. Mindy peeked at herself in the oval beveled mirror above the pedestal sink and squeaked in horror. She was lucky Quinn hadn't run at the sight of her! Or driven her straight to the hospital!

With wet fingers, she tried to finger-comb her hair into some semblance of order, then turned the taps to icy cold and splashed her face. The result wasn't much of an improvement. She still looked puffy and pasty, and her hair needed a good cut and the help of a hair dryer and some gel.

The baby chose then to somersault in her belly, and she smiled and splayed her hands over the shimmer of movement.

"Hey, kid," she murmured.

He—she—flipped again as if in response, and she laughed. Ah, well. What difference did it make what she looked like? Quinn had never been impressed anyway, she thought, just a little ruefully.

When she padded into the living area, Quinn was taking something out of the oven. He glanced up. "I was just going to wake you. Are you supposed to be on your feet?"

"A couple of hours a day are okay, the doctor said. I figured I'd use them to shower and eat and make my nine million daily trips to the bathroom."

A grin lightened his face. "Junior nestled a little too close to your bladder?"

"Junior," she informed him, "is using my bladder as a trampoline." Then she felt heat touch her cheeks. Maybe this wasn't an appropriate topic of conversation.

Then again, they lived together now. He'd hear her going to the bathroom every hour, on the hour, all night long.

They lived together, Mindy thought again. How weird was that?

She perched on a wicker-and-iron stool and rested her elbows on the counter. "What are we having for dinner?"

"London broil and baked potatoes." He deftly sliced the meat. "You'll discover that my repertoire is limited."

"You can serve that every night if you want." Her mouth watered. "It smells fabulous, and I didn't cook it."

He leveled a stern stare. "And you won't cook while you're here. Right? Don't get any idea about helping out or surprising me with dinner."

"Bossy," she said without heat. Then she gave him a sunny smile. "But, hey, you want to spoil me, go right ahead."

"I intend to make sure you follow the doctor's orders," he corrected.

She bit her lip. "Quinn, I really do appreciate what you're doing for me. I mean, I know it's for Dean, but still."

"Maybe you're the one I'm worried about." Those very blue eyes lingered on her face for a moment. Then his dark head bowed and he went back to slicing meat.

"Well, I know that, but I just wanted to say that even if it's because of Dean, I still…" *Oh, give it up!* she decided. What did she want him to say? *No, no! Dean has nothing to do with me sweeping you up and bringing you home with me?* Of course Dean had everything to do with it! They both knew that. "Thank you," she finished. "That's all I really wanted to say."

Quinn glanced up, expression unreadable. "You're welcome."

Just like that. Her own mother wouldn't take her in, and Quinn, hardly more than an acquaintance, said,

You're welcome, as if what he was doing for her was nothing big and no more than she should have expected.

"I called my friend Selene, too," Mindy said. "You met her at the funeral?"

He nodded.

"She has a new roommate. Selene would have let me have her bedroom, but the couch in the living room where she'd have had to sleep isn't even a pullout, and she has a boyfriend who stays over a lot." Mindy traced the grout between the tiles on the countertop. "Me being there would have been awfully inconvenient."

"Your situation is life and death. What's convenience compared to that?"

"She did offer." It seemed important for him to know that she had a friend who cared enough to do that much.

"Accepting help doesn't seem to come easy to you." Quinn opened the refrigerator. "What do you want to drink?"

Surprised by the mundane question on top of his observation, she said, "Milk, if you have it."

He set a quart on the counter and reached in the cupboard for glasses.

Watching him pour, she burst out, "Are you suggesting I don't *want* anyone to help me?"

He gave her one of those glances she found to be infuriatingly impassive. "I'll bet it just about killed you to ask your mother and Selene for help."

"Not Selene," she heard herself say, then pinched her lips together when she realized what she'd admitted.

"But you couldn't accept her help unless giving it

meant she wasn't making any sacrifice." He picked up the platter of sliced London broil and a second one with two baked potatoes, and carried them around the end of the breakfast bar to the table. "Time to eat."

Mindy carried the glasses of milk to the table while he went back for a bowl of steamed broccoli.

Sitting at the place he indicated, she said, "I could tell she felt obligated to offer but was relieved when I didn't take her up on it. I didn't turn you down, did I?"

A glimmer of a smile showed in Quinn's eyes as he sat across from her. "But you wanted to."

"Of course I wanted to!" she snapped. "I've already spent enough time on the receiving end of your 'help.' You were always irritated with me and impatient when I didn't do things the way you'd have done them. I couldn't cope in my own way. Oh, no, I had to cope *your* way. So, yeah, I'm a little nervous about throwing myself on your mercy again!"

The minute she finished her tirade she was appalled. He was being wonderful and what did she do but lob grievances that should have been forgotten.

She squeezed her eyes shut. "I'm sorry! That was really low of me."

Into the silence he said, "No. You're right. I was a jackass."

Her eyes popped open.

"Being in charge, controlling, might have been *my* way of coping." His breath sounded ragged.

"You mean, so you didn't have to grieve. So you were too busy to grieve."

His shoulders jerked. "Something like that."

Mindy bit her lip. "I should have seen that."

"How could you?" he said simply. "I didn't." He turned a table knife over and over between his thumb and finger. "Once you kicked me out…" Quinn cleared his throat. "That's when it hit me."

"He was gone," she whispered.

"Yeah." He tried to smile. Almost succeeded.

Damn it, her eyes were watering again. "I was even more sad after you were gone, too. You were the only other person who loved him. Without you around, it was as if Dean had never even existed. You know? Sometimes I'd have to get out of bed in the middle of the night to look through a photo album. Just to…to make him seem real."

They looked at each other across the table without the defenses they usually erected. She saw that Quinn looked older than he had four or five months ago. The lines between his eyebrows and carved from nose to mouth were more pronounced. She had always thought of him as solitary by choice; now she saw through his aloofness to the loneliness beneath.

Or perhaps that was only wishful thinking.

She gave him a crooked smile. "This is going to sound awfully self-centered of me, but… Can we eat?" She wrinkled her nose. "I'm starved."

A brief laugh escaped him. "Yeah, I'd hate to waste the effort."

They served themselves and ate in silence but for Mindy's murmurs of pleasure and appreciation. Not until she was full did she say, "You know when I told you to get lost? I wasn't that mad at you." She made an apologetic face. "I knew I'd start showing any day. I didn't want you to notice I was pregnant."

"Why?" He frowned at her. "Did you think I'd try to snatch the baby?"

"No, I thought you'd undermine my confidence in being a mother. I was afraid you'd disapprove of everything I did."

Voice gravel that was painful on the thin skin of her guilt, Quinn asked, "Were you ever going to tell me?"

"Of course I was!" She paused. "After he was born and I knew what I was doing."

Quinn's gaze lowered to her belly. "Is the baby a he?"

"No. I mean, I don't know. It's just awkward to always say 'he or she.'"

"Do you have a preference?" he asked with seeming interest.

Mindy shook her head. "I like babies. And kids."

His expression was brooding. "I've never been around either."

"They're not some weird, exotic species, you know. Kids *want* to like you." She shrugged. "Mostly, they give you the benefit of the doubt."

His eyes met hers again, and she was surprised to see humor in them again. "Unlike me?"

"Um…I didn't say that."

His grin stole her breath. "You didn't have to." He nodded at her plate. "Are you done?"

"I'm stuffed," she admitted.

Quinn pushed back his chair. "Maybe you'd better go back to bed. Or I can pull out the sofa bed if you'd prefer."

"I can't let you clean up, too." She stood and reached for her plate. "At least let me…"

He circled the table and took the plate out of her hand, then firmly turned her and gave her a nudge. "No. Bed rest. Remember?"

"But you'll be waiting on me hand and foot," she protested.

He shook his head. "Am I going to have to cuff you to the bed?"

Once more, her mouth ran away with her. She teased, "That sounds kinky," before her brain could put the brakes on.

Quinn only laughed. "So it does," he agreed, sounding lighthearted.

As she fled, Mindy realized that she'd heard his laugh before—floating up the stairs after she'd gone to bed, leaving him and Dean alone. Feeling oddly gratified to have succeeded in making him laugh herself, she went to get her toothbrush and toothpaste.

FUNNY HOW DIFFERENT LIFE was when you had someone waiting for you at home.

Mindy had eaten breakfast with him that morning, refusing his offer to scramble eggs or make pancakes.

"I always have cereal anyway. Maybe this weekend, when you don't have to go to work."

She took a section of the morning newspaper and read with concentration that furrowed her brow while she ate her cold cereal with a banana sliced on top. Pretending to read the front page of the *Times,* Quinn watched her.

She hadn't bothered to get dressed—and why would she? Instead, she had thrown her terry-cloth robe over her pajamas. The pajamas had probably come from a maternity store; the robe hadn't. It refused to meet over her belly, leaving a three-inch gap through which he could see a powder-pink knit top. It occurred to him that he'd never seen her in pink before.

She looked up. "What?"

"Did I say something?"

"You're staring."

He came damn close to blushing. "I just had the thought that I've never seen you in pink." He nodded at her front.

Mindy glanced down, then made a face at him. "It's the maternity clothes! Most of them are *cute.*" She said the word with loathing. "You know. Baby on Board with an arrow pointing at the stomach. I mean, you can find more elegant stuff, but it's expensive. Mostly I got my maternity clothes at the thrift store. It's not like I'll be wearing it for long."

"*You're* cute." Okay. Where the hell had that come from?

"Me?" She blinked at him.

"Yeah. I mean, you're little and blond and..." He shrugged helplessly. "You can do cute."

"But I don't want to." She frowned severely at him. "I'd rather be...quirky."

He thought of some of the getups he'd seen her in and said, "I guess you'd qualify."

"My mother is big on pink," Mindy admitted. "She dressed me like a doll. She didn't take it well when I started wearing T-shirts with skulls on them and torn jeans."

He grinned. "Did you really?"

Clearly offended, she scowled at him. "That's funny?"

"Only if you dyed your hair black and wore a dog collar with spikes."

"I put a temporary dye on my hair once." Her face relaxed at a memory she obviously relished. "Freaked Mom out."

"You never mention your father."

"He died when I was fourteen." Subject closed. She bent her head again and immediately became engrossed in the newspaper—or pretended to become engrossed.

Interesting.

Quinn swallowed the last of his coffee and said, "I'm off. You have my cell-phone number. Call if you need me. Okay?"

She sketched a mock salute. "Yes, sir."

He raised a brow.

This smile dripped with sweetness. "Have a good day. Think of li'l old me waiting at home."

He was laughing when he went out the front door.

And damned if he hadn't been thinking of her ever since.

Over lunch Carter said, "What the hell are you smiling about?"

Wiping the smile from his face, he snapped, "Nothing."

He called her twice to be sure she was okay. The first time she didn't answer, and he assumed she was sleeping. Nonetheless, worry edged his mood until she answered in the early afternoon.

"Fine. And, yes, I've been good," she assured him without being asked. "I'm watching *Days of Our Lives* right now. I've never watched a soap opera before."

Once upon a time, he'd doubted she had the smarts to be interested in much but soap operas. Now he said, "So what do you usually watch?"

"Oh…movies." Her voice became more animated. "*Friends*. I loved *Friends*. I cried during the last episode."

He had the impression she cried a lot. Although in fairness, this last six months hadn't been her best.

"Some of the BBC programs on PBS," she continued. "I like British accents."

What a reason to watch.

"Mostly, I'd rather read."

"Explore my bookshelves," he told her.

"Thanks," she said. "Now go back to work. Catch some bad guys."

"Can't find this bad guy." Marvin was still eluding them.

"Really?" Her voice softened. "You found me."

"By chance," he reminded her.

"If you're looking for something, sometimes you stumble right over it." Her laugh rippled out. "Maybe I should go into the guru business."

"Maybe. Listen, I'll rent some DVDs on my way home."

"Would you?" She sounded hopeful. "Thank you, Quinn."

Carter settled heavily into the chair across from Quinn's desk. "Who was that?"

He guessed he couldn't avoid telling a few people. He just didn't want anyone to read the wrong idea into the fact that Mindy was living with him.

"Mindy Fenton. She's hit a bad patch and is staying with me."

"Bad patch?" Carter rubbed his chest absentmindedly in a way that was making Quinn nervous. He'd been nagging his partner to get a checkup. His retirement was going to be a short one if he ignored angina pains. Carter kept insisting he had heartburn. Too much coffee, he always insisted. Ate a hole in the esophagus.

"She's pregnant. With Dean," Quinn added hastily. "She's due next month. But she's got preeclampsia, which is some kind of hypertension thing that happens to pregnant women. The doctor wants her doing nothing but resting. That's tough to do when you're living on your own. I offered my spare bedroom."

"Dean's kid, huh?" Carter gave his chest a final pat. "He'd have really liked having a baby, wouldn't he?"

"Yeah. He would have."

They were silent for a moment, remembering a man who was still half kid himself.

Carter heaved a sigh. "What's the plan for this afternoon?"

"Hell if I know."

"Maybe we should put some more pressure on Abdul. I think he knows where his good friend Marvin is."

"Yeah, why not?" Quinn shrugged and rose.

Marvin was their primary suspect in a drive-by shooting. A few other names had come up, but Marvin's disappearance from his usual social scene didn't proclaim his innocence.

They revisited several people, making them nervous per intention, but learned nothing new. Quinn watched his partner press his hand to his chest several times and surreptitiously pop antacid tablets. At five o'clock, he said, "Let's hang it up. Damn it, Carter, make a doctor appointment!"

"Mind your own business," Ellis Carter said without heat.

"For God's sake, if you have heartburn you need something more effective than Tums!" Quinn glowered at Carter. "If you've got something else going on, you need to know it. I'm not in the mood for another funeral."

Face flushed with rare anger, Carter said, "You never let up, do you?" and stalked out.

Quinn didn't move. He sure knew how to make friends and keep 'em.

Thirty seconds after Carter had left, he reappeared in the doorway. Scowling, he said, "All right! I'll make the damn appointment! Are you satisfied?"

Quinn smiled. "Yes."

"Don't smirk," his partner snarled, before vanishing again.

Quinn walked out to his car feeling good. His step seemed lighter than usual. Pulling into the parking lot of the video store, he caught himself whistling.

He grabbed a few new releases almost at random, since he had no idea what she enjoyed. He skipped the horror and the blood-and-guts action stuff, choosing a British import, a romantic comedy, a weird-sounding independent film and Tom Hanks's latest, which he'd been meaning to watch himself.

The house was quiet when he let himself in. He carried the cartons of Chinese takeout he'd stopped for into the kitchen, then turned to see her standing in the door in her pajamas.

"You're home!" Mindy's nostrils flared. "And you brought dinner."

"Bored?"

"Not too bad yet. But getting there. And hungry."

"Here, take some of these and go sit down." He nodded toward the dining area. "I'll get plates and we can serve ourselves."

"Cool."

She was happily peeking to see what he'd bought when he laid out plates and forks.

"Spring rolls. Heaven."

"You're easily pleased," he said with amusement.

"Now that I'm not nauseated all the time, I'm hungry instead." She took the glass of milk he'd poured from him. "Thanks." When he pulled up his chair, Mindy asked, "Did you find your guy?"

"Guy?" For a moment he was blank. "Oh. Marvin.

Nah." For no particular reason, he added, "His mother doesn't believe he'd have shot anybody. She doesn't like guns and is convinced he feels the same, even though he's gotten into things she doesn't like."

"Drugs?"

"Definitely drugs."

She paused after a swallow of milk. "Is it possible he didn't shoot anybody?"

Riveted by the sight of her tongue sweeping her upper lip, he had trouble making sense of what she'd said. "I guess anything's possible."

"Well, you'll find him." She gazed expectantly at Quinn. "Is that what you did all day? Look for Marvin?"

"Pretty much," he admitted. "Nagged Carter into seeing a doctor."

"Doctor?"

He found himself telling her about his partner's "heartburn" and stubborn refusal to get it checked out. That got them off on health care, the costs for someone like her who wasn't insured, then on to politics. Quinn surfaced to realize over an hour had passed.

"Hey, you need to lie down."

She made a face. "I suppose."

"I rented some DVDs."

"Really?" She brightened. "What did you get?"

Mindy claimed to be delighted with his choices, and the next thing he knew the Tom Hanks movie was in the DVD player, Mindy was lounging on the couch and he was slouching in an easy chair.

It wasn't bad, but he found himself enjoying watch-

ing her face as much as he did the movie. Her express-
iveness was part of why he'd always seen her as young,
he realized; she had childlike wonder in her eyes when
she saw something that delighted her, some of a kid's
inability to hide her surprise and worry and unhappiness. Now, he hoped she never acquired a more sophis-
ticated veneer. What kid wouldn't like to grow up with
a mom with a giggle like that?

After she'd gone to bed, he washed their few dishes,
giving her time to use the bathroom first.

Turning out lights, Quinn realized he hadn't enjoyed
an evening this much in a long time. He didn't even mind
that his bathroom had been taken over by a woman, and
an untidy one at that. His mood was too good.

This was going to work out, he thought. For both
of them.

CHAPTER NINE

"WHAT IN HELL do you think you're doing?" Quinn couldn't believe his eyes. His day had gone south with a frantic call from a mother who'd found her kid beaten to death. Fortunately—or unfortunately, depending on your point of view—finding and arresting a suspect hadn't taken as long as booking him. Still, he was two hours late home. He'd stopped to pick up a pizza and was just walking in the door.

Mindy was apparently just on her way *out* the door. Clutching a pillow.

"Pizza." She looked at the box with longing. "I can warm some up when I get back."

He ground his teeth. Did the words *bed rest* mean nothing to her? "Back from where?"

"My Lamaze class is tonight."

"Lamaze." He had the vague impression that Lamaze had something to do with puffing and panting. The purpose escaped him.

"Yes. You know." One of Mindy's hands fluttered. "Getting ready for childbirth?"

"Won't your doctor be doing a C-section?" He'd done some research.

Mindy shook her head. "She'll induce labor as soon as she thinks it's safe. But she'd rather the baby be born naturally."

Quinn didn't move from his position blocking the door. "You can't go out."

"Yes. I can." She looked steamed. "Quinn, I'm a big girl. You've been wonderful, but I don't need a daddy to tell me what to do."

His jaw tightened. "Expressing a little common sense makes me overbearing?"

She let out an exasperated puff of air. "I've been in bed all day. I even ate lunch in bed! I won't be gone an hour and a half. I'll be fine. I promise."

"I'll drive you," he heard himself say.

Her expression softened. "You don't need to. Really."

Had she looked at herself in the mirror lately? Her stomach was so enormous, she waddled. He'd seen her struggle just to get out of a chair.

"I don't know how the hell you'd reach the gas pedal by the time you put your seat back enough to get that belly behind the steering wheel." He was wary enough to recognize the mutinous flare on her face. Quinn cleared his throat and moderated his tone. "I'll feel better if you let me drive."

"*I* feel like a teenager who's been grounded." Her lower lip looked as sulky as a teenager's, too. She sighed again. "Fine. But we have to go now."

"I'll stick the pizza in the fridge." He hoped she didn't hear his stomach rumble.

He half expected her to bolt, but she was waiting

when he hurried back to the front door. He gestured her out onto the porch and locked the door behind them. For a minute, he thought she was going to protest when he opened the passenger door for her, but all she did was mumble, "I feel like a beached whale," as she set the pillow on the floor, gripped the door frame and lowered herself to the seat.

He followed her directions to a community center housed in a retired school building on Beacon Hill. The parking lot for El Centro de la Raza, surrounded by a ramshackle chain-link fence, was full of shadows behind Dumpsters and in stairwells. He parked by a cluster of other cars at one dimly lit end of the old school.

"I should have suggested you bring something to read." Looking contrite, Mindy opened her door. "I'll be about an hour."

"I'll walk you up." Quinn didn't give her a chance to argue. The damn place was almost deserted and the neighborhood not the best. Anybody could be wandering the halls in that place.

She was still trying to heave herself out when he arrived at her side of the car. He gripped her arm and pulled. She came faster than he'd expected and bumped right against him. Her stomach did a lurch and roll as if the kid inside was protesting—or trying to cut and run. It was the weirdest damn sensation, feeling that against his stomach.

"Thanks," she said, straightening away from him. "Wow. I have a couple more classes, but I don't know if I'm going to be able to make them."

He restrained himself from saying, *You shouldn't be at this one.* Instead, he took her elbow in a firm hand and gave her his support as she laboriously climbed the steps to the first floor.

Most of the hand-lettered signs on the doors and on the walls of the wide halls were in Spanish. Quinn seemed to remember that this school had essentially been seized by the community back in the radical sixties or seventies. Now, several of these old school buildings in Seattle housed community centers.

Mindy turned into an open classroom. Voices and light spilled out. Quinn started in behind her.

Chairs had been pushed against the walls. Eight—no, nine—couples stood around the room. The women ranged from maybe no more than six months along to one that—God help her—had to have twins in there. Triplets, maybe. Or else she was eleven months pregnant. Quinn could barely tear his incredulous gaze from that grotesquely enormous belly. And he'd thought Mindy was huge.

He came to himself when someone closed the door behind him and then clapped to get attention. He turned to see a dark-haired woman who had the body of a thirty-year-old, streaks of gray in her hair and a wide, beaming smile.

With apparent delight, she said, "We're all here, so let's get started. Mindy! You brought a partner. Wonderful!"

Alarmed, Quinn backed toward the door. "I'm, uh, just here to observe. Or… I'll wait in the hall." He had his hand on the knob when hers closed on his forearm.

"Nonsense! You *did* come with Mindy?"

"I drove her," he admitted.

"And did you have plans for the next hour?"

He hesitated.

She beamed. "Well, then, why not give her a hand?" She chuckled. "Literally. Gentlemen, flex your fingers! You're going to give our mothers-to-be back rubs. Ladies, lie down."

Looking like a suspect caught in a high-intensity beam, Mindy stood stock-still. "Lorraine, Quinn is just a friend. He's not, um… I mean, he was a friend of my husband's."

"Don't be shy," the Lamaze instructor told her with a gentle hug. "He doesn't mind." She turned a piercing gaze on him. "Do you?"

He could see the whites of Mindy's eyes. Did she *want* him to bow out? But he could also see that every other woman in this room had a man kneeling beside her. He hated knowing that Mindy had been coming by herself from the beginning.

"No," he said. "I don't mind."

"Splendid!" Lorraine went to the front of the room. "Now, a relaxed woman stays in control. Your job," she told the husbands, "is to help her relax between contractions."

"Quinn," Mindy said in a low voice, "you don't have to do this."

"I really don't mind." He smiled, a little ruefully. "Besides, I'm scared of her."

He was rewarded with a tiny chuckle.

"Come on. Lie down."

As she set down her pillow and lowered herself to a mat on the floor, Quinn thought about stripping off his jacket but remembered that he still wore his holster and weapon. Wouldn't want to send those mothers-to-be screaming into the hall.

As the instructor talked about finding the tension in his partner's back and rubbing gently, he knelt, took a deep breath and laid his hands on Mindy.

Her shoulders felt incredibly fragile, the bones so fine he was afraid to squeeze too hard. There was definitely tension there—her body was so rigid, he guessed he could lift her above his head with one hand and she'd stay stiff.

He kept kneading as the instructor circulated, giving encouragement and chiding a few guys who were apparently ham-handed. Neck, shoulders, down her spine and finally to the small of her back. Mindy made a tiny sound when he put the heel of his hand against her lower back and pressed.

Quinn yanked his hand back. "Did I hurt you?"

"No." She gave him a brief, shy smile over her shoulder. "It felt good. You found the spot that's been aching."

"Oh." Okay. He went back to work, rubbing, kneading, loosening.

She sighed, murmured, moaned. She sounded a hell of a lot like a woman who was being...

Quinn slammed the door on that thought, appalled at the near miss. But a whisper seemed to slip under the crack at the bottom.

Pleasured. She sounded like a woman being touched in a different way.

He gave his head a hard shake. No, damn it! He couldn't think of her like that. She was Dean's wife. Right now, she needed a friend. And what was wrong with him anyway? The woman was eight months pregnant!

He was half relieved, half reluctant when the instructor suggested moving on to breathing exercises.

"Ladies, lie on your side or back, however you're most comfortable."

While the others ran through familiar exercises, she gave Quinn the five-minute lesson. Four shallow pants, one exhale.

"Count for her. Be firm. Look into her eyes. During labor, you need to compel her attention. You can't let her focus slip."

Feeling like an idiot, he counted and Mindy panted. Finally, Lorraine called a halt to the exercise and had the women sit up. Everyone pulled chairs out and listened as she talked about breast-feeding. Quinn was almost as unnerved by the discussion as he'd been by stroking his hands from Mindy's neck to her tailbone. He kept stealing glances at her rapt face as she listened and then to the swell of her breasts above her ripe belly. She was definitely more buxom than she'd been. He found himself imagining the sight of her breast as she opened her bra for the hungry mouth of her baby. The image was enough to make him move uncomfortably.

The class over, they walked out to the car in silence. For the first time, he was thinking about her alone in labor, trying without any help to maintain her focus on the pattern of breathing rather than the pain. Damn it, he thought, why hadn't she asked a friend to do this with her?

During the equally silent drive, he also started to think about *after* the baby was born. She wasn't intending to go back to that dank apartment, was she? He'd have to make it clear that he wanted her to stay at his place for a few weeks. Or longer. Having her there wasn't the hardship he might have expected it to be.

"You think that stuff works?" he asked.

The car was dark, but he knew her head turned. "The breathing, you mean?"

"Yeah."

"I don't know." She was quiet for a minute. "I hope it does. I'm actually a little scared." Her voice hurried. "I mean, of labor. I think it must hurt a whole lot."

He'd been a young patrolman when he'd had the memorable experience of helping a woman give birth. The young husband leaned over the front seat of the car holding her hand and giving encouragement as she screamed and pushed. He remembered crouching between her legs and watching in horror and fascination as a head crowned and then popped out. The baby, slick with mucus and blood, had slid right out into his hands. He'd just about quit the job after that one.

"Women survive it all the time. And then they do it again."

"I know." She was gazing straight ahead, her profile lit in flashes as they passed under streetlights. "It's just, the first time… And having something already wrong."

He took her hand, which went still in his for an instant before she gripped hard. "You're a lot stronger than I ever gave you credit for," he said. His voice sounded hoarse. "You'll do fine, and I know you'll be smiling when they hand you the baby."

She sniffed. "Thank you, Quinn."

He didn't let go of her hand, and she didn't let go of his. Not until he pulled into the garage and had to set the emergency brake. Then he went around and helped her out. She seemed to be moving slower, more heavily, tonight than even two days ago. He waited until they were in the house before he said, "You seeing the doctor again soon?"

"Wednesday. Visits are weekly this last month."

"Good," Quinn said with relief. "Are you hungry?"

"Starved!"

"Listen, you go lie down and I'll warm up the pizza."

She disappeared into the bedroom, but reappeared a couple of minutes later in pajamas and lay down on the couch with a sigh. She kept a pillow and throw there now.

Quinn brought her two slices of pizza and a glass of cranberry-apple juice. He figured he deserved the beer he opened to go with his own pizza.

As usual, Mindy started strong but couldn't even finish the second slice. Quinn supposed the baby was crowding her stomach as well as her bladder. She hadn't been kidding about the regular visits to the bathroom during the night. The first couple of nights, he'd come wide awake every time he heard the bathroom door close, however softly. Now her quiet footsteps, the bathroom door opening and closing, the toilet flushing, were part of the night sounds he hardly heard. They were almost…comforting.

"The Howies invited us to Thanksgiving." Disconcerted by how that "us" sounded, Quinn set down his empty beer can. "I suggested they come here instead. Either you'll have a newborn, or you'll want to be close to the hospital just in case. And still on bed rest."

Mindy bunched her pillow and rolled to her back. "Have you ever cooked a turkey?"

That part was worrying him a little, but, "How hard can it be?" he said with a shrug.

"The first time I cooked one, it was awful. It was still too frozen when I started, so it wasn't done when dinnertime came. I swear that thing cooked for eight hours. And then it was so dry it was inedible."

He laughed. "Thanks for the pep talk."

"Fortunately, I now make fabulous stuffing and have mastered the turkey thing." She smiled back. "So, whaddaya say, Quinn? Can you take orders?"

"Damn straight."

She made a contented sound. "That was nice of you tonight. Staying at the class, I mean."

"I meant it when I said I didn't mind." Well, okay, he'd been lying at the time, but now he was glad he had stayed. "You shouldn't have to go alone."

"I should have asked Selene. She's just…we're good friends, but she's not that reliable." The pinch of worry made Mindy look pale and plain. She stayed quiet for a minute. "Have you ever delivered a baby?"

His expression gave away something, because she started to sit up. "You have! Oh, God. Was it horrible?"

"Lie down," he ordered. "Yeah, it was horrible, but mainly because I was twenty-three and completely unprepared. Hell, the couple wasn't much older or any more ready. The woman woke in the middle of the night thinking she was having a few twinges of false labor, or maybe just gas." He gave a rough laugh. "The husband got nervous, insisted they go to the hospital. They didn't make it. They pulled over, he flagged me down in the rain." The guy had looked like a maniac, soaking wet and waving his arms frantically, his eyes wide and staring. "I knelt on the street and, uh, caught the baby when it popped out. Easiest labor in the world. Me, I'd only had sex with a couple of girls at that point, and somehow this was more than I wanted to see."

Mindy giggled. "It didn't make you eager to be a father?"

He shuddered again.

"They showed us a film at the Lamaze class last week." She wrinkled her nose. "It was pretty graphic. I couldn't help thinking yuck."

"Yeah, but you should have seen the look on those parents' faces when I wrapped the baby and laid it on her breast." Funny, he'd forgotten that, but the scene came back to him as if it had taken place a few months ago instead of ten years ago: the father hyperventilating and making strangled sounds of joy, and the young mother smiling so softly, with such awe.

"Do you suppose he'll look like Dean?" Mindy laid

her hands over the mound of her stomach and looked at it. "Maybe with freckles?"

Wow. A little Dean. The idea made something twist uncomfortably in Quinn's chest. To compensate, he joked, "If it's a girl, let's hope she looks like you. Dean's nose. Not so good."

Mindy giggled again, color back in her cheeks. "You didn't have any sisters or brothers, did you?"

He shook his head. "Just me." Until Dean came along. "You?"

She shook her head, too. "I don't think Mom was crazy about pregnancy, childbirth or motherhood."

"What about your dad?"

Her smile trembled. "He was great. He'd get down on the floor and play board games with me. I have this picture of him playing Twister. You know. One foot on the blue spot, one on the red, a hand behind him on the yellow…"

Quinn nodded. He'd seen ads.

"His hairline was receding even then, and he wore glasses with thick lenses. I think he was a geek. Big surprise, since he was a software designer. I don't know why my mother married him." She tried to smile again. "I…really missed him when he died."

"I never knew my father." Quinn was startled to realize the words had come from him. Stranger yet, they kept coming. "I never even knew who he was. I'm not sure my mother knew."

Quinn didn't look at Mindy. He didn't want to see her pity.

"Do you have any pictures of her?"

"No." His voice sounded harsh now. "I doubt anyone ever took one."

"I'll bet you could find a high-school yearbook, or something like that."

Now he did meet her eyes, his own hard. "Why would I want to?"

She didn't back down. "Curiosity? Don't you wonder sometimes if the way you remember her is really the way she looked?"

"I don't think about her." He still sounded cold, but he knew he was lying. And he could see that she knew it, too.

"Dean didn't tell me very much about what happened to you. He said I should ask you sometime."

"There's not much to tell." Quinn managed a shrug. "She was a drug addict. Sometimes she fought it, but she always lost."

Mindy asked tentatively, "Did she try to be a good mother?"

Had she tried? Quinn gave a sharp, painful nod. "Yeah, in her own way. She never shot up in front of me, and she didn't have parties at our place. I don't think she left me alone until I was—I don't know—maybe five. Not for long enough to really scare me, anyway. She put me in school, even went to a few open houses. But, God, she got skinnier and skinnier and her hair lank and her eyes…" Dead. They'd been dead, long before she was. He'd looked into his mommy's eyes and known.

"She really did that? Just left you alone?"

"She'd disappear. At first it was just overnight, but then she'd go for a couple of days. Sometimes a week, or even two weeks. She'd say, 'Now you be good and go to school,' but I wouldn't. I'd just…huddle."

Why was he telling her this? Quinn had no idea. Nonetheless, he finished the story, voice raw. "The last time, the police came instead."

"Oh, Quinn," Mindy whispered.

"Not what you'd call a stable childhood."

"And I complained about my mother!"

"With good reason. Didn't she understand that you might lose the baby if you didn't have some help?"

"I don't know if she *wanted* to understand." Mindy bit her lip. "Because taking care of me would have been inconvenient."

Quinn growled an obscenity.

"I wish…"

When she didn't finish, Quinn prodded. "Wish what?"

"Oh…" Her eyes shimmered. "Just that we'd been friends sooner, I guess. It bothered Dean that we weren't."

Yeah, it had. Quinn had known at the time how much Dean wanted his best friend and his wife to like each other, but Quinn hadn't really tried. He hadn't figured out yet why.

"I'm sorry, too."

Both were silent for a long moment. Then Mindy said, "Maybe he knows. I mean, now. That…you're doing what you can, and that we're talking."

"Talking?"

"Instead of just being polite."

That's what they'd done. They'd been civil for Dean's sake to hide…what? He'd always believed it was disdain on his part, but now he wasn't so sure. And for the first time, it occurred to him that she had never, even from the get-go, been as easy with him as she was with other people. He wondered why.

"You didn't like me, did you?"

Her gaze shied from his. "I wouldn't say…"

"Come on. We're being honest."

She took a deep breath and met his eyes again. Her cheeks were flushed. "Okay. No, I guess I didn't like you." Her forehead furrowed. "Although it wasn't quite that. I mean, I didn't, because you looked at me like… like I was a hooker Dean had brought home."

Quinn winced.

Absorbed in untangling her recollections, Mindy didn't seem to notice. "Somehow you always made me uncomfortable. I'm not sure that was your fault. Maybe—I don't know—you reminded me of someone." She gave a fake-sounding laugh. "Maybe you gave me a traffic ticket. I was actually a little scared of you, which I resented. So I suppose I was snippy to hide it." She stirred. "We blew it, didn't we?"

"Yeah, we did." He gave her a wry smile.

"Why *did* you look at me that way?" she asked un-expectedly. "Did you think I was out for his money or something?"

He rolled his shoulders, feeling tension he hadn't known was there. "No, it wasn't that." *Then what the hell* had *it been?* he asked himself. "Dean always had a woman around," he explained. "I hardly paid attention. They came and went."

"Isn't that normal for a bachelor his age?"

"Well, sure, but…" Quinn struggled for the right words. "He had a pattern. Until you came along. He'd fall in love. I mean, everyone around him would be rolling their eyes. She was all he'd talk about. There'd be this escalation as he courted her, and then maybe a couple of months of contentment once he had her. Then…" He shrugged. "His interest would wander. She wasn't exciting anymore. Suddenly, someone else would be. The last woman was gone, he was in love again. It was as if he needed that first excitement."

"The way he always wanted new things," Mindy said slowly. "He'd only had his pickup truck a year when he decided he had to have a new one. He needed an extended cab, he claimed. He lost so much money when he traded the last one in. I tried to argue, but it was like he didn't even hear me. He *wanted* that truck. He spent weeks doing nothing but reading reviews of pickups."

So she'd noticed. "With women, it was pretty much the same. He coveted, he was flushed with triumph when he got whatever it was he wanted, and then he was bored with it. Or her. After a while, I quit taking him seriously when he claimed to be in love. Then, out of the blue, he announced that he was marrying you."

"And you thought…"

"That you were holding out for a ring," Quinn said bluntly.

"Thus the scathing way you'd look me over."

For the second time in this conversation, he winced. "I didn't realize I was that obvious."

"It never occurred to you that he might really be in love?"

"I guess in a way I wasn't sure he was capable of it. Not the 'till death do us part' kind."

She challenged, "So you would have looked at any woman he married the same way."

What in hell did she want him to say? *I didn't think you were up to his weight?*

"I thought you were too young."

"You mean too shallow, don't you?" Eyes spitting fire, she struggled to sit up again.

There she was, shaped like a pygmy goat, in her flannel pajama bottoms, a white T-shirt cut like a tent and decorated with a spot of pizza sauce, her hair disheveled, and she was fighting mad.

Before he could answer, she snapped, "Well, did it ever occur to you that *Dean* was shallow? I loved him, but, honestly, the man didn't even read the newspaper! He didn't care about world events, or politics, or ideas. He didn't *want* a wife with any depth! I didn't know…"

With a small gasp she stopped, as if she'd said something she hadn't even known she was thinking.

"Are you saying you fit the bill?" Quinn paused, then finished with quiet intensity, "Or that you didn't?"

"Oh, God!" She struggled the rest of the way upright. "I loved him! I did!"

But maybe, Quinn diagnosed, she wouldn't have *kept*

loving Dean. Maybe *she* would have gotten bored. And right now, she didn't want to believe that.

"It's okay," he said.

"No, it's not!" Using the arm of the couch, Mindy pushed herself to her feet. "I shouldn't have said something I didn't mean. It's you," she said with venom. "You always goad me. I don't know why." Tears sparkled in her eyes. "Good night."

"Mindy…" Feeling sick, he rose, too.

"I don't want to talk about it anymore." She gave him a last look, full of grief and knowledge she couldn't evade and hatred because *he* was the one to trigger unwelcome awareness. Then she walked out and a moment later he heard the bathroom door open and close.

Alone in the living room, he closed his eyes and let the wave of self-revulsion crash over him.

CHAPTER TEN

MINDY LAY AWAKE staring at the dark square of window. She napped in snatches all day, making it harder and harder to fall asleep at night.

And tonight… Oh, she'd been awful to Quinn! Mindy punched her pillow. He hadn't said anything, only asked a simple question.

Are you saying that you fit the bill? Or that you didn't?

Squeezing her eyes shut, she saw her big, lanky husband with his easy grin and disarming freckles. He was strong, funny, gentle and ambitious. So, okay, she'd begun to notice that his interests were pretty limited, that he just didn't care about anything outside his immediate sphere. Well, so what?

She moaned and turned her face into the pillow. Quinn hadn't implied a thing. *She* was the one to freak when she heard what she'd said. She hated knowing she had started to get bored when Dean had gone on and on about the riding lawn mower he'd decided he needed despite the fact that their yard wasn't big enough to justify it, or the fishing trip she'd skipped, or which player's

RBI was piss-poor this year. She'd give anything now to go back and really listen instead of going, "Uh-huh," while continuing to read the newspaper out of the corner of her eye.

She'd never thought Dean was dumb, or less than her intellectual equal. Look at the business he'd started! How many small businesses succeeded on the scale Fenton Security had?

But his tastes had been so different from hers. He'd liked shoot-'em-up movies with flashy special effects or long chase scenes. Sports. *Any* sport. Whatever was on TV was okay. He could get excited about curling if that was all that happened to be on.

From the time she was little, her dad had taken her to exhibits at the Seattle Art Museum or funny little foreign films, or they'd gone for the whole day down to the Seattle waterfront, visiting the aquarium and then spending two hours at the Elliott Bay Bookstore. She'd loved climbing in the castle in the children's room at the bookstore when she was really young, and then reading in it when she got older. Her dad had bought her books, subscribed to magazines for her. Dean hadn't read anything but *Sports Illustrated* and the sports page.

Her mother hadn't been much of a reader either—another of the mysteries of why her parents had gotten married in the first place and then had stayed together. Mindy had loved college, where she had friends to talk to about books and art and the odd things she sometimes wondered about. She'd kind of thought that marriage meant having somebody to talk about those things with forever.

Dean had listened to her when they were dating. In those early days, he'd seemed to enjoy arts-and-crafts fairs and prowling plant nurseries and window-shopping in Pioneer Square. But not long after they'd married, he'd started making excuses. Oh, gee, he'd already promised Colin to go fishing. Then she'd started making excuses, too. Maybe he wasn't the only one who'd pretended. Or maybe when you were first falling in love, you genuinely *were* fascinated by everything the other person thought and did and enjoyed. Maybe it was natural to have that fascination wear off.

It just would have been nice, she'd thought wistfully at the time, if they'd been left with more interests that they truly had in common.

What she hated to think—what had scared her tonight—was that they'd both been just a little dissatisfied with their choice. What if Dean had fallen in love again—with some other woman? What if having a child together hadn't been enough?

But he was dead and she'd never know. So why did the whole idea upset her so much?

Maybe, she thought with disquietude, because Quinn *didn't* bore her. Quinn's house was filled with books. He didn't drive the latest-model car. The music in his collection was eclectic. The house itself had charm, but it wouldn't impress anyone. Dean had really, really loved to impress people.

Quinn mowed his small lawn with an old-fashioned push mower that had no engine at all. She'd peeked in the garage the other day and seen it, along with Dean's

Camaro and a tidy workbench and tools that made her itch to play with them.

She liked talking to Quinn, too. The other night they'd spent an hour arguing about the ethics of big business after watching the documentary *The Corporation*. She'd never have even gotten Dean to sit down and watch a film like that.

"Who wants to see talking heads?" he'd have said dismissively.

But the talking heads had had interesting, scary, provocative things to say. Quinn seemed to think so, too.

She'd been so sure she didn't like him! Or so sure she didn't *want* to like him. Mindy wasn't sure which.

Except, a niggling feeling inside told her she *did* know. She just didn't like the answer. She didn't like her secret suspicion that her husband's best friend had unsettled her because… No! Why even think it? Quinn was being nice now for Dean's sake, not hers. He'd be horrified if he knew that, despite her ponderous body, she was having stirrings of… Darn it, there she went again. The point was, all she'd do was confirm his initial belief that she'd been too young and…and flighty to have deserved Dean's love and vows.

And maybe, she thought unhappily, he was even right.

SHE STAYED IN BED the next morning until Quinn had left. His footsteps paused once in the hall outside her bedroom, but he didn't knock and she would have pretended to be asleep if he had.

By evening, she'd decided she had just been silly the

night before. All widows probably wondered whether their marriage would have endured if their husband had lived. There were a lot of "if onlys" that wandered through your mind, when you couldn't go back and change anything or see what really would have happened.

She'd made the firm decision not to compare Quinn and Dean. It was pointless. She was lucky Quinn was being so nice and that they were able to enjoy some of the same movies and that they could have a good discussion or a rousing argument, since he was determined to take care of her for Dean's sake. Staying here was…nicer, since he wasn't glowering at her all the time anymore.

When she heard him arrive home, she detoured to the bathroom to peer at herself in the mirror and brush her hair before she went out to say hi.

He was already setting a bowl and casserole dish on the stove when she sat on a stool at the breakfast bar.

"Hey."

His gaze swept unreadably over her. "How are you feeling?"

Mindy made a face. "Bored. As if I weighed three hundred pounds. How was your day?"

He grunted. "We found Marvin. Dead."

"Oh, no! His poor mother."

"Telling her was no picnic."

"Does that mean he was your guy? Or not?"

"Probably was." Quinn grabbed olive oil from a cupboard and set out spices. "He must have become a liability. Either he had a big mouth or he was panicking."

"Oh, dear," she said again. "Where was he found?"

"Lake Union. Marina owner spotted him."

He talked a little more about his day as she watched him slice potatoes.

Finally she asked, "What are we having?"

"Hmm?" He glanced up. "Oh. Oven-fried potatoes, garden-burgers and a fruit salad." Apparently satisfied with the quantity of potatoes, he sprinkled them with olive oil, rosemary and other spices. Then he spread them in the casserole dish and put them in the oven.

"Quinn." Mindy took a deep breath. "Tomorrow's my doctor appointment."

"Right. I hadn't forgotten. I plan to drive you. What time?" He was now assembling fruit and had pulled out a second cutting board.

"Ten. Um… What I was wondering is if you'd like to come in with me."

His hands stilled. "In with you?"

"Yes. I mean…" She gripped the edge of the countertop. "To hear the baby's heartbeat. And…well, to talk to the doctor. Since you'll probably be driving me. When I go into labor. Or when she decides to induce."

One brow lifted. "Probably?"

"You might be caught up at work. I could call a cab."

She could tell he didn't like that idea. Frowning, he mulled it over.

"You have my cell-phone number. I'll be available."

"Okay," she agreed, not pointing out that he might be in the middle of, say, inspecting a body that had just been pulled from Lake Union.

After a moment, he began chopping an apple. "Sure," he said as if he didn't recognize how momentous her offer had been. "I'd like to hear what this doctor has to say."

So it was that the next morning, he sat next to her in the waiting room at the women's clinic, looking as out of place as—she tried to think of the right analogy—as a jaguar strolling by a swing set in a suburban backyard. Dangerous, and not quite domestic, she thought, stealing a look at him frowning and flipping through the notebook he invariably carried.

She tried to see him with other eyes. After all, *she* knew he wore a holster and gun under that worn black leather coat and that his reactions were, according to Dean, scary fast.

But however hard she tried, she still saw the qualities that had unsettled her when she'd first met him. To start with, he was six feet tall or maybe a little more, broad-shouldered and obviously fit and strong. Compared to him, most men looked…soft. The black slacks and jacket didn't help, but really it wasn't his wardrobe so much as a grimness about the set of his mouth coupled with a stillness and sense of containment, as if he was both guarded and hyperalert. His eyes, a startling blue, had a laser intensity when he looked up at an arriving couple. Mindy suspected he was very, very good at interrogation.

But he also had that air of suppressed sadness, of melancholy, that she'd found as disturbing as anything. Sometimes, when he didn't realize she was looking, his eyes were so bleak it sent a shiver through her.

Brendan Quinn, she had always suspected, was a lonely man, but one who would never accept pity.

And now he sat next to her in the waiting room as if he were any husband or father, when the idea of him changing a baby's diaper was impossible to bring into focus. Slamming a suspect against a wall, sure. Cooing in response to a toothless smile…probably not.

But, to his credit, he was here, and he stood promptly when the nurse appeared in the doorway and called, "Mindy Fenton?"

Mindy was no sooner through the doorway when the nurse handed her a cup.

"You know the drill!" she said cheerily.

Quinn looked at it as if it were an incendiary device. "You have to…?"

"How do you think they found protein in my urine?"

"Ah." Then, unexpectedly, a grin tugged at his mouth. "I don't suppose you ever have trouble producing some."

"Smart-ass," Mindy muttered, turning in to the restroom. The closing door shut off his laugh.

When she was done, he waited in the hall while the nurse weighed her and then took her blood pressure. Finally, Mindy was left alone to take off her maternity pants, heave herself onto the examining table and wrap her lower half like a mummy in the white drape.

"I'm ready," she called, and Quinn stepped in, looking cautious.

"You know, men have it easy," she told him.

He eyed the metal stirrups on the table with thinly disguised horror. "Yeah, we do."

At a knock on the door, he turned.

Dr. Gibbs swept in, Mindy's chart in her hand. "Hello," she said briskly, holding out a hand to Quinn. "You are…?"

"Brendan Quinn." He shook. "Mindy's husband was my best friend."

"I'm staying with Quinn," Mindy explained. "He was nice enough to offer, and now he's paying the price. I'm being waited on hand and foot."

The doctor's assessing gaze became approving. "Good for you."

"He even went to the Lamaze class with me the other night. I thought he might like to hear the baby's heartbeat."

"Good idea. Let's have you lie back." Dr. Gibbs supported Mindy as she lowered herself. Then she lifted her maternity shirt to expose the huge, pale mound of her belly. "You're certainly looking pregnant."

Despite her self-consciousness, or perhaps because of it, Mindy laughed. "You think?"

As they all looked, a knob poked up, then disappeared. Her belly shifted, as if a whale had passed under the surface of smooth water.

"I'm glad to see the baby so active." Dr. Gibbs smiled and took her stethoscope from around her neck. "Let's have a listen."

After she'd located the baby's heartbeat, she signaled for Quinn to come closer. He was staring at Mindy's belly with something, she thought, of the same faint shock with which he'd regarded the cup. But he put the stethoscope to his ears.

"Hear anything?"

Frowning, he shook his head.

The doctor moved the diaphragm a tiny bit, then a tiny bit farther, stopping when she saw his eyes widen.

He listened raptly, his expression stunned. Mindy's heart gave a bump at the wonder on a face she'd thought too closed, too cynical, ever to show such vulnerability or surprise.

After a long moment, he removed the stethoscope from his ears with seeming reluctance. "It's so fast," he said, still staring with fascination at her belly.

"Babies have a much faster heartbeat than adults."

"I guess I knew that," he admitted. "From CPR. But it's really racing."

Dr. Gibbs chuckled when Mindy's stomach bulged and shifted again. "Well, the little guy—or gal—seems to be doing gymnastics right now. Your heart would probably race if you were doing somersaults, too."

Quinn's laugh had a rusty sound. "Yeah, I suppose it would."

Dr. Gibbs sent him into the hall while she did a quick exam, then left Mindy to get dressed. Both returned to the room when Mindy was slipping on her flip-flops. It might be November, but she had no intention of putting on shoes—especially since there was no way she could get close enough to her feet to get socks on first.

"You're looking good," the doctor informed her. "Your blood pressure is down, I don't see the puffiness around your ankles or face, and the baby is obviously active. I recommend we continue to wait."

"Would the baby survive if it was born now?" Quinn asked.

"Yes, many are born far more prematurely than this. Nevertheless, I don't believe in hurrying labor unless we have no choice. Preemies are more likely to have problems, and you could run up some serious bills if he or she had to stay in the neonatal unit for any length of time."

"I can pay the bills if that's the safest course for the baby." Those vivid eyes briefly rested on her face. "And for Mindy."

"That's good to know," Dr. Gibbs said. "But I'm still of the wait-and-see mindset." She fixed a stern gaze on Mindy. "You're following my instructions?"

Mindy nodded. "I get up only to go to the bathroom and to eat. And I did go to my Lamaze class Monday night."

The doctor pursed her lips. "That should be fine as long as you've been resting in bed all day. Well." She flipped the chart closed. "Any questions?"

"Do you think my due date is still accurate?"

"Yep. I give you two more weeks tops. And that's assuming your blood pressure stays down." She rose from her stool, nodded, said, "Glad to meet you, Mr. Quinn. Mindy, be sure to make an appointment for next week," and left the room.

The examining room seemed very small in her wake. Mindy stood, eager to escape its confines. "Well, that was exciting, wasn't it?"

"It was interesting." Quinn let her precede him out the door and down the hall, then waited patiently while she scheduled the next week's appointment.

Outside, he held the car door while she got in, then went around to his side. With the key in the ignition, he paused. "Hearing the heartbeat..." His shoulders moved. "I guess the baby didn't seem real until now."

"Well, it does a little more to me since I'm the jungle gym." Mindy patted her belly. "But I know what you mean. Hearing the heartbeat makes you realize there's really a whole separate being inside me."

"Yeah." He seemed to tear his gaze from her stomach. "Yeah, that's it." Giving himself a little shake, he started the car and then turned to look over his shoulders. "It won't be just the two of us pretty soon."

She liked living with him. Liked it a whole lot. But pride made her say, "You know, once the baby is born, I won't need the help. No more bed rest. You won't want a baby keeping you awake at night. I can leave you in peace."

Quinn braked hard enough at the street to jolt them both. "You gave notice on that apartment, didn't you?"

"I had to. But I'll have to find a different place. Eventually, I mean. And it's not as if I can afford anything better! Maybe the Sanchezes won't have rented it out again yet..."

"Damn it, Mindy, that's no place for a baby!"

"He won't be crawling for months! What difference does it make where the playpen and crib are?"

"He'd develop asthma from the mold." Quinn glowered at her. "Why are you determined to move out of my place?"

"Um..." Very carefully, Mindy said, "I wouldn't say I'm determined to move out."

"Then what the hell are we talking about?"

"Quinn, you offered me your spare bedroom because I was desperate! I won't be desperate anymore once the baby is born. Your offer didn't include postnatal care."

"Well, now it does." He cast an irritated glance at the rearview mirror and she realized that another car had been waiting behind them. "Yeah, yeah," Quinn muttered, and turned onto the street. "I'd feel better," he said, his tone oddly formal, "if you'd plan to stay for a while."

She hadn't cried in at least a week. A recent record. But she immediately felt teary. "Thank you, Quinn."

"Good, it's settled." His shoulders seemed to relax.

It occurred to Mindy that he had just insisted, once again, that she do what he thought best, and she had once again submitted docilely. Where was her pride? Her sense of independence? She should resent his high-handedness! Why was he so convinced she needed to be taken care of?

She tried to fan a spark of resentment to life. She might even have succeeded, if just then Quinn's fingers hadn't flexed on the steering wheel and he hadn't said, "I don't usually put a Christmas tree up. But this'll be his first Christmas. We ought to do it right."

Her heart melted, dousing the spark. This big, tough, lonely man was worried about her newborn baby having the kind of Christmas Quinn himself hadn't had when he was a child. Never mind that the tree would be no more than a blur of color to an uncomprehending baby, that Mindy would have to unwrap any presents.

Doing Christmas right meant something to Quinn. And that made her heart ache.

"Just think." She gently rubbed her belly and smiled at him. "A baby by Christmas."

HE'D SPENT THE PREVIOUS Thanksgiving with Dean, Mindy and half a dozen other friends of theirs. Quinn would have escaped as soon as he'd eaten except for the football game. The women had hung out in the kitchen, the men in the living room.

Most years he volunteered to work on holidays. Let the guys with families have 'em off, he figured.

This year, he was up at eight groping inside the turkey, pulling out semi-frozen gizzards. Mindy, sleepy-eyed and bundled in her fuzzy robe, sat at the breakfast bar to supervise. Once he'd stuffed the turkey, wrapped it in aluminum foil and put it in the oven, she yawned, said, "I'm going back to bed," and disappeared.

Grateful for two ovens, Quinn mixed up pie crust and got out the rolling pin. Damn, wasn't he domestic?

The Howies arrived at noon, shivering as they stepped in. The rain, they reported, was mixed with sleet, and the news said the snow level was down to a thousand feet.

Quinn helped them out of their coats. "Mindy is in the living room. Why don't you go on in? I need to check on the turkey."

"Don't stand up!" Nancy ordered as Mindy started to struggle up. "Is Quinn taking good care of you?"

Without hesitation, without a glance his way, she

said, "The best. He'll deserve sainthood by the time he gets rid of me."

"Oh, my goodness." Nancy sat next to her. "Dean's child. What a shame he isn't here. You must think about him every day."

From the kitchen, Quinn missed Mindy's answer. The comment was a punch to his stomach. When was the last time he'd really missed Dean? Having Mindy here, expecting Dean's baby, maybe he *should* be caught at every turn by a memory, but the truth was he'd almost quit thinking of her as Dean's wife. She was just…herself. A mop-headed, pretty woman with more than her share of pride, a quick mind, and a softness when she talked about the baby. Even the baby…damn it, Quinn knew it was Dean's, but in Quinn's mind the kid had become his own person, too. Or maybe her own person. Someone distinct. Someone who mattered aside from her parents.

He guessed he didn't much like the idea that Mindy was still moping all day for Dean. Wishing like hell she didn't need him because she had Dean.

Okay, he thought with dismay; that was pretty damn pathetic. She wasn't supposed to miss her husband because now she had him. That wasn't even the kind of relationship they had! Or that either of them wanted.

He frowned. Okay. Maybe, if Dean's ghost wasn't between them, and they were just meeting now… But she was his best friend's widow… Well, that wasn't the kind of thing you forgot.

So what right had he to be bothered if she was still

deep in mourning for Dean? Damn it, he should be *glad* she'd really loved his buddy!

Not… Oh, hell, face it. Not jealous.

God help him, he was a lousy excuse for a human being.

"Can I help?" Nancy asked brightly, from right behind him.

He jumped a foot. "Sorry. I was…" Brooding. What he'd been doing was best left undescribed. "No, I think I've got everything set. All I have to do is turn the potatoes on—" he suited action to words "—and then heat the rolls and broccoli."

"Oh, it smells so good!" Her face glowed. "It was so nice of you to ask us, Quinn."

"I'm just sorry we haven't made it a tradition." He realized he meant it. Maybe he'd never let himself love them, but they were still the closest thing to family he had. "I figured you'd want to get an early glimpse of your first grandchild."

"Oh!" She sneaked a peek toward the living room, where George was laughing at something Mindy had said. "Do you think she'd mind if we thought of ourselves that way? Since you boys were our only children…"

He'd wondered sometimes how they felt about him. He guessed that was his answer.

Throat thick, Quinn said, "I think Mindy will be thrilled. She's not very close to her mother, you know."

"What a shame!" Nancy shook her head. "We couldn't have children, you know."

He hadn't.

"It wasn't that we didn't want any," she continued. "But those were the days before people rushed off to fertility clinics and then spent a year's income on some treatment. We just hoped, and let time go by."

Why was she telling him this?

"By the time we accepted that it wasn't going to happen, we were too old to start with a baby." She gave a small laugh. "We didn't even want one anymore! We planned to adopt an older child when we called the agency. They gave us Dean and then you."

"Probably not quite what you were imagining," Quinn said dryly.

"But you see, you were exactly what we'd imagined. Two boys who needed us." She reached out a hand and gripped his with startling strength, even as he felt the tremor. "You brought us such joy even as you broke our hearts by showing us how much you'd missed. We always thought…" She stopped.

He laid his other hand over hers, feeling its fragility. "You thought?"

"Oh, that we could make up for the childhood you hadn't had." Her smile was sad. "But I guess it was too late."

"Maybe not," he heard himself saying. This felt awkward as hell, but necessary. "I didn't want to believe in all the little things you did, but lately I've been realizing how much they meant to me anyway."

"Really?" She searched his face.

"I guess it's losing Dean that made me think."

Her fingers bit into his hand.

"Most of my memories of him are mixed up with you and George. And home. Trusting you never felt safe." He frowned. "That doesn't sound right."

"I know what you mean."

He'd tended to retreat from physical closeness aside from sex. Even when he was seeing a woman regularly, he wasn't much for waking up in the morning to find her draped over him, or holding hands, or having her cuddle during a movie.

But somehow this was easier to say when he looked down at their clasped hands. This woman had bandaged his wounds, nursed him when he'd been sick, smiled when he'd brought home good report cards and wept with pride at his high-school graduation. She'd been his mom, however carefully he'd always told people, "I live with the Howies."

"The thing is," he continued, "looking back, I realize that I *did* trust you. Maybe not the first couple of years, but at some point I quit thinking you'd ditch me if I did something wrong. It just…never crossed my mind that you and George wouldn't be there for the long haul."

He seemed to have a gift for making women cry lately. Her eyes welled with tears. "Oh, Brendan. We hoped. We always hoped."

"And Dean's baby…" He hunched his shoulders. "I want for him what you gave us. Not what we had before."

If possible, she squeezed his hand even harder. "Even if Mindy never remarries, I think that baby will have everything he needs and all the love in the world. You two will make sure of it."

He was pierced with the words, *if Mindy remarries...*

If she remarried, she sure as hell wouldn't need him. Neither would her child. He'd have no place in their lives. Quinn didn't understand why, but he hated that idea.

"Oh, dear!" Nancy said, letting go of his hand. "The potatoes are boiling over! I guess we'd better pay attention to business."

He swung around and lifted the lid from the pot, then turned the heat down. Shaking his head, he said, "Looks like I could use some help, after all. Would you turn on the broccoli and put the rolls in a bag to heat while I take the turkey out?"

"Of course. I'd be delighted to help!" She beamed at him even though her eyes still looked misty.

It didn't come naturally, but he kissed her cheek anyway. "Yeah. You always have been. I've just been too dumb to realize what a lucky guy I was."

Nancy patted his shoulder. "Dear Brendan, dumb is one thing you've never been. Scared, maybe. Of course you were scared!" she added, as if chiding herself. "But what a fine man you've turned into." She nodded, turned to the stove and laughed softly. "All that worrying for nothing! How foolish of me."

"Worrying?"

But she didn't hear him, or had no intention of answering. She smiled beatifically. "Brendan, dear, I do believe these potatoes are done."

"If you'd mash them..."

"Of course I will. Now, you concentrate on the turkey. My, it all smells good! What a perfect Thanksgiving this will be!"

Yeah, Quinn thought in some surprise. She was right. As holidays went, this one wasn't going to be half-bad.

CHAPTER ELEVEN

THE NEXT WEEK, Quinn went to the Lamaze class with Mindy as if it were a given. He was pleased when she didn't argue. Afterward, as they walked out, he said, "We're a pretty good team in there."

Looking ponderous and very, very tired, she said, "Uh-huh."

He'd been hoping for more. Something like an invitation to continue the partnership through labor. But the idea apparently hadn't occurred to her.

After a minute, he said, "You're not going to make it to another class, you know."

Pausing at the head of the stairs, Mindy nodded. She reached for the railing and carefully stepped down.

Quinn hovered at her side, ready to catch her if she fell. She took one step at a time, clinging to the railing. He was glad her doctor's appointment was upcoming so soon; just the last couple of days, she'd become quiet and broody and *bigger*.

He'd noticed that the woman who looked like a house last week wasn't at the class tonight. Someone else asked, and the instructor beamed.

"Tammi had a nine-pound-eight-ounce boy last night."

The kid was almost ten pounds? He'd stolen a look at Mindy's swollen belly and tried to imagine a baby that big in there.

Now she sank into the car with a sigh of relief.

Once in on his side, Quinn asked, "Are you okay?"

"Hmm?" She gave him a distracted glance. "I'm fine."

She didn't sound fine. She sounded as if her response was automatic, her mind a million miles away.

Or turned inward.

"Damn it," he growled, "that doctor had better decide to induce labor when she sees you."

Mindy turned a surprised face to him. "Why?"

"You can't go on like this!"

"Of course I can." Her attention drifted away. "Women do."

"Not all women have preeclampsia."

"Quinn, I'm pregnant. No one ever said the last few weeks were easy."

She was silent then, gazing out the side window, her thoughts God knew where. And wherever they were, they were inaccessible to him. He wanted to say, *Damn it, I'm worried!* but kept reminding himself that he was no more than a buddy, someone helping her out when she needed it. Did he have a right to be scared?

In the house, she said good-night right away and disappeared into her bedroom, firmly closing her door behind her. He didn't sleep well, with an ear listening for her bathroom trips. The next day, he called twice. The first time she didn't answer, and he worried until she did an hour later.

"I'm fine, Quinn."

He was getting tired of hearing that. "No labor pains yet?"

"I've been having a few," she admitted.

"What?"

Half the diners in the sub shop turned to stare at him.

"I called the doctor's office and they said it's normal to have…well, warm-ups. The pains are too far apart to be real labor. For goodness' sakes, I shouldn't have told you!"

He wished she hadn't. No, that was a lie; he hadn't liked not knowing what she was thinking or feeling. But, damn it, now he wanted to check up on her every half an hour. Knowing she'd get ticked, he didn't. He just pulled his cell phone out every fifteen minutes or so to be sure he hadn't missed a call.

He broke a few speed limits getting home. Once there, he was intensely frustrated to find her bedroom door closed.

"I'm home," he announced, not quite loud enough to wake her if she was asleep, just letting her know.

No response.

She hadn't been eating much these past few days, but he put on dinner anyway, then paced. Should he wake her when dinner was ready? She'd said she was having trouble sleeping nights. Getting comfortable was hard. If she really was sound asleep…

He heard her door open as he took the casserole out

of the oven. She went to the bathroom first, then into the living room without bothering with a robe. The T-shirt stretched over her belly. Her hair, he noticed, was imprinted by the pillow but dandelion fluffy, as if she'd showered that morning. He wished she wouldn't when he wasn't home. What if she slipped?

"Did you get some sleep?" he asked.

"Not so much I didn't hear your footsteps going back and forth in front of my door," she said, a little tartly.

"I was worried about you."

"Quinn, there's nothing to worry about yet!"

She was making him crazy. "You're having labor pains, but I shouldn't worry?"

"It's normal!"

"Well, I've never done this before!" How the hell had they come to be yelling?

"I haven't, either! And you're not the one doing it!"

That was a low blow. He turned away so she couldn't see his reaction.

After a minute, he said, "Okay. I'm sorry. I'm just not used to…" What? "I don't know. Really caring about somebody."

"Oh, Quinn." Her voice melted, buttery soft. "The baby is okay. Really. And…he's going to be glad you care."

"I'm more worried about you than I am the baby." He didn't know what possessed him to tell her that. They were probably both better off with the pretense that he was in this because she carried Dean's kid. But it irritated him, this assumption she refused to discard that he didn't give a damn about her.

She met his gaze, hers startled and shy. He thought she blushed.

"That's nice of you to say, Quinn. But we're *both* fine."

If he heard that one more time… But he said only, "Are you hungry?"

Mindy made an apologetic face. "Not very, but I'll try."

She ate only a few mouthfuls, although he noticed she moved food around on her plate with her fork as if to keep him from noticing. He didn't comment when he cleared the table and scraped most of her dinner into the trash.

On a sudden inspiration, he asked, "You want to play cards? I have a cribbage board around somewhere."

Her face brightened. "That sounds like fun. I'm awfully tired of watching TV."

Since he hadn't been much of a television watcher to start with, he had no trouble understanding that. He remembered seeing the cribbage board in a drawer when he'd been looking for something else, so he was able to retrieve it quickly.

He set the board on the coffee table and put the pegs in the first holes, then glanced up to see her lying stiff on the couch, her eyes wide and staring.

Fear punched him. "Mindy?"

She didn't answer for a minute, then exhaled slowly and relaxed. "I was just having a twinge."

"A *twinge?*"

"Well, okay. Stronger than that, but it's the first one I've had in at least an hour, so we don't need to panic."

Who was panicking?

"You want me to deal?" she asked.

She was taking all this calmly. If she could be laid back about it, so could he.

"I'll do this hand."

She won the first game and crowed about it.

"Two out of three," he insisted.

They talked idly as they played. Once she giggled at a story he told her about a stupid crook, and he realized he hadn't heard her do that in a long time. It was an infectious sound that made him smile. The kid was going to pop out expecting to hear his mommy giggle.

He let her win the third game, so she went to bed satisfied. Then he finished cleaning the kitchen and read for a while before he went to bed.

Quinn usually slept in his boxer shorts or naked, but he'd taken to wearing pajama bottoms since Mindy came to stay with him. As he pulled them on, he patted his stomach, thinking it was getting a little soft. When was the last time he'd been to the gym? Or even run? Dumb question—he knew the answer. He'd been so damned eager to get home every day since Mindy had come to stay with him that he hadn't hit the gym in a month.

He heard her get up to go to the bathroom a time or two. The distant sound of doors opening and closing and the toilet flushing was part of the rhythm of the night now. But some time later, he came awake abruptly with the knowledge someone was standing beside his bed.

"Quinn?"

Swearing, he jackknifed up. "Mindy?"

Her voice was very small. "I think it's time."

"You're sure?" Stupid question.

"The contractions are five minutes apart."

"Wow." He shook his head, trying to clear the cob-webs. "Damn. Okay."

"Oh!" She gave a strangled gasp.

He switched on the lamp and gripped her hand. "Breathe! Come on. Pant. One, two, three, four, blow. Okay, that's it. Three, four, blow." He kept counting until he saw in her face that the contraction was subsiding. "That was closer together than five minutes, wasn't it?"

She nodded. "I'd better get dressed."

He threw on clothes and followed her, to find her sit-ting on the edge of her bed panting. She'd managed to get into a T-shirt and denim jumper before the next con-traction hit.

Quinn found her flip-flops and the suitcase she'd packed in advance. "Do you need your toothbrush and toothpaste? Anything else from the bathroom?"

They waited for one more contraction to come and go, then he hustled her to the car. She was panting again when he got behind the wheel. He waited until this one passed, then rocketed out of the garage and into the street. For the first time, he noticed the time: 4:08 a.m. Thank God the roads were empty at this time of night.

Her next contraction came at 4:12. Three and a half, four minutes apart. He wished she'd woken him sooner.

He reached for her hand and held it during the short drive. "You're doing great," he kept saying, meaning-lessly. At the hospital, he slammed to a stop in the emer-gency entrance. Mindy rode out another contraction before E.R. personnel eased her out of the car and into a wheelchair.

"I'll be right back," he promised, and drove off to park the car. He ran back to the entrance, then followed signs to the Obstetrics ward.

At the nurses' station he said, "Mindy Fenton?"

The middle-aged nurse smiled kindly at him. "We're just getting her settled in a delivery room."

"Her doctor?"

"Is on her way in."

By the time they let him in to see Mindy, she was in bed wearing a hospital gown and a monitor. He could see the baby's heartbeat pattering in electric green across the screen.

"Is that normal?" he demanded.

The nurse who had been taking Mindy's pulse smiled. "Yes, it looks just fine." She patted Mindy's hand. "I'll be right back."

"How close are the contractions together now?"

"Less than three minutes. It's happening really fast." She gave him a brave smile. "I'm so glad you were home and I didn't have to wait for a cab."

A cab. *God.*

"Yeah." He saw the change on her face. "Okay, here we go. One, two, three, four, exhale." He kept counting, barely aware of a nurse appearing, giving an approving smile and withdrawing from the room. "Good girl," he murmured, when Mindy sagged. He smoothed her hair from her clammy forehead. "Hey, you're handling these really well."

"My cheerleader." Her voice came out as a small, dry croak.

He handed her a glass of ice chips and steadied it as she took a few into her mouth.

When she'd swallowed, she said, "Will you wait, Quinn? I mean, if you want to go home…"

He'd have been mad as hell if he hadn't seen the anxiety in her eyes. "I'm not going anywhere."

"Oh." The hand still clasped in his relaxed. "You'll have to ask the nurse where to wait…"

"No." He met her eyes. "I mean, I'm staying right here. You're not doing this alone."

Mindy stared at him. "You mean that?" she whispered.

"You thought I was just going to lounge out there somewhere reading a good book while you went through labor alone?"

"I…"

He didn't let her finish. "You need a labor coach. I'm it."

Her eyes filled with fat tears that immediately spilled over. "Oh, Quinn."

"Hey." Out of the corner of his eye, he saw a change on the monitor. "Here comes another one."

He helped her breathe through it, then said, "Roll onto your side."

"What?" She started to roll toward him, but he shook his head and pushed her the other way. He untied the neck of her hospital gown and began to gently knead her shoulders. Mindy gave a throaty moan.

Her muscles were taut under his hands, and he

guessed fear was part of it. Showtime had arrived with a bang. *She'd* probably been worrying about whether she had a ten-pound baby in there, too, and how the hell she was going to get it out.

He was probing tense muscles beneath her shoulder blades when she stiffened. He kept rubbing gently as the contraction crested and then ebbed. Without a word, he deepened the massage, moved down to the small of her back.

The world seemed to narrow to the two of them, to the monitor and the nurse who checked on Mindy every little while, to the shrinking minutes between contractions and their murmured conversation.

"You'll call the Howies? And my mom?"

"The minute we know whether you have a boy or girl."

"I should have chosen a name, and I haven't. Except…if it's a boy, I thought maybe Dean."

Normally he wasn't a fan of juniors. But in this case… "Yeah. That'd be nice."

"But if it's a girl… Oh!"

"Breathe," he reminded her, when a small sob escaped her. "That's it, that's it."

He was exhausted. He'd had no idea how unrelenting this process was once it began. Nature could be ruthless. And Mindy's labor was progressing fast, from what he'd learned in the Lamaze class. What if she had a contraction every five minutes for forty hours?

The doctor arrived somewhere in there and kicked him out while she did an exam. "Six centimeters dilated," she announced, when he returned. "We're well on our way."

"You don't think you should do a C-section?"

She was kind enough to do no more than give him a pat on the arm. "Mindy is doing just fine. Don't worry."

"Ohhh!" Mindy wailed and he rushed to her side.

Framing her face with his hands, he made her look at him and talked her through this one, the most intense yet.

The contractions came faster and faster, until they were right on top of each other, one barely easing before the next roared in its wake. Her eyes never left his; she gripped his hand so hard he lost all feeling in it. The doctor coaxed Mindy to put her feet into the stirrups and draped a white cover over her knees.

"Try not to push yet," she cautioned, when sinews stood out in Mindy's neck and her back arched with a powerful wave of contraction.

And finally she said, "Oh, yes! I see the top of the head. Now, as you reach the top of the contraction, push! Yes, like that. *Push!*"

The effort was enormous, primal. An agonized, guttural cry came from Mindy's throat as her body arched from the narrow bed.

She collapsed briefly, then did it again, and again, the doctor singing encouragement, Quinn gripping her hand and watching something amazing.

Finally, Mindy cried out in triumph and the doctor crowed, "Yes! Here she is!"

"She?" Quinn croaked.

"She?" Mindy whispered.

"You have a little girl." Dr. Gibbs lifted a scrawny, red, mucus- and blood-covered creature that let out a squall and flapped arms and legs as Quinn gaped. "Let us clean her up, and she'll be happier with her mommy."

The nurse accepted the newborn from the doctor, who encouraged Mindy to push again. A few minutes later, the nurse brought a small, white-wrapped bundle to the bed and gently laid it—her—in the crook of Mindy's arm. The face was red and puckered and ugly as sin—and yet Quinn might as well have been reeling from the slam of a bullet, so wrenching was the pain under his breastbone, an onslaught of love for a baby that wasn't his but *felt* like his.

Damn it, she wasn't ugly, she was beautiful—tiny, perfect features, a miniature rosebud of a mouth, perplexed blue eyes and a fuzz of moonlight-pale hair that had a hint of red in it.

"She's a strawberry blonde," Mindy whispered in wonder. She looked up at him, her eyes awash in tears, her smile tremulous. "Isn't she gorgeous, Quinn?"

"Yeah," he heard himself say, in a voice that wasn't his. "As pretty as her mommy."

In his dumbfounded state, Mindy had never looked prettier. Her face glowed with joy and a love so gentle and profound, it deepened the ache in Quinn's chest.

"Oh, sweetie, are you hungry?" As if it were natural, she pulled the neck of the gown down and he realized she was going to expose her breast.

Quinn shot to his feet. "I'll go make those calls."

"Oh, yes!" That glowing smile rewarded him. "Thank you, Quinn. You'll come right back?"

So naturally, she was tugging that gown from her shoulder to free her breast.

He bolted.

In a central waiting area, he had to sink to a chair and lower his head to keep it from spinning. What had happened to him? Why did he feel this powerful bond to a woman and child who weren't his?

It was just the moment. The experience. It had to be, he thought desperately. It couldn't be anything more lasting, more threatening to the even tenor of his life.

He couldn't let it be.

Eventually Quinn pulled himself together enough to go to the bank of pay phones. He'd been carrying the two numbers in his wallet for the past couple weeks.

He called Mindy's mother first.

A man answered, asked who he was. A moment later, Mrs. Walker came on. "You're that friend she's been staying with?"

What woman didn't know who her daughter lived with?

"Yes, Brendan Quinn," he repeated. "Mrs. Walker, Mindy asked me to call you. She's had her baby."

He heard a squeal.

"Is it a boy? A girl?"

"A girl. She's cute. Her hair looks…" What was it Mindy had called the color? "Strawberry blonde. And her eyes are blue. I guess all babies have blue eyes, don't they?" Actually, he had no idea. "But she looks like hers really are."

"Oh, my goodness." Her mother sounded genuinely staggered.

Man, did he know the feeling.

She wrote down the name of the hospital. Quinn

couldn't tell her how long Mindy would be staying. He promised to get in touch once he knew more.

Then he called the Howies.

Nancy was wonder-struck as well. "A little girl!"

He described her again.

"Well, Dean was a redhead," Nancy said practically. "Oh! Has Mindy named her yet?"

"No, during labor she said she hadn't thought of a name if she was a girl yet. If the baby had been a boy, she was going to name him Dean."

"You know, Dean's mother's name was Jessamine. Isn't that pretty? Do you remember how much he talked about her?"

She was always going to come for him. He didn't know what was holding her up, but even after his faith had eroded inside, he became enraged when anyone suggested that she might be dead or just plain not interested in returning for the kid she'd discarded. Not that anyone put it so bluntly, but Dean had known what they were saying. Quinn had envied him the ability to love and trust someone so unshakably, even if that person didn't—or couldn't—live up to the trust.

"Jessamine." He sounded out the name. "I'd forgotten her name. I'll mention it to Mindy."

"Oh, she may want to name the baby after her own mother or grandmother. Don't put pressure on her."

"No. I won't." He shifted, resting a shoulder against the wall. "Listen, why don't you and George plan to come over next week some day? I've talked Mindy into staying with me for a while, at least. Once she's got the hang of this motherhood thing, I know she'd love to have you visit."

They promised they would, and he made one last call, this time to Ellis Carter.

"You sound beat," his partner sympathized. "Hell, I remember what it was like. Did I ever tell you about the time…"

"Yeah, you did," Quinn interrupted. Carter loved to tell the story about his wife's first labor, which had—or so Carter liked to say—gone on forever. She'd been dilated three centimeters, had a further hour of vicious labor pains only to be told she was now dilated only two centimeters. According to Carter, she'd risen from the delivery table like a Valkyrie and gone for the nurse-practitioner's throat. He'd had to bodily hold her back.

"A girl, huh?"

"Yeah. Dean has a baby daughter."

"Wow." Carter cleared his throat. "Damn."

"You'll let everyone know?"

"Sure, sure."

"I won't be in today."

"You must need to hit the sack."

Quinn guessed he did. Right now he was still too wired. Too shaken. But he knew that when weariness hit, it would be hard. One minute he'd be fine, the next he'd feel as if he'd walked into a wall. That was how it worked.

He went back to the room and poked his head in warily. Mindy had restored her gown to its place, he saw with relief. He wasn't ready yet to face the fact that she'd be nursing regularly, that women were prone these days to doing it anywhere. That eventually, he'd probably see her breast before the baby's mouth latched on.

"She's asleep," Mindy whispered.

His heart did another tumble when he saw her face, frowning in sleep. She made a snuffly sound and burrowed against her mommy's breast.

"Isn't she amazing?"

"Yeah. Yeah, she is." He pulled up a chair and sat beside the bed, his gaze captured by that funny red face.

"Did you call everyone?"

"Huh? Oh, yeah. Your mom sounded blown away. I think I got her up. I'm guessing she'll be tearing in the door here any minute."

"Really?" Mindy looked vulnerable. As if she didn't want to hope her mother cared, but she couldn't help herself.

"She was excited. Nancy was, too. She and George are hoping to come over to see the baby once you're ready."

"Oh, good."

"Nancy had a thought for a name, too. Did Dean ever talk about his mother?"

Mindy nodded. "He thought she must be dead. He said he knew she'd have come back for him otherwise."

"Yeah, he was always so sure she'd be showing up any day. We'd make plans, and he'd say, 'Except, if my mom comes, I might not be here.'" Quinn shook his head, remembering. "Just a few years ago, I offered to search for her. He blew his top. Finally he admitted that he'd rather imagine her giving him up because she knew she was dying of cancer and didn't want him to watch than find out she'd been raped and murdered in some alley, or become a junkie."

"How sad!"

"He really believed in her. He wanted to keep believing." Weird how Quinn found he could understand Dean feeling that way better now than he'd been able to when Dean was alive. "Anyway, Nancy reminded me that her name was Jessamine. She thought it was so pretty."

"Jessamine." Mindy looked down at her tiny daughter. Her voice had gone soft again. "Dean would love that, wouldn't he?"

"He would, but if you don't like the name…"

"It's beautiful. Just like her. Jessamine." When Mindy lifted her head, her eyes sparkled with tears. "Thank you, Quinn."

Alarmed, he said, "Thank Nancy."

"No, I didn't mean for the name. Well, for that, but mostly for everything else. I don't know what I would have done without you."

"You're strong," he said, and meant it. "You'd have done fine."

She gave a funny laugh. "Did that choke you?"

He grinned, a little ruefully. "Nah. It just came right out."

Face sobering, Mindy said, "I'm not so sure I *would* have done fine. This time, I really, really needed help."

"You know, being here for this…" He moved his

shoulders, uncomfortable with expressing emotions but feeling compelled. "Today. I wouldn't trade it."

Gaze on her sleeping daughter, Mindy's smile went back to glowing. "I was scared, but you were right. It was all worth it."

The nurse popped in to say that the doctor had decided to keep Mindy overnight because of her condition, even though her blood pressure was good. Mindy was whisked to a room and the nurse took tiny Jessamine off to the nursery so that her mom could get some sleep.

Dr. Gibbs, looking in on Mindy, scrutinized Quinn. "You look like you need some, too. Go home. Come back when you can stand without swaying."

A minute later, Quinn stood outside the entrance, wondering where he'd left the car. Across the parking lot, Mindy's mother, trailed by some guy, hurried toward the hospital entrance. Too tired to make the effort to intercept her, Quinn turned vaguely in the direction from which he thought he'd come that morning.

His feet stopped when they found the car. He got in and drove home in a semiconscious state. He kept hearing Mindy's guttural cry, seeing the exultation on her face, the tiny flapping arms of the being who had emerged from her body.

And Mindy's wondering, loving smile. Had Dean's mother looked at him like that when he'd been born?

Quinn's thoughts took an inevitable, sideways jump. Had his *own* mother ever looked at him like that? Had she wanted a baby at all? He could close his eyes sometimes and remember being held and swung into the air and rocked. Or perhaps the fleeting images weren't memories at all, but dreams. Childish fantasies, cooked up when he hid in the back of the closet in the dark, filthy apartment, because he'd thought he heard footsteps stop outside the door, the knob rattle. *Mommy, where are you?*

But from what he remembered more clearly, she *had* tried. So maybe, when he was younger and her addiction less fierce, she'd been the loving mother from those whispered memories.

For some reason, Mindy's surprise that he hadn't wanted a picture of his own mother popped into his mind. Her face had become increasingly hazy in his memory. Maybe, if he actually found a photo of her when she was young and still hopeful, he'd remember more of the good times, before her addiction had become more powerful than any love she felt for him. Finding out what high school she went to wouldn't be hard.

He drove the car into the garage at home, right next to Dean's shiny red Camaro, turned off the engine and sat unmoving, unable to summon the will to make himself get out and go into the house.

Tomorrow morning, he'd set up the bassinet Mindy had ordered online. On the way to the hospital, he'd pick up some other things—diapers, maybe a couple of those tiny sleepers that didn't look like they'd fit a doll. He'd ask a clerk what Jessamine would need. He didn't think Mindy had bought much yet.

Tomorrow morning, he'd be bringing mother and child home. A month ago, he hadn't known where

Mindy was. Hadn't known she was pregnant. Now, he couldn't imagine not having witnessed the birth of Dean's daughter, couldn't imagine going back to his lonely life.

But he'd have to. He had no right to want more, to ask for more. And no reason to think Mindy would give it.

Finally, moving stiffly, feeling as if he'd had the crap beaten out of him, Quinn shut the garage door, patted the fender of Dean's car and made it to his bedroom, where he fell face down on the bed into a sleep filled with dreams and confusion.

CHAPTER TWELVE

MINDY CALLED QUINN on his cell phone the next morning and said, "I haven't bought a car seat yet! The hospital won't let me take Jessamine without one. I hate to ask, but...."

"I just bought one," he said. "Set up the bassinet this morning, too."

Relief washed over her. "Oh, thank goodness! I suddenly had this image of me trying to wrench Jessamine from somebody's arms."

"I'd arrest 'em if they tried to stop you."

Her heart gave one of those funny little hops that he seemed to provoke so often these days. Who'd have thought grim Det. Quinn could be so sweet?

When he picked her and Jessamine up, she discovered he'd bought the Rolls Royce of car seats, a convertible one with parts that could be added on and removed to see a baby through kindergarten and the booster-seat stage. Right now, it sat facing backward and had a simple harness to buckle Jessie in.

In the car, Mindy said, "The hospital sent me with a couple of diapers, but I suppose…"

"I took care of that, too." He started forward with as much care as if he were transporting someone who was badly injured. "I bought a few other things, too, that I thought you might need. I asked for help."

Who had he asked? She pictured him in the baby aisle at the grocery store, staring baffled at the rows of diapers of different brands, some for girls, some for boys, in half a dozen different sizes. He must have looked cute stopping some woman with her cart and asking her to tell him what a newborn would need.

Mindy wondered what else he'd bought. Bottles and nipples? Pacifiers? Strained peas Jessie wouldn't need for six or eight months?

Smiling, she vowed not to tell him if he'd bought useless things. She just hoped the diapers weren't toddler pull-ons.

At home he let her lift Jessamine out of the car seat and then escorted them in. She stopped in the doorway to her bedroom and gaped. "Quinn!"

"Did I go overboard?"

Several downy baby blankets were draped over the side of the bassinet. A mobile with bright-colored faces and shapes and even a mirror dangled above it. On the bed were more diapers than any baby would use in weeks and a couple of bags from Nordstrom.

"You didn't have to do this." In a dream, she laid Jessie, still snugly bundled in a receiving blanket, down in the bassinet, gently covered her with a fuzzy pink blanket with a woolly sheep embroidered on it, and turned to the bags. "What did you buy?"

Still standing in the doorway, he said, "I just noticed you didn't have any clothes for her yet."

Amazed and touched, she pulled one small sleeper after another from the bag, some thin knits, others thick, warm fleece. In the second bag were tiny undershirts, a mint-green knit cap embroidered with a white-and-yellow daisy, a rattle and a quilted sack with arms and a hood that looked like it would keep Jessie warm on the way up Mount Everest.

"With the weather getting cold..."

Quinn never showed emotion, exactly, but she realized he was waiting with apprehension for her reaction.

"Oh, Quinn." Blasted if she wasn't crying again. "This is the nicest thing anyone has ever done for me. I mean, it's for her, but..."

"Don't start that again."

Okay, she was wrong. He *did* show emotion. He looked seriously irritated.

"'Thank you' will do," he growled.

She blinked away moisture and said obediently, "Thank you, Quinn."

"Are those okay? The receipts are in the bag if you want to take anything back or get something different."

"Everything you bought is perfect. Beautiful." Her face wanted to crumple.

He shook his head, disappeared from the doorway and reappeared a moment later with a tissue in his hand. "Here," he said, thrusting it at her.

She blew her nose, mopped her cheeks and smiled at him. "I think I need a nap."

He nodded toward the bassinet. "Will she let you nap?"

"She actually hasn't cried much yet. I think she's too traumatized by the noisy, bright world. I did nurse right before you picked me up."

He looked vaguely alarmed, probably at the idea of Jessie squalling, and left her to her own devices. Mindy sat on the edge of the bed and gazed at her sleeping daughter, still awed by her perfection. No, by her very existence.

She was surprised, too, by the love that was so sharp it might have been pain. It was fierce and instinctive, awakened the minute she'd seen her daughter, bloody and trailing the umbilical cord. She couldn't imagine *not* feeling this way. It left her puzzled because she knew her own mother had never loved her so intensely. For the first time, instead of hurt she felt pity for the joy her mother had missed.

"Daddy," she whispered, "I wish you could have seen Jessamine."

She woke an hour later to a piercing cry. She was on her feet in an instant, lifting Jessie and cuddling her.

"Sssh, sssh, it's okay, Mommy's here." She looked up to see Quinn in the doorway and realized she'd never shut the door.

"Is everything okay?"

"I think someone is hungry," Mindy murmured. "Or wet. Is your diaper wet, sweetheart?"

He nodded and retreated again. She wondered in gentle amusement what he would have done if she'd slept through Jessamine's cries. Tried to change her diaper himself? Or woken Mindy?

But then it occurred to her he had yet to hold Jessie. Or even, she thought in surprise, touch her.

She knew when she nursed that Jessie wasn't yet getting much milk, but she seemed satisfied by the act of suckling. Since she didn't immediately fall asleep again, Mindy carried her out to the living room.

Quinn rose from his chair, the newspaper crackling in his hands. His gaze was fixed on the bundle in her arms.

"Here," she said. "I thought you might like to hold her."

"Hold her?" He looked…well, she couldn't quite decide. Horrified? Unwillingly fascinated by the idea?

"She won't break."

"I've never held a baby."

"One was born right into your hands. You kept her safe."

"I passed her off to her mother as quick as I could."

"Coward," Mindy teased. "Come on. Put down the paper."

With obvious reluctance, he did.

"Now, sit."

He sat.

"Wow. If I'd known you'd follow orders so easily…"

He gave her a dark look.

She laughed at him and laid Jessie in his arms. His head bent, and he and the baby gazed in equal bemusement at each other.

Mindy curled one foot under her and settled on the end of the couch, a few feet from Quinn's chair.

The very sight of him in jeans and a black T-shirt, powerful muscles flexed in his upper arms as he sat frozen holding the tiny, pink-bundled infant, was enough to give Mindy that familiar twist in her chest. Jessie wriggled one arm free of the receiving blanket and waved it, causing Quinn's eyes to all but cross as he studied the minute hand.

"She's so…little."

"Not that little. She was almost eight pounds. Imagine having a five-pound preemie."

"Can she see me?"

"I think things are pretty fuzzy. It takes a few weeks for a baby's eyes to figure out how to focus."

Jessamine let out a squawk. Quinn jumped. "Nothing wrong with her lungs," he muttered.

Mindy smiled. "Nope. I'm afraid you'll be hearing a whole lot from her in the middle of the night. Not only does she want to nurse every couple of hours, but I have a suspicion she's nocturnal."

"Isn't that normal?"

"Yeah, there's a reason new parents look haggard for the first couple of months." She bit her lip. "Quinn, you've let yourself in for an awful lot. I can start looking for an apartment right away if you want."

His head lifted and he pinned her with a glittering stare. "I said I wanted you to stay and I meant it."

"O-kay." She waved her hand. "Down, boy."

He looked astounded.

"You don't have to intimidate me. I'm just asking. And telling you. You won't hurt my feelings if you ask me to start apartment hunting."

"I don't intend to kick you out!"

Jessamine opened her mouth and screamed bloody murder.

Mindy laughed at his aghast expression. "You scared her."

He swore, then said, "Damn it, I didn't mean... Oh, hell. What do I do?"

"Just lift her to your shoulder." She mimicked the action. "Support her head with your hand. Like that. Good. Then pat her back and murmur soft things to her. Or sing. She likes it when I sing."

"She wouldn't like my singing." He cleared his throat. "It's okay. You don't have to cry." His big hand engulfed Jessie as he awkwardly patted. "Hey, don't cry. Don't cry."

As if by instinct he began to jiggle her, and his voice softened, took on a singsong rhythm Mindy had heard herself using as well.

Jessie quieted.

Mindy smiled. "I think she likes that."

"Yeah." He stole a glance down. "Yeah, I think she does." His amazement was comical.

"Would you mind holding on to her while I take a shower?" Mindy stood, taking his assent for granted.

There was a hitch in the rhythm and Jessie's head bobbed. "What if she..."

"Talk to her."

The hot water beating down on her felt unbelievably good. Drying herself afterward, Mindy looked ruefully at her still-soft belly. She was going to have to keep wearing her maternity clothes for a few weeks, at least. How long did it take to get your figure back?

Finger-combing her wet hair, she went back to the living room to find that Quinn hadn't moved, but Jessie had apparently fallen asleep against his shoulder.

"Afraid to twitch?"

"Won't she wake up if you move her?"

"Haven't you ever seen puppies and kittens and little kids sleep?" She reached for her daughter.

He let her take Jessie. "I've never had a puppy or kitten."

She stopped. "You're kidding."

"Why would I kid?"

"Not even the Howies?"

"They had an old dog. Buster." He looked momentarily reminiscent. "Buster was a beagle. A great dog. He died when I was a junior in high school. They never replaced him."

"Wow. We took in a pregnant cat when I was a kid. We found homes for most of the kittens. We kept the mom and one kitten. Mom still has them. I remember the way the kittens slept in a heap. One could climb right on top of the pile and the others wouldn't even stir." She leaned a cheek on the pale fuzz of her daughter's head. "I think Jessie is like that."

Putting Jessie down for her nap, Mindy thought, *At least he had a pet.*

What the Howies had done for Dean and Quinn was extraordinary. They hadn't just given them a home. They'd given them a childhood neither had had. Even Dean, much as he'd worshipped the memory of his mother, had admitted that she'd taken him from one dump to another. They'd lived in women's shelters some of the time. He'd remembered long days of kicking his heels while he sat on plastic chairs in government offices while she applied for food stamps and welfare and subsidized housing. As fast as he'd grown, he'd never had clothes that fit. The jeans had always been too short, his bony wrists had always stuck out below the cuffs of shirts.

"I wanted the things other kids had." He'd looked with satisfaction around his living room, at the leather couches and crystal and wrought-iron lamps, at the ten-thousand-dollar painting that hung over the fireplace. He'd always made sure everyone knew how much he'd paid for that painting. "I haven't done half-bad at getting them."

He would hate to know she hadn't been able to get anywhere near that much money when she'd sold the painting.

In the early days, she'd enjoyed his childish pleasure in his success and in new possessions, but had also found it a little sad. What she hadn't realized was that he never would have been completely fulfilled. That car or boat or fancy lawn mower wasn't an end, but…oh, more like a piece of chocolate popped in the mouth of someone who was ravenous. It tasted good, it spiked the blood sugar and brought temporary contentment—but then it was swallowed and the blood sugar plummeted and the stomach was still empty. Dean was always hungry.

Mindy wondered whether Jessie would have been like that bite of chocolate for Dean, or whether she would have satisfied a deep need in him for love. She *wanted* to think he would have been a great father.

Over the next few days, she kept thinking about Dean and about Quinn in contrast.

Why didn't Quinn covet the newest, shiniest, most dazzling possessions? He hadn't had it any better than Dean. Worse, in some ways.

And why had one man tried hard to be loved by everyone, while the other became a loner, skipping most human connection by choice?

Why, she wondered, had Dean, who'd known that he was loved, been so restless? Shouldn't he have been *more* able to make long-term commitments than Quinn, who'd never had anyone make one to him until the Howies came along?

More and more she speculated on whether her marriage would have lasted. Would *she* have satisfied Dean, or would his unending hunger have caused him, sooner or later, to start dreaming about replacing his wife with a newer, more spectacular model?

She felt horribly cynical even to be thinking that way, or to be wondering whether she would have remained content in the marriage, but part of her needed to know.

And she knew why, although she wasn't ready to think about that yet.

One night, after Jessie was asleep and she and Quinn were cleaning up the dinner dishes, Mindy said, "You didn't have much when you were growing up, either. Why is it that you aren't like Dean? I mean, always wanting something newer and better?"

Quinn paused with his hand on the handle of the faucet. If he was surprised at the way she'd jumped in with both feet, given the fact that they'd been talking about a scandal in the state attorney general's office, he didn't show it.

"I don't know," he said finally. "I just never cared that much about possessions. In fact…"

He braked so suddenly she was intrigued.

"In fact what?" she prodded, when it was clear he wasn't going to finish.

His face took on that closed look she was so familiar with. For a moment she thought he wasn't going to answer. Then he shrugged, turned on the water and poured soap into the sink.

"I was going to say, if anything I was suspicious when someone wanted to give me something. It felt like a bribe. I always assumed strings were attached."

Disturbed by the sad picture of a boy who didn't believe in pure goodwill, she asked, "Why?"

"Why?" He turned off the water, not looking at her. "I don't know. No, that's not true. My mother always had a man. When they gave me presents, they were trying to buy something from *her.* I knew that, even when I was really young. And when she gave me a special treat, I knew to brace myself. She did it when she felt guilty. Usually it meant she was going to take off for a few days, or she'd spent her welfare check on heroin without going to the grocery store first." He shrugged, his appalling story matter-of-fact.

"How awful," Mindy whispered. On automatic, she

accepted the pan from him that he'd just rinsed and began to dry it.

"I survived."

"Has anyone ever given you a present you really loved and kept?"

He looked surprised. "I don't know. Yeah, probably. I guess some of the CDs in my collection were given to me." He turned off the running water and looked directly at her. "The Camaro."

"It wasn't a gift. You insisted on paying for it."

"I think of it as one. As something of Dean's you wanted me to have."

"I did want you to have it. But I wanted to *give* it to you." It still frustrated her, remembering his stubborn refusal to accept anything from her. "You know, I think that's when I lost hope that we could stay friends. When you wouldn't even let me do that."

"I couldn't let you give me something that expensive."

"But you meant so much to Dean, and so did the car. It just seemed important that you had the best piece of him I could give. Don't you understand?" She felt as if she were begging. "It wasn't really from me. It was from Dean."

Hands in the soapy water, Quinn said, "I didn't take presents from him, either. Nothing big."

"A CD was okay, but not a car."

His mouth twisted. "Something like that."

"Did you really believe *Dean* would want something in return?" She studied Quinn's hard, unreadable profile.

The breath he drew was ragged. "No. My reaction was…instinctive. He got that."

"And I didn't." Mindy tried to smile, but felt her lips tremble. "You and I didn't even know each other that well, and I expected you to take this huge gift from me because we'd both loved this guy." The realization stung. "That was…really self-centered of me."

"You didn't know."

"But I did. Kind of. Dean tried to tell me about you. I knew that when you left the Howies, you took only the things you'd actually bought with your own money from your job. Dean was laughing when he told me, like, see, Quinn has this weird quirk. He might have respected your wishes, but he *didn't* get it. Not really. He just thought it was funny."

Quinn made a rough sound in his throat. "He was humoring me."

Belatedly, she understood she might be hurting him by telling him this. "Maybe I'm wrong…"

"No. You're not. I knew he didn't really understand. 'Why not take everything you could get?' was his attitude. I don't mean that in a bad way," he added quickly. "Just…we were opposite sides of the coin."

"Do you suppose…" Mindy gazed out the kitchen window. "Do you suppose his mother wanted nice things desperately? Or that she always promised him that someday they'd have all the things they wanted? Or the last thing she said was that when she came back for him, she'd buy him some toy?"

"I don't know." Quinn rotated his head, as if to loosen tight neck muscles. "What I do know is that he was hardwired to be the way he was."

"And you to be the way you are."

"Maybe. Aren't we all?"

She frowned. "I'm not sure I believe that. I think we have some choice. We may be pulled one way or another, but we can dig in our heels and say, 'I'm not going to be like my mother.'"

Where in heck had *that* come from? Was that how she saw her quest as a human being? To *not* be like her mother?

Quinn gave her an odd, thoughtful look. "You're not, you know."

"I didn't mean that. It was just an example. Pulled out of a hat."

"Uh-huh."

She swatted him with the dish towel. "Mr. I-Will-Never-Trust-Another-Human-Being."

The mask slid over his face again. "Is that how you see me?"

Feeling bold, she stuck to her guns. "I think that's how you see yourself."

"I trusted Dean."

"But not so far as to accept something from him that might have strings attached."

He pulled the plug from the drain and faced her, voice flat. "You don't know what the hell you're talking about."

"Maybe I don't." Her boldness was swirling away with the dishwater. "But I want to."

"What difference is it to you what makes me tick?"

Her breath caught in her throat. At something he saw on her face, he went still. They stared at each other.

"I…" Her words squeaked to a stop.

The muscles in Quinn's jaw flexed. Then his lashes shielded his eyes and he said, with seeming indifference, "Jessie's crying."

"Oh!" She pressed her fingers to her mouth. She hadn't even heard her own baby crying! "Oh, dear. I'd better…" She backed from the kitchen. "She must be hungry…."

He was putting away the pans she'd dried and didn't even seem to notice when she fled.

THAT ONE CONVERSATION in the kitchen seemed to change everything. Until then, it had never once occurred to Quinn that Mindy might see him as anything but Dean's friend. She was so damn determined to believe that everything Quinn did for her was really for Dean, how was he supposed to think differently?

But the way she'd poked and prodded, as if it *did* matter who he was, and then the startled knowledge and guilt on her face when he'd confronted her… The way color had run up her neck and blossomed on her cheeks as she'd sucked in air. For a minute there, as they'd stared at each other, he was afraid he'd given away more than he'd ever meant to, as well.

It was the next day that Quinn let himself put into words the truth that had been eating at his gut.

He wanted her.

God help him, he couldn't remember when he hadn't. Maybe from the beginning, although he hadn't known why he always felt uncomfortable in her presence, why he didn't like to watch Dean nuzzle her neck or wrap a possessive hand around her hip or pull her onto his lap. Guilt tasted like bile in his mouth, corroded his stomach, but even he knew it made no sense. If he'd come on to Dean's wife when his buddy wasn't around, he'd deserve to burn in hell. As it was, he'd done the best he could: buried even the knowledge that she attracted him, stayed away from her, frozen out her attempts to draw him into a warm family circle, as if they could be sister- and brother-in-law.

He'd just been too stupid to know why he was doing it.

When he'd first met her, Quinn remembered thinking that she wasn't Dean's type. Dean liked women that were more like his Camaro: sexy, well-endowed, just a little obvious. Mindy wasn't exactly Quinn's type, either. He'd tended to go for women whom Dean called "high society," ones who were subtle, smart, sleek.

Mindy was like a bunch of daisies picked in the field. Effortlessly pretty, sweet, cheerful.

So why was it, Quinn wondered, that she'd somehow drawn both men?

He grunted in amusement. Maybe the qualities that had irritated him the most had also first attracted him. That infectious giggle. Her bare feet. Her short tousled hair that always made him think of the head of a dandelion. Her childlike pleasure in simple delights.

Perhaps it had been much the same for Dean. She'd been fresh, charming, without artifice, fun. Dean had clearly basked in the way she glowed with admiration for him.

Quinn hadn't let himself get to know her well enough to discover that she was also smart, well read and, in her own way, as lonely as he was.

He swore aloud, something that caused no heads to turn at the station. You'd have to invent a new obscenity if you didn't want to be background music here.

Carter was still booking Marvin's shooter, while Quinn was writing up a report. His mind kept wandering, because the truth was that they'd got lucky. A drug bust and the resultant charges had apparently scared the hell out of a barely eighteen-year-old member of the gang, who offered to testify about the murders he'd witnessed to get out of jail time. The arresting officer had called Quinn.

Quinn hoped the kid was planning to move after the trial, because if he stayed in Seattle he was dead.

Carter wandered in, a pint of milk in his hand. He peered over Quinn's shoulder. "You haven't finished yet?"

"There's no challenge," Quinn complained. Then, "You're drinking *milk?*"

Carter patted his stomach. "I didn't get a chance to tell you today. I have an ulcer. Can you believe it? The doctor recommends I give up coffee among other things."

"An ulcer, huh." Quinn couldn't help laughing. "I'm the one who should have the ulcer. You're too good-humored to have earned one."

"I suppress the angst," his partner said with dignity. Then he grinned, too. "Doctor said it may have nothing to do with stress. He's got me on some kind of antibiotic. Go figure."

Quinn clapped him on the back. "That's good news. I was expecting a five-way bypass."

"You were expecting to bury me." Carter took a swallow of the milk. "Unlike you, I'm done for the day. Don't stay too late."

Quinn tossed a wadded up piece of paper after him. Carter danced to the side and, laughing, walked away.

The bare-bones report written at last, Quinn escaped in turn. He arrived home to find the Howies' car in the driveway. He opened the door to the smell of dinner cooking, the murmur of voices and the sound of Nancy's laugh. His stride checked and he paused, still unnoticed. Quinn hadn't heard her laugh like that in years.

He walked in unnoticed. George and Nancy sat close together on the couch in the living room, heads bent over the baby. Wearing sweats and a pair of fuzzy slippers, Mindy was in the kitchen, stirring something on the stove, humming tunelessly and swaying in time to her own music. To his biased eye, she looked cute.

What in hell was wrong with him?

"Hey," Quinn said.

She turned from the stove, spoon suspended above the pan, face brightening. "Quinn! Look who's here!"

"I saw." Ridiculously warmed because she seemed so glad to see him, he strolled into the living room. "Nancy and George. What do you think? Isn't Jessamine the most beautiful baby ever?"

"Oh, Quinn." Nancy accepted his kiss on the cheek. "She is darling!"

Jessie lay on Nancy's lap, limbs flailing, her mouth

pursed and her vague gaze wandering from face to face. Quinn reached down and lifted her to his shoulder.

"Hey, little one," he murmured.

Her head wobbled as she tried to see his face. He liked holding her, now that he was getting the hang of it. The other night, he'd spent a couple of hours with her snoozing on his chest, him reading police reports. He'd ignored every itch and muscle twitch for the pleasure of having the feather-light weight over his heart, her baby smell in his nostrils.

In the past, he'd been disbelieving when tough cops he knew had wandered in to offer It's a Boy cigars, their faces invariably wearing dopey, happy grins. Now, he understood. And Jessie wasn't even his child.

So far, he was trying real hard not to think about what that meant. So he didn't appreciate it when, over dinner, George said, "Well, Quinn, are you going to miss that little doll when Mindy gets her own place?"

Mindy laughed at him. "You mean, is he looking forward to getting a good night's sleep?"

He couldn't summon a joke. "I'll miss her." Even to his own ears he sounded curt.

There was an awkward little silence before Mindy started telling about how Quinn had gotten shanghaied into attending her Lamaze class. "But he turned out to be a great labor coach," she concluded, beaming at him. "I don't know what I'd have done without him."

The Howies gazed at him with identical expressions of shock. Did they disapprove because he'd been present at the birth and Mindy wasn't his own wife?

But then George nodded with seeming respect and approbation, while Nancy smiled with delight. "Quinn! I didn't know you were actually in there with Mindy! How wonderful that she had your support. Of course you and Dean always were willing to do anything for each other. I should have known you'd step in for him."

Out of the corner of his eye, Quinn saw Mindy's smile dim a little. Or maybe he was imagining it. His flare of anger took him by surprise. Why did everyone assume that every decent thing he did was either a tribute to his dead friend or a duty imposed by their friendship? Was it impossible to imagine that he'd *wanted* to be with Mindy when she'd needed him, that he could love someone besides Dean?

In shock of his own, he thought, *Love?*

They were all staring at him, so he buttered a roll and said, "I can't believe Dean would have expected me to hold his wife's hand during labor. Heck, *he'd* have probably fainted."

They all laughed.

"Mindy and I have gotten to be friends." He made it sound matter-of-fact and casual at the same time. "I wanted to do this with her."

"You know Quinn's delivered a baby before, don't you?" Mindy jumped in.

"No!" Nancy exclaimed.

He had to tell the story again, distracting them from the idea of him sitting at Mindy's side during labor as a sort of embodiment of a dead man. The idea repulsed him.

After the Howies left, Jessamine began to cry and

Mindy went to get her. He stayed in the kitchen when she sat on the couch, discreetly freed her breast and helped Jessie latch on. He knew what she was doing, but he never let himself look. Quinn didn't know if she'd noticed how he avoided her when she was nursing—he hoped she hadn't. But he couldn't seem to make himself just sit down and keep chatting as if she didn't have her shirt lifted and her bra open to expose a breast. He wasn't sure whether he was made more uncomfortable by the fact that he was turned on by the idea of an eager mouth on her breast, or by the tenderness he could see even across the room.

Quinn froze in the act of opening a kitchen cupboard. He was just full of revelations tonight, wasn't he? But why in hell would the tenderness between mother and child bother him?

Because he felt excluded.

The answer came to him without even a pretense of a struggle. He'd already known. Just hadn't wanted to admit it.

Mindy wasn't his, and Jessie wasn't his. If he got too close, he'd be kidding himself. Some kind of invisible force field surrounded them, and he couldn't cross it.

Quinn shook his head, stunned by the devastation that lay inside him, as gray and lifeless as the land buried in ash after Mount Saint Helens had erupted.

He'd always felt the same way when he saw kids with their parents, mothers with babies, fathers swinging toddlers onto their shoulders or shooting baskets with their teenage sons on the driveway outside their houses. From the time he was little, he'd watched other kids run to meet their parents after school, babbling about what Teacher told them and eager to show off schoolwork, and he'd felt…invisible. A watcher who would never be enclosed in one of those shimmering bubbles. Even at the Howies', he'd been the one who hadn't fit, the silent, solitary extra at the table, as if he were forever a guest.

By then, he'd told himself he didn't care. Now, standing in his kitchen watching across a great distance as Mindy nursed her baby and cooed softly to her, he knew he'd lied to himself. He did care. He'd cared then, and he cared now, with a searing pain that roared in his ears like a wildfire that had leaped the fire line.

He wanted to be loved.

And the agony came from knowing whose love he wanted, and could never have.

CHAPTER THIRTEEN

INFECTED WITH A SENSE of urgency about the future, Mindy waited only until the evening after the Howies' visit to ask Quinn if she could use his tools in the garage. He had a well-equipped workbench, she'd discovered on further exploration, with a table saw she itched to get her hands on.

Even though she knew he'd seen some of her work, he seemed surprised when she told him that, before Dean's death, she'd actually been selling wall plaques and signs that said Welcome or My Secret Garden in gift shops. Either he thought her stuff was nothing special or he'd assumed her woodworking was no more than a hobby. His surprise left her feeling insulted. Or maybe hurt was a better word.

But he did shrug and say, "Sure. Use anything you want. Just let me know if you need help. The table saw can be dangerous if you don't know what you're doing."

The next morning, after he'd left for work, she headed out to the lumberyard and the hardware store, Jessie in a cloth carrier on her stomach. She came home with several thicknesses of plywood, enough lumber to cut out the bits and pieces she had in mind, paint and sheets of copper and galvanized steel, miscellaneous mosaic tiles and wooden dowels, springs and intriguing pieces of hardware. On impulse she stopped at a junk store that had caught her eye on the way to Lamaze class and bought old signs, buttons, a broken stained-glass window and a hideous collage someone had once made after a beach vacation. She'd need more. Lots more. But this was enough to get her started.

Mindy was going to make birdhouses.

She'd seen a few quirky ones in leafy neighborhoods of the city, hanging from tree limbs or sitting atop fence posts. Back when she'd first suspected she was pregnant, Mindy had seen one that looked like a gingerbread cottage. Meticulous and charming, it had made her smile—and think. There were almost limitless possibilities. She could build a miniature southern plantation house, or a tiny church. She could use an old wooden game board, or paint and age plywood to look like one. She imagined gingerbread trimming eaves; a deep blue, star-spangled birdhouse; a small log cabin.

She hadn't yet made a single one when Dean had died. After that, well, the whole idea had seemed like a dream.

But looking out at that enormous old maple in Quinn's backyard, she'd started picturing a birdhouse hanging from one of the branches. It would have to look as if it might have been hanging there since this house had been built, but it would also have to be witty in some way. She wanted a birdhouse that would make Quinn smile.

All those wonderful tools *were* sitting unused out in the garage. She had time. And Mindy really thought the fantastical birdhouses she was imagining would sell. What better time to experiment?

What's more, if she made even one really great birdhouse, she'd have a Christmas present for Quinn. Something made by her own hands.

The next two weeks, Jessamine napped contentedly in an oval wicker laundry basket in the garage while her mommy sawed and hammered and painted and cursed when she figured out flaws in her designs.

Mindy got books from the library and read about Pacific Northwest birds. Some preferred perches, others holes; some open-air accommodations, others dark interiors as if they'd found a hole in a rotting cedar tree. Many of the birdhouses she imagined would probably decorate a porch or even a living room and never be inhabited, but she wanted to design them so they could be.

She split tiny shakes for the roof of her first one, a rough-hewn cottage decorated with stars cut out of an old tin sign she'd found at a junk store. But when, as an experiment, she set it outside in the rain for a couple of days, to the side of the house where Quinn wouldn't see it, she discovered the roof leaked. She had to cover the seam at the ridge. After some experimentation, she bent a strip of the same tin sign and tacked it on. In faded red letters, it advertised some long-forgotten brand of soda pop. She liked the effect.

Her favorite was a Northwest Indian style longhouse, with the door opening beneath the legs of a bear she painted in red and black. That was one of the first she took to the gift shop in Belltown that had once carried her signs.

The owner, a woman who wove baskets for sale in the shop, leaped up to coo over Jessamine. "Ha! Well, now I know why you disappeared. Do you have something for me again?"

"I do. I don't know if they'll appeal to you, but…"

The owner followed her out to the car. The minute she saw the row of birdhouses in the trunk, she said, "They'll be gone in a week. Christmas shoppers are already getting frantic. What are you thinking we should ask?"

They discussed price, and Mindy left those first birdhouses at the shop. Three days later, the store owner called to tell her they'd all sold and to ask when she could have more.

"'Tis the season," she reminded her.

Mindy started making two or three birdhouses in a similar style before she moved on. It would make sense, she realized, to alternate simple ones, perhaps painted in a checkerboard of white and red and then distressed, with more ambitious undertakings. The latest of those was a doozy. Working from a photo, she was trying to capture the soaring spire of the Smith Tower, the tallest skyscraper west of the Mississippi when it was built early in the twentieth century.

Quinn came down to the workshop a couple of times and admired her efforts. "So you're selling them, huh?"

"Yes, and they're going fast."

"Good for you." He grinned at Jessie, nestled

against his shoulder. "Your mommy is an artist. Did you know that?"

Jessie opened her mouth and wailed. She neither knew nor cared what Mommy did with saws and hammers. She just wanted a snack. Laughing, Mindy took her from Quinn and followed him into the house.

As she settled down in the living room to nurse, Quinn backed away, his expression remote. "I think I'll go to the gym. Will you be okay?"

"Of course I'll be okay." She flapped her hand at him. "Go."

He emerged a moment later from his bedroom with a gym bag, cast a single, distracted glance at her and went out the front door.

He'd been distant lately, Mindy thought with dismay. He seemed to enjoy Jessamine, but mainly when he could have her to himself. He never hung around when Mindy was nursing or changing diapers—although, the diaper part she could understand. Not that Quinn hadn't changed a few diapers himself. He seemed happy on his days off to take care of Jessie for a couple of hours while Mindy worked in the garage or did errands.

What was missing was the closeness she'd felt with him those last couple of weeks before Jessie was born, and even at first after she had been. Mindy couldn't quite pinpoint when he'd changed. It hadn't been abrupt, more like a gradual retreat.

Did it have anything to do with the Christmas season? She couldn't remember whether he had seemed any different last year. She had noticed that, despite Quinn's talk about making Jessie's first holiday special, he hadn't even hung strings of lights from the eaves like his neighbors. Three days before Christmas, and he hadn't suggested putting up a tree. Did he even have ornaments?

She sighed. Blaming his mood on holiday-induced depression was wishful thinking on her part. Christmas had nothing to do with his mood. *She* had everything to do with it.

Her sad conclusion was that the closeness had been an illusion. When he thought she'd needed him, he'd been there. Of course they'd talked—they'd spent an awful lot of time together that had had to be filled somehow. Now she didn't need him, and he was following his preference, which seemed to involve avoiding her.

Mindy knew she should be looking for a place to live. She *had* been looking—halfheartedly.

He'd spoiled her. She'd been okay with scrimping until she'd come to live here. Now, her determination to save a substantial portion of Dean's estate to put Jessie through college was flagging. After listening to Quinn's bleak stories about his and Dean's childhoods, she'd decided that she had to worry first about giving her daughter a sense of security neither man had had. She didn't want Jessie learning to crawl on dirty indoor-outdoor carpet laid over a cold cement floor, or paddling in a rusty bathtub. She especially didn't want Jessie ever to be embarrassed about where she lived or feeling somehow *less* than her playmates. College…well, they'd worry about that when it came.

Mindy had been looking through the classified ads

in *The Times* and circling possibilities. She'd even called on a few. Secretly, she was relieved when they were already rented or had some feature that ruled them out.

Now, looking down to find that Jessie had fallen asleep, her mouth slipping from the nipple, Mindy thought, *We have to find our own place.* Quinn was trying to tell her he wanted his life back. She shouldn't make him come right out and say it. She wasn't sure she could bear it if he did.

She and Jessie would have Christmas with him, such as it was, and then move.

SHE CIRCLED ADS IN THE PAPER and made a dozen calls, dismayed at discovering that all she could afford were apartments in complexes where she wouldn't be able to set up a workbench a thin wall from someone else's bedroom or kitchen. Nonetheless, she made appointments to see several.

Would Quinn let her keep using his work area? she wondered with a flutter of hope. If she came only when he was gone, so she didn't intrude, he might be willing. At least for now.

At the sound of his key in the lock, she hastily folded the paper and put it on the chair next to her. She wanted to find a place and actually have a date set to move before she said anything. If Quinn saw she was looking, he'd feel obligated to tell her there was no hurry, and that would hurt when she could see he didn't mean it.

"Hi," she said when he walked in.

He must have showered at the gym, because his hair

was wet and slicked back and his gray T-shirt clung damply to his chest. Mindy tried not to stare obviously, but he had such a beautiful body. He was muscular without being bulky like a weight lifter or stringy like a runner. He wasn't super hairy, either, which she liked. Although his jaw was shadowed with evening bristle, he had only a dusting of dark hair on his forearms and no thick mat creeping from the collar of his shirt.

"Hey," he said. "Jessie asleep?"

"Mmm." She nodded. "I was tempted to try to keep her up, but she sleeps with such determination."

His expression softened. "Yeah, the way she scrunches up her face, I'd be afraid to try to wake her up."

"Won't it be wonderful when she smiles?"

"Yeah. A smile will be good."

He stood there, gym bag over his shoulder, and she sat at the table without even a book in front of her, as if she'd been staring into space.

"Selene called," she lied, indicating the phone.

He nodded. They avoided meeting each other's eyes for another awkward moment.

"I should go to bed," she said. It was almost nine. She might get a couple of hours of sleep before Jessie woke with an empty tummy.

"Listen, I was thinking. Do you want to go pick out a Christmas tree?"

"Oh! That would be fun." Mindy hesitated. "Um…do you have ornaments? And lights?"

"No, I thought we could buy some of those, too. Unless you kept Dean's?"

No Christmas decorations at all, she marveled.

"No, he had sort of a designer tree with mauve and silver. I could never have hung a plastic spoon Jessie decorated with glitter in preschool on that tree. Anyway… Christmas ornaments didn't seem like the kind of thing I needed to cart from apartment to apartment. So I sold them."

Embarrassed, even feeling a little guilty, as if she were tacitly criticizing Dean, she waited to see how Quinn reacted.

He didn't sound as if he'd even noticed her momentary discomfiture. "Makes sense."

Getting back to the point, Mindy said, "We'd better hurry up and do it or there won't be anything left but scraggly trees and plain glass balls."

Quinn's face was a study in conflict. He probably didn't give a flying leap what kind of ornaments or tree they bought, but didn't want to say so. After all, for whatever reason, he was determined to do this right.

"Tomorrow? When I get home?"

"That'll be fun," she agreed, without the slightest idea whether it would be.

Another awkward pause ensued. "I'd better throw my stuff in the wash," he said finally.

She rose, phone in hand. "Sure. I'd better hang this up."

He shifted the gym bag on his shoulder and turned away.

A minute later, she was heading for the bathroom when Quinn emerged from his room.

"Going to bed?"

Mindy nodded. "Do you want the bathroom first?"

"No, go ahead."

She started toward it just as he came down the hall. They bumped right into each other.

His hands gripped her upper arms.

"I'm sorry..." died on her lips.

Something flared in his eyes, and for an instant his fingers bit into her flesh. Then he all but pushed her away and went on down the hall.

Breathless and shaken, she sagged against the wall. What had just happened?

Nothing, she decided, on a wave of depression. She'd been imagining...well, she didn't even know what she had imagined. Quinn was just in a mood. Disconcerted because she'd charged at him, maybe.

She was the one who resonated at his touch and remembered the strength of his hand holding hers while she panted in labor, his gentleness massaging her back. She was the one who realized how careful he had been *not* to touch her since. Even handing Jessie back and forth, he seemed to try not to let their hands do more than brush.

Swallowing, she continued into the bathroom.

"DO YOU LIKE LITTLE LIGHTS that blink on and off, or bigger ones?" Mindy's tone was one of exaggerated patience.

Quinn wondered if she'd already asked him. He knew his mind had been wandering.

"Not blinking. Otherwise, whatever you like is fine."

"But...it's your house."

He didn't say, *With you gone I won't be putting them up next year.* That would kill the Christmas spirit.

"I've never bought any. I don't know what I like."

She gave him a strange look, then wordlessly chose a box of lights from the shelf.

The whole expedition was weird. They were in Fred Meyer. Mindy carried Jessamine in the denim sling and Quinn pushed the cart. They undoubtedly looked like any family out shopping.

"Okay," Mindy said, in a determinedly cheerful voice, "what about ornaments? Do you like a color theme, or a hodgepodge?"

A picture flashed before his eyes: a tree decorated with what his adult eye realized was no aesthetic sophistication whatsoever, probably ugly by most people's standards, but the child who remembered the tree was dazzled and thrilled. *He'd* helped string popcorn and wrap the string around the branches. And tonight was Christmas Eve! Santa would leave presents under it for him to find in the morning.

"Quinn?" A hand squeezed his forearm. "Are you all right?"

He shook his head to clear it. "Popcorn."

"What?"

"Nothing." He pretended to look at the boxes of ornaments. "I just remembered…" A long, long ago Christmas. Before his mother's addiction had consumed her, when he still believed in childish fantasies like Santa Claus.

Had there been presents under that tree in the morning? No memory of them surfaced, but neither did a ghost of the crushing disappointment that boy would have felt. Maybe, that year, his mother had managed a holiday to satisfy a child.

Funny that he hadn't remembered, hadn't known there'd ever been a Christmas like other people had.

"These," he said, grabbing a box at random. Plain red glass balls.

"Jessie would think those are pretty," Mindy agreed, probably humoring him. "And shall we get some gold ones?"

They finished selecting enough ornaments to dress a tree, a stand and the skirt to cover it, and a couple of rolls of wrapping paper and ribbon.

He hadn't bought Mindy anything yet and had no idea what she'd like. Dean had been a champion gift giver. Quinn couldn't top the BMW. Anyway, she'd just had to get rid of most of what Dean had bought her.

"I've gotten a couple of things for Jessie," he said. "The other day, I was in Pioneer Square. There's a toy store there." Embarrassed, he shrugged. "I guess she doesn't need toys yet, but I asked what was good for a baby."

Mindy smiled at him. "That's sweet, Quinn."

Sweet.

She laughed at him. "You don't have to look as if I'd just insulted you."

"Yeah. Don't let anyone hear you say things like that."

Her laugh rang out again, and despite himself his mood lifted.

"Let's pay for this stuff and go find a tree."

He'd passed a tree lot a block off California Street that day, and despite Mindy's dire warnings there seemed to be plenty left to choose from.

The night was dark and chilly. Forget the idea of having a white Christmas; Seattle was about to have another gray one.

Garish lights made the lot as bright as day. He lifted Jessie from her car seat and inserted her into the snowsuit he'd bought as Mindy held it out. Then he zipped and put the bundle of baby and suit into the sling. Jessie was clearly awake now and probably needed a dry diaper, but she wasn't yet squalling. She looked enthralled by the bright lights and strange shadows.

Mindy stopped in front of some bushy trees that looked as if they'd been sheared.

"I like those better." He pointed toward crude racks of ones that were labeled noble and grand firs.

"But they're really expensive."

"Think of it this way. I've saved up my money from all those holidays when I *didn't* buy a tree."

Her mouth pursed. "Oh. Well…I guess that's true." She wasn't convinced, which amused him. "They are pretty."

He pulled trees out, one at a time, and Mindy circled them.

"This one," she said finally. "It's perfect."

"We'll take this one," Quinn told the lot attendant, who proceeded to wrap the branches with twine and then helped Quinn load it in the trunk. Quinn paid and tied down the trunk while Mindy settled the baby in the car seat.

At home, Quinn said, "Do you want to wait until tomorrow night to set the tree up? Or shall we do it tonight?"

"Tonight," Mindy said instantly, like a child unwilling to be denied a treat. "If you can wait while I nurse Jessie."

While she sat on the couch with Jessie cradled against her, Quinn laid a tarp on the hardwood floor, then carried the tree in and set it in the stand, tightening the screws until the tree stood upright. He filled the cavity with water, then wrapped the red quilted skirt around to cover stand and tarp.

Satisfied with his effort, he turned instinctively to see what Mindy thought—just in time to see Jessie's mouth slip from her mother's breast. Transfixed, he froze where he was, one knee on the floor.

Her breast was perfect. Small, round, soft after Jessie's ministrations, the nipple erect and glistening pinkish brown.

He'd never gotten hard so fast before. He actually groaned, and Mindy looked up, startled. He thought she was, anyway. In truth, he couldn't tear his gaze from her bare breast.

"Oh!" she gasped, and swiftly pulled her shirt down. "Um…sorry."

"It's okay," he said in a strangled voice.

It wasn't okay. *Damn, damn, damn,* he thought viciously. He wouldn't be able to look at her now without imagining her bare-breasted. Without longing to weigh those breasts in his palm, without imagining his mouth, someday, where Jessie's had been.

God help him, he was jealous of a baby.

"I...I'll put Jessie down." Mindy rose so quickly she almost tumbled back onto the sofa, then turned and fled.

Still half-kneeling, Quinn flattened a hand on the floor and bent his head. He was breathing as if he'd just run a race.

Calm down, he ordered himself. He couldn't think about what he'd just seen. What he wanted. What he couldn't have.

Christmas tree. Think about making Mindy and Jessie happy.

Gradually, his pulse steadied. The painful swelling under his zipper subsided. He shoved himself to his feet and went back to the car for the bags of ornaments.

When he returned, Mindy stood uncertainly halfway into the living room, her eyes wide and spooked. He had a feeling it wouldn't take much to make her race for her bedroom.

"Did we remember hooks?" he asked, even though he knew they had.

"Yes, thank goodness." Still hanging back, she did follow him to the tree.

"Lights first?" he remembered.

"Yep. You'd better do it, since you're taller."

He plugged in the string they'd bought to make sure they worked, then untangled it and began wrapping from the top down. When he was done, they made adjustments, then clipped the small bulbs to branches.

Quinn noticed Mindy was keeping the tree between them. Just as well.

The Howies had always made decorating the tree an occasion. A couple of times, he'd tried to get out of it, but they'd been firm. He could hear George saying, "This is something we do as a family." Quinn could remember making an effort not to feel anything. They could force him to be there, but they couldn't make him get into the stupid Christmas spirit. He'd known, deep inside, that they were trying to breach his guard and that he was vulnerable.

Carefully hanging a gold ball on a lower branch, Quinn wondered how different his life would be if he'd let himself succumb. Maybe he'd be married by now and have kids.

Maybe he wouldn't have to imagine that Dean's wife and child were his.

"Will you put the star on top?" Mindy asked.

He summoned a grin. "You couldn't do it without a ladder."

"I can get a kitchen chair," she said with dignity. "I'm not *that* short."

"Uh-huh."

She tossed a pillow. He flung up his arms to defend himself. The atmosphere felt almost normal.

She plugged in the lights while he found the box with the gleaming gold star. When he turned from putting it atop their tree, he saw her gazing at the tree in delight.

"Oh, Quinn!" she breathed. "It's beautiful."

He turned to look. She was right; it was pretty, especially considering they'd bought the ornaments tonight.
They *had* more or less stuck to a color theme of red and
gold, with a few striped and multicolor balls here and
there. Mindy had hung a dozen white snowflakes that
were made like Victorian doilies and then starched stiff.

"Hey, we're good," he said.

Mindy laughed, with a funny choking sound at the
end. "Yes, we are."

Why, he wondered, did he have the feeling she was
sad as well as happy?

Later, after she'd gone to bed, he left the Christmas
lights on and sat on the couch, gazing at the tree and trying to figure out why something as ordinary as celebrat-
ing a holiday evoked such a complicated swell of
emotions in him.

Frowning, he tried to separate these strands, as if
they were strings of lights tangled after being in a box
together for too long.

Grief, for his mother and for Dean and because he'd
missed so much, some by his own choice. Images of
other Christmases kept flickering through his con-
sciousness. Quinn's last Christmas before his mother
died, when he'd sat alone in their apartment and looked
at the blur of other people's holiday lights out the window and felt afraid, because he knew she was slipping
away and he didn't know what would happen to him.
That first Christmas at the Howies', and Dean's huge
grin as he ripped the big bow from the handlebars of the
bike and climbed on it. Drinks on Christmas Eve with

Dean. An uncomfortable Christmas dinner or two at the Howies'. Pathetically decorated trees at the station, mistletoe in doorways, invitations tossed in the trash, murders committed on Christmas Day.

And finally, last year, when he hadn't been able to say no to Dean and had had dinner with him and Mindy. He'd felt stiff and uncomfortable, an outsider, and longed to be able to go home.

Now he had all this new stuff knotted with the old: these feelings for Mindy, Jessie's birth and his powerful love for her, this sense of his home and life being filled for the first time ever.

And, most of all, the crushing awareness that it was all temporary, that one of these days Mindy would take Jessie and move out, that she might even remarry. When she created a family of her own, he'd be left forever outside the circle of her affection, with no right to have a part in Jessie's life.

Finally, feeling older than he had since he was that boy waiting for his mother to die, Quinn unplugged the Christmas lights and went to bed.

CHAPTER FOURTEEN

JESSIE SMILED for the first time on Christmas Day.

Mindy said she hadn't, that she wouldn't be able to smile until she was six weeks old, but Quinn knew a smile when he saw one.

He tickled Jessie's toes. "You're just jealous because you missed it."

"I didn't have to see it. It was gas. A burp. A grimace. When she really smiles, she'll light up."

"Jealous."

From the other end of the couch, she kicked him. "Am not."

Lazily content, he kicked her back. "Jealous."

Her big green eyes laughed at him, though her mouth was pursed primly. "Just wait until she *really* smiles."

Her hair wasn't a tousled mop anymore, he realized; chin length, it was more of a shining cap, somehow befitting her status as mom. He suspected it was still lighter than air, downier than Jessie's pale strawberry fluff.

Nancy let out a gentle snore from the easy chair. Quinn had given George and Nancy his bed last night and slept on the couch. Nancy had insisted she'd tossed and turned because she was so excited.

"A real Christmas!" she'd declared last night, eyes shining.

Quinn had vanquished his guilt for shutting them out by resolving it wouldn't happen again. For better or worse, they were his family.

They'd cleaned up the wrapping-paper disaster before eating, but a couple of bows still reposed beneath the coffee table, he heard tissue paper crinkling when he shifted and ribbon trailed over the back of Nancy's chair. The mess was somehow reassuring. It meant Nancy was right; this was a real Christmas.

His gaze kept wandering back to the birdhouse Mindy had made for him. Every time, a smile would tug at his mouth. She'd constructed in miniature an old-fashioned jail, with little iron bars on the windows. But the barred door, flung open, seemed to be hanging from one hinge—though when Quinn poked it with one finger it was solid—and to the side a decrepit scaffolding now served as the support for a flowering vine painted in intricate detail. Maybe she was trying to say something about him. He wasn't sure. But the darn thing was clever.

He noticed she was still wearing the necklace he'd given her, too. The pendant was a daisy, tiny diamond petals surrounding a yellow topaz center. Pretty and sunny. Her face had lit when she'd opened the package, so he hoped she really liked it.

A faint odor drifted to Quinn's nostrils, rousing him from his contented stupor. "Diaper time," he said.

Mindy stirred.

"I'll do it," he said. "Merry Christmas."

"Isn't he sweet?" she asked the room in general.

George laughed at Quinn's response. Stretching, George said, "I suppose I should wake Nancy so we can think about getting going."

"You could stay another night," Quinn suggested as he stood, Jessie's stinky butt resting in the crook of his arm. "Avoid the ferry lines. We can snack on leftovers later."

"I feel bad taking your bed another night."

"It's been great having you here. I don't mind the couch." Funny how easy it was to say that, when not that long ago he'd relegated George and Nancy to the category of distant acquaintances. Dean's family, not really his. "Think about it," he said, and went off to change Jessie's diaper.

The Howies did stay. Even Quinn got roped into playing pinochle during the evening. He discovered once again that he and Mindy made a damn good team.

The sleeper couch was supposed to be a good one, but it still wasn't comfortable for someone of Quinn's bulk and height. But he really didn't mind. The day had been a good one. He wished it wasn't over.

In the morning he saw Mindy's light under her door, and she came out looking heavy-eyed and cranky.

"You know that saying about sleeping like a baby? Don't believe it."

He slid the mug of coffee he'd just poured for himself across the breakfast bar and reached into the cupboard for a second mug. "I didn't hear her crying."

"That's because I didn't want her to disturb the Howies. I leapt up every time she squeaked. The poor kid was probably just talking in her sleep, and I kept snatching her up to nurse or to check her diaper or to rock. What do you want to bet she's as exhausted as I am today?"

"You can both nap once the Howies leave."

"You'd better believe it," she agreed with fervency.

He took a swallow of coffee, cursed when it burned his mouth, and said, "I'd better take this with me."

Sitting there in her bathrobe, bare toes curled over the rung of the stool and her hands wrapped around the mug, she said, "Have a good day."

A man could get used to having a pretty woman get up to see him off in the morning and be there to greet him when he got home.

This one had better not get too used to it.

"Yeah, you have a good day, too," he said, and left.

For most of the next week, he felt more natural with Mindy again. He could almost forget the sight of her bare breast and his own primitive response. The holiday and all those warm, fuzzy feelings had cast a spell that briefly canceled out darker emotions like guilt and lust.

They celebrated New Year's Eve by watching the party in Times Square on TV, talking about other years, trips to New York City, how Jessamine hadn't even been thought of a year ago. Mindy said that in astonishment, as if no Jessie was unthinkable. At midnight, they clinked their glasses of champagne together, took a few sips and went to bed. He'd never enjoyed a New Year's Eve more.

Lust made a roaring comeback two nights later when Quinn met Mindy in the hall after he'd thought she was in bed. He wore nothing but pajama bottoms. She had on a short T-shirt and skimpy royal-blue panties. His stunned gaze took in long, perfectly shaped legs and the swell of hips that weren't as boyish as he'd imagined from seeing them clothed.

Her gaze collided with his chest and never lifted to his face. Color washed over her face as she retreated. "Oh...um...I'm sorry. Jessie peed on my lap."

She slipped into her bedroom and closed the door. His last glimpse was of the pale curve of ass barely covered by the French-cut panties.

Quinn stifled a raw groan so she wouldn't hear him.

The next evening, he went to the gym and worked out until his muscles groaned and his vision blurred. He walked in the house, heard her giggle float from the living room, and got hard. Gritting his teeth, he thought, *I can't live like this.*

"Quinn? Is that you?"

"Yeah, I'm home," he called back. "Let me throw my stuff in the wash."

She sat cross-legged on the sofa in flannel pajama bottoms and a sweatshirt, Jessie against her shoulder. She gave a firm pat, and Jessie belched.

He couldn't help smiling. "Hey, she's going to be able to burp those boys under the table when she gets to school."

Mindy gave him a laughing look over her shoulder. "Oh, great."

"They'll all have a crush on her."

"Who was the first girl you remember having a crush on?" Mindy nuzzled the baby's neck.

He didn't have to think. "Rebecca Kane. Fifth grade. She was hot."

"You mean, she was getting breasts."

"Right," he agreed, sitting in his easy chair, a safe distance from her. "That's a fifth-grade boy's only requirement."

Mindy made a face at him. "I had no figure at all until I was in eighth grade."

He pictured her, a stick of a girl with big gray-green eyes and that defiant haircut. No, maybe she'd had pigtails and been meek. He could imagine her just a little shy, not yet having come into her own.

Thinking about Mindy's figure was not healthy for him. "I'm going to hit the sack," he said, standing. "You two stay up and play all night if you want."

Mindy lifted Jessie so he could give her a smack on her small button nose. Then he grinned at her. "Sleep tight, kiddo."

She smiled. Her whole body smiled. Her arms flapped and her face lit with delight.

Pierced to the heart, Quinn said, "Mindy. Did you see that?"

"See what?" She looked up at him in alarm.

"Turn her around. Smile at her."

"What?" She set Jessie back in her lap, her hand cradling Jessie's head. "What's that man talking about?" she crooned, smiling and tickling her tiny daughter's stomach.

Jessie turned it on like a light.

"Oh, Jessie! Quinn! Oh!" Mindy almost sounded teary. "Did you see? Look at her!"

"I'm looking."

He couldn't tear himself away. He hung over the back of the couch grinning at the baby like some idiot just so she'd grin back. Mindy laughed and told Jessie she was the most beautiful baby ever born.

"You are very, very clever to make your mommy and…" She visibly checked before continuing, "And Quinn so happy. Isn't she, Quinn?"

Mindy sounded breathless, as if she'd almost said *daddy. Your mommy and daddy.*

Damn it all to hell.

"Yeah." Even to his ears, his voice had changed. Become remote. "She's a smart baby. But I'd still better go to bed."

A man could lead himself to bed, but that didn't mean he'd sleep. Not when he felt as if he were flying over paradise, craning his neck to look down from that airplane window, wanting to storm the cockpit and yell, "Land here!" even though he knew there wasn't a runway.

He just couldn't imagine Mindy looking at him with anything but shock and loathing if he hit on her. Even if he was wrong, even if miraculously she turned out to feel the same way he did, how could he look at himself in the mirror knowing he had what should have been Dean's?

What *would* have been Dean's, if not for a bullet.

SHE'D ALMOST SAID *daddy.*

She couldn't stay, Mindy thought in panic. She felt

as if they were a family, but they weren't. She'd seen the look on Quinn's face, seen his instant retreat. She had scared him, thinking that way.

Steeling herself, the next night at dinner Mindy said, "You know, I can't stay here forever."

His gaze sharpened. "There's no hurry."

"I know. But, well, what I was wondering is, if I rent an apartment where I can't set up a workshop, could I maybe pay you a little a month…"

His expression became forbidding.

"Or something," she continued, more raggedly, "to keep using yours?"

He scowled. "I'm not using it. Of course you can! You know I won't take money from you."

"I had to offer!" she retorted.

"Well, you have an answer. The damn garage is yours when you need it. Because we're friends, and I'm not using it right now anyway."

She bit her lip. "Thank you."

"You're welcome." Subject closed.

But he stayed moody for the rest of the evening and retreated to his bedroom early.

The next day, she looked at two apartments. She hated the first, and the second was nice but didn't feel secure with ground-floor windows and no reassuring landlord upstairs.

A week later, she found one she liked. It was in West Seattle, within walking distance of Safeway. The building had only four units, and a tenant in the one that would be below hers had a toddler, according to the owner. Maybe they could exchange babysitting, Mindy thought hopefully. With two bedrooms, Jessie could have her own.

The neighborhood was nice, so Quinn couldn't complain, and it wasn't more than a mile or two from his house, so if he wanted to visit Jessie he could easily.

"I'll take it." She pulled her checkbook out of her purse. "How much do you need?"

She put off for several days telling Quinn that she'd actually rented a place, finally vowing that tonight would be the night. Her resolve faltered when Quinn came home with deep creases between his eyebrows. He looked battered and soul-weary.

Mindy had started dinner earlier, a bean-and-rice casserole, and had just put corn bread in to bake. Seeing him standing in the kitchen doorway, she said, "You look exhausted! Did you have a bad day?"

"Stepdad beat a two-year-old to death, then tried to bury the body." He rubbed a hand over his face. "Son of a bitch."

"Oh, Quinn," she breathed.

"The kids are always tough." He seemed to give himself a shake. "Smells good. Where's Jessie?" He spotted her lying on a quilt, her hand tightly clutching a red plastic rattle Mindy had put in it. "There's my pretty girl," he murmured, lifting her into his arms.

He set her down again while he went to take off his jacket and weapon, then said, "Shall I make a salad while you nurse?"

"Bless you," Mindy told him, and carried Jessie to the living-room couch.

Quinn was dishing up when she came back from putting Jessie down for her evening nap.

"A two-year-old." She poured them both milk. "I can't imagine."

The creases deepened. "Yeah."

She touched his arm and felt the muscles tighten. "I'm sorry, Quinn."

"Crappy day." He shrugged. "It happens. How was yours?"

"It was fine. Jessie had a good nap."

As they ate, Mindy sensed he would have preferred to retreat into silence. The knowledge that he would rather have been alone emboldened her at last to push her empty plate away and say, "Quinn, I rented an apartment."

"What?"

"I can't move in until the first, so you're stuck with us for a couple more weeks, but you did keep saying there wasn't any hurry."

"You're moving out." He sounded stunned.

"Yes, but not far away." She told him about the apartment, hearing herself talking faster and faster in an artificially cheerful voice. "There's even covered parking!" she said, as if claiming a sunken Jacuzzi tub or a hot tub on her deck.

"Why the decision to move?" Quinn set down his fork, his voice harsh.

"Jessie is six weeks old. I've been here for two and a half months now."

Muscles flexed in his jaw. "So?"

"So I think it's time to prove to us both that I can be independent." Mindy moistened her lips. "Quinn, what you did for me is amazing. But I'm not contributing in any way. I'm guessing if I offered you rent you'd say no." His expression told her she was right. "There must be days when you'd give anything to be able to come home to an empty, peaceful house."

"Have I said that?"

"No."

"Then don't make assumptions." He looked at her with a flat gaze. "But obviously you're ready to strike out on your own and that's okay. God knows it would be awkward if you lived here and wanted to date."

Date? The idea had never even occurred to her. She couldn't imagine ever wanting to flirt and go out to dinner with some man who wasn't Quinn.

Then, feeling dense, she realized what he was really saying. "You haven't been dating, either, have you? Of course you haven't! It would have been hard to explain Jessie and me, wouldn't it?"

He sounded ticked. "That's not what I'm saying."

"You do date?"

"I haven't since Dean died."

"Oh," she said softly. "Oh, dear. We're a pair of cripples, aren't we?"

Some emotion flared in his eyes. "I'll go find my goddamn crutch." He shoved back from the table. "I'll hope I don't need it the day you're moving."

She stared after him, her chest feeling hollow.

She'd hurt him. She could tell she had. But he couldn't want her to stay forever. Could he?

No. Her eyes welled with tears she refused to let fall. Maybe she'd annoyed him, but that was all. It was time for her to go, just as she'd planned.

THE NEXT TWO WEEKS reminded her of the final weeks of pregnancy. The days had seemed to go on forever, and yet she'd dreaded them ending.

Quinn was unfailingly polite and distant with her while remaining affectionate with Jessie. He reiterated several times that Mindy was welcome to continue to use the garage. She thanked him repeatedly. She hated every minute with this pleasant stranger, and then knew in the same minute that she'd miss him more than she had Dean.

Guilt sliced her at that thought, causing her to miss something Quinn had said and earn a slightly lifted brow.

"Is something wrong?"

"No! No. I'm sorry, I just…my mind was wandering."

"I was saying that Benson in fraud says he and his wife want to get rid of some baby stuff. He mentioned a crib and a playpen and some kind of swing that hangs in a doorway."

"Oh." She recalled herself to the moment, tucking the guilt away to be examined another time. "That would be great."

"Benson said his wife is home days if you'd like to go pick out anything you want before they have a garage sale."

Mindy took the name and number of the fraud detective's wife and thanked Quinn. He assured her she was welcome. She could almost see him mentally x-ing off another day on the calendar when he said goodnight. Five days to go.

Then four. And three.

They got even more polite, more *careful* with every word spoken. A growing sense of loss made her chest feel as if it were encased in lead. Drawing a deep breath became hard. She woke every morning aware of the heaviness.

With only two days to go, her mother dropped by. No surprise there—she'd visited at least weekly since Jessie had been born.

Mindy knew better than to think her mother was there to see her. Maybe, she thought unkindly, Jessie was appealing because she could still be dressed up like a doll. In pink.

It was all Mindy could do not to roll her eyes at the sight of her mother, of all people, cooing and babbling nonsense at Jessie, who lay on the middle cushion of the sofa, kicking and flapping her arms in delight at the lady bending over her making silly faces.

"Can I get you a cup of coffee? Tea?"

"Goochy goochy goo!" Her mom tickled Jessie, who grinned.

More loudly, Mindy said, "Looks like you're enjoying being a grandmother."

Her mother glanced at her. "You don't have to sound surprised."

It had to be her mood, because Mindy was shocked to hear herself say, "Well, you never seemed too thrilled with motherhood."

That did it. Her mother straightened. "Exactly what is that supposed to mean?"

"Nothing," she muttered, like a sulky teenager.

"You know, our relationship is a two-way street."

Anger flared in her. "Was it a two-way street when I was five? Six? Ten? I never remember you tickling me and laughing! Are you saying I didn't give enough back to keep you interested?"

Her mother actually jerked, as if Mindy had hit her. But then she squared her shoulders and lifted her chin. "I suppose being a mother didn't come to me naturally. As it turned out, my…abilities or lack of them didn't much matter. You were Daddy's girl from the beginning."

"What?" Mindy whispered.

"He adored you, you adored him." Cheri Walker gave a brittle smile. "I was the outsider in our family. The guest who smiled and pretended she felt perfectly at home."

"Are you serious?"

"It hardly matters anymore." She picked up Jessie and bounced her against her shoulder, as if the subject were over and done with.

"It matters." Mindy was still reeling from her mother's revelations. "We both loved you."

Patting Jessie's back, her mom said, "I know your father loved me. I…miss that."

"So much that you had another man in your bed before Daddy was even cold?" Mindy was horrified at how caustic she sounded, how cruel.

Spots of color touched her mother's cheeks. "So you did see him."

"How could you?" she asked, with all the heartbreak and shock of her fourteen-year-old self.

Her mother very carefully laid Jessie down. Head still bent, she said, "Do you remember the funeral? When I tried to hold you and you tore yourself away from me and cried, 'I want Daddy!'?"

Mindy shook her head, then said, "No. I...really don't remember much about it."

"If I'd died instead, you'd have been sad but not distraught."

"That's not true!"

Her mother gave a sad laugh. "Let's not kid ourselves. But it doesn't really matter whether it's true or not. It's what I felt. That you didn't really love me, and the one person who had was gone."

"So you went looking for a quick substitute?" More cruelty, but she'd needed so desperately to say this.

Her mother flinched again. "I'm afraid so." She was quiet for a moment, her eyes unfocused. Very softly, she said, "I've been looking ever since."

"You always have a man madly in love with you!"

"Love? You're an adult now, Mindy. You know better than that. What the men in my life do give me is an illusion of love. Most of the time, that's enough."

Past a knot in her throat, Mindy managed to say, "I did love you." She drew a breath. "I do."

Her mother's composure seemed to crack. "Thank you for saying so."

"You don't believe me." What mother didn't believe her own daughter loved her, even if their relationship wasn't perfect?

"I suppose…" Her mother faltered. "I always believed I forfeited your love when I had such a hard time, oh, knowing how to *be* a parent. I can tell it comes easily to you, but I felt so awkward from the beginning. Just holding you felt…strange."

Perhaps her primary emotion should be hurt, but instead it was pity. Mindy tried to imagine not knowing how to hold Jessie, not having the instincts she'd discovered had lain dormant just waiting for that moment when the nurse had handed the bundled, red-faced baby to her.

Trying to understand, she asked, "Do you know why that was?"

"You never met your grandparents." Her mother gave another of her brittle laughs that Mindy had always taken as uncaring. "You didn't miss a thing. My father wasn't physically abusive, but he was so critical I never felt as if I'd done anything right. I never had the chance to think, Dad is proud of me. And my mother was always in her bedroom weeping. I realize now that she was suffering from clinical depression, but then…then it felt as if she couldn't be bothered to tear herself from her own unhappiness enough to care about my report card or to shop for a prom dress for me or…" She stopped, gave a funny little shrug. "Well, I suppose it's easy to psychoanalyze myself now. But I always thought, I won't be like her. And then I was."

"No." Face wet with tears, Mindy scooted from the easy chair to the coffee table. "You weren't. I did know you loved me. I just…wanted to be closer to you. Especially after…after Dad died. I needed you so badly."

Her mother sniffed and dabbed at her eyes. "You're ruining my makeup."

Mindy gave a watery laugh. "Maybe you should quit wearing it, like me."

Her mother shuddered. "I look *old* without it!"

"You know perfectly well that you're beautiful."

Sounding much as usual, she retorted, "I know no such thing."

But Mindy only laughed and used her shirtsleeve to mop her own tears. "Okay, so tell me. This Mark guy. You don't think he's really in love with you?"

"Actually…" Was she blushing? Was such a thing possible? "I think he might be. He's a very nice man, Mindy. I know you don't want to meet him, but…"

"What on earth would make you think I don't want to meet him? Of course I do!"

"Oh." For a moment, she appeared flustered. "He's not anything special to look at."

"Do I care?"

"You have that lovely Quinn."

"Mom, I'm moving out the day after tomorrow." The reminder was a stab of pain. "Quinn isn't mine. He felt obligated, because of Dean. That's all."

"You're sure?"

Her throat felt thick. "I'm sure."

"What a shame. Such a nice house, and he seems to have plenty of money, and so handsome…" She sighed with seeming regret.

Mindy couldn't summon her usual irritation. So, okay, her mother was being her usual shallow self. But then, she didn't know Quinn. Not really. And that was Mindy's fault, because she never invited her mother over when Quinn was home. She was ashamed to realize it hadn't even occurred to her that Mom might want to be included at Thanksgiving or Christmas.

"I love you," she said again, impulsively.

Her mother didn't seem to hear her. "Dear, I'm afraid Jessie has done something nasty. Did I mention that diapers were my least favorite part of being a mother?"

Mindy only laughed again, surprised them both by hugging her mother, and lifted her baby girl from the couch.

"Yup. She does stink. Can you wait while I change her and nurse? I could make sandwiches."

"Certainly." Her mother smiled at her, sniffed, then said, "Oh, dear. I must have a lash in my eye."

FRIDAY NIGHT, her last in this house, full-fledged panic set in. Mindy wanted Quinn to say, "Don't go. Stay with me," but she knew he wouldn't. He could be madly in love with her, and he wouldn't say it. His pride would never let him.

And who was she kidding? He'd probably close his bedroom door tonight and do a little tap dance, because he'd have his house and his life to himself again.

He'd brought home Chinese takeout. She had made an effort to look more presentable. Instead of sweats, she had on jeans, a long-sleeved, form-fitting turtleneck and real shoes.

Peeling off his leather jacket and unbuckling his shoulder holster, Quinn nodded toward her feet. "I didn't know you owned any shoes."

"I actually have several." She scrunched up her nose. "I just tend to trip when I wear them."

A shadow crossed his face. Guessing that he was recalling the funeral, she felt tactless.

"I remember." Holster and gun in hand, he said, "I'll be right back."

He always took the gun into the bedroom. She didn't know whether he locked it up, or just dropped it with the holster onto his bedside table. She was just as glad he didn't make a habit of tossing it onto the counter. Guns made her nervous.

The evening was colored by the excruciating knowledge—to her—that tomorrow night she'd be in her own apartment and Quinn's house would be his again, as devoid of her presence as if she'd never been here at all. He was quiet tonight, but more relaxed, as if he didn't feel he had to be as careful since she'd be gone so soon.

They talked about baby milestones and how soon Jessie would be rolling over, then sitting.

"She changes every day. I go to work and come home to find she's grown up a little more while I was gone." Quinn was silent for a moment, head bent as he gazed at the cup of coffee he cradled in his hands. "I'll miss seeing her as often."

What about me! Mindy wanted to cry. *Will you miss seeing* me?

"She'll miss you, too."

His mouth twisted into a semblance of a smile. "Thanks for saying so."

"You don't think she will?"

"Yeah." He sounded both sad and resigned. "I think she might."

Don't let us go, she begged silently. *Ask me to stay forever.*

But she didn't want him to ask when it was Jessie he loved, Jessie he'd miss. Not her. So, after a minute, she said with difficulty, "You can visit whenever you want, you know."

He gave her a distracted glance. "Thanks."

With coffee for him and herbal tea for her, they moved out to the living room. Quinn sat at one end of the couch, Mindy at the other, the distance between them feeling symbolic to her. If they'd been the friends they pretended to be, she'd have sat next to him, perhaps rested her head on his shoulder. She had always liked to touch. Only with Quinn did she feel so…restrained.

And contrarily, so hungry for touch.

She kept stealing glances as if she would never see him again, studying his mouth and wondering what it would feel like on hers. And his hands—large and strong, they were always gentle with Jessie, and yet so *safe*.

Only, the sight of them didn't make her feel safe. Instead, a shiver of pure sexual need ran through her at the idea of those hands framing her face, stroking down her throat to her breasts and her belly and then lower yet.

Mindy desperately fixed her gaze on the coffee table, trying to keep her breathing shallow. What was she *doing?* He'd be horrified if he even guessed what she was thinking!

Or…would he? She lifted her mug to her mouth and glanced at him over it.

His knuckles showed white where he gripped the mug. Despite his easy posture, she would swear he was sitting as stiffly as she was. The creases in his cheeks were deeper than usual, and as she looked he rotated his head just the smallest amount, as if he didn't want her to know his neck was tight.

He might just be bored. Tired. Unhappy about something that had nothing to do with her. She was dreaming to think otherwise.

But…what if?

Then he could *do* something. Say something, she thought. But he hadn't, and he wouldn't. Close to tears, she closed her eyes and struggled for composure. It was a very, very good thing that she wouldn't be living with him anymore. This was too hard.

She groped with her feet for the shoes she'd slipped off. "I think I'd better go to bed. Tomorrow's going to be a long day."

"Right." He set down his coffee mug, swore. "Mindy…"

Those damn tears were starting to make her vision

blurry. She swiped at her eyes. "I know you hate being thanked, but I have to do it one more time."

He stood. She did, too. The couple of feet between them didn't feel like so much now. She must have taken a step. Or maybe he had. Because all of a sudden, his arms were closing around her and she was hugging him fiercely.

"Mindy," he said, in a ragged voice she'd never heard, and she tilted her head back to see his face.

Something unfamiliar came over her then. Ignoring every warning she'd given herself, every deep-rooted inhibition, Mindy rose to tiptoe and pressed her mouth to Quinn's.

For a moment he was completely still. She might as well have been kissing a statue. A sob escaped her and she was starting to pull back when a sound seemed to be wrenched from Quinn and one of his hands came up to cup the back of her head. The next instant, he kissed her, or accepted her kiss, she didn't know. It didn't matter. She was too utterly lost in sensation, in intense gratitude because now she knew what being in his arms felt like, and it was magic.

Her lips parted and his tongue drove in. One hand gripped her buttock and lifted her, pressing her against him so she couldn't miss his arousal. Her body throbbed with awareness, with need. She gasped for air when his mouth lifted, then hummed with pleasure as she sought his mouth again.

But his lips weren't there to meet hers. His body had gone rigid; his arms dropped from her and he strained away.

Her own hands fell to her sides. She hated, oh, hated, to see his face, because she knew what it would show. Revulsion, shock, anger. Please not pity.

There was no pity, but every other emotion she'd feared blazed on his face as he backed away from her. In a thick voice, he said, "Dean hasn't even been dead a year. God, I'm sorry, Mindy. I'm sorry."

He was sorry because he had to reject her. Sorry because he'd been tempted even for a moment to kiss her back. Most of all, he was sorry for her, because she was...was...

She pressed her hand to her mouth. Her stomach roiled. She was like her mother. Oh, God, just like her. A sad widow who wanted another man in her bed with indecent haste, because she couldn't bear to be alone.

"No," she whispered. "No, no, no."

Quinn's expression changed, but she was hardly aware. "Mindy..."

"No!" she cried, half fell over the coffee table, and ran for the bathroom, where she lost her dinner and her self-respect.

She had never been so grateful in her life as she was to see that the lights were out and Quinn's bedroom door was shut when she emerged.

She'd have to face him in the morning. But not now. Not now.

CHAPTER FIFTEEN

"ANOTHER STORE AGREED TODAY to start carrying my birdhouses," Mindy said.

Quinn lay stretched out on her floor with Jessie on his chest. "Great!" he said, and lifted the baby to swoop her through the air like an airplane.

She laughed in glee. Quinn was way more fun than Mommy.

He laughed back at her, his often somber face as bright with merriment as baby Jessie's.

Mindy shook her head in bemusement. Who'd have ever thought the word fun would apply in any way to Brendan Quinn?

Settling Jessie back on his chest, Quinn asked, "You'll let me know if your money gets short?"

In mock offense, she retorted, "I'll have you know I'm becoming quite prosperous!" Then she made a face. "Okay, I'm not making enough to live on yet, but I'm getting there."

And she was. Mindy was amazed at her success. She'd apparently found a niche. Country-style decorating was still hot and magazines increasingly touted the allure of "outdoor rooms." Seattle had half a dozen stores that specialized in garden art and pottery. Three of them now carried her birdhouses, as did a couple of gift shops. A plant nursery she'd approached the other day had expressed interest. If her birdhouses kept selling the way they had been, she would soon have trouble producing them fast enough.

"Someone suggested a Web site." She sat cross-legged next to Quinn, her back against the couch. "But I don't know. I'd have to pay someone to build it and maintain it. And then I might have to make a whole bunch of identical birdhouses. And that seems boring."

"But profitable," he pointed out, swooping Jessie again.

"Mmm." She mused for a moment then said, "Oh, well. It's just something to think about. Can you stay for dinner? I thought about ordering a pizza."

He didn't often stay; usually he stopped by for an hour after work, or later in the evening on his way home from the gym. He'd say hi to her, then lavish attention on a delighted Jessie.

Tonight, he surprised her by agreeing, "Sure. Sounds good."

They'd been going on this way for a month now. She and Jessie entered through the side door to his garage every day, after he was safely gone to work. There, Mindy worked in fits and starts as Jessie allowed. She'd found an old chaise hanging on the wall, which she sat in to nurse. Much of the day, Jessie napped contentedly in the playpen Mindy had bought from the Bensons. Fortunately, she seemed impervious to the whine of the saw and the drill and even the wham of her mom pounding with a hammer.

About an hour before Quinn usually got home, Mindy tidied the work space and she and Jessie slipped out. She was trying very hard to be unobtrusive.

When she'd first moved out, he'd gone several days before stopping by. After he'd all but flung her from his arms and she'd fallen over the coffee table running away, moving day had been horrible. With Selene and her boyfriend and another friend helping, Quinn and Mindy had managed to avoid looking each other in the eye. Which had made the first time he'd stepped into her apartment more than a little awkward. She'd thought about saying something blithe like, "Wow, that kiss! Wasn't it silly?" but face to face with him, she couldn't do it. The kiss was the farthest thing from silly.

So they just didn't mention it. And in avoiding the subject, it loomed like Mount Saint Helens letting off bursts of steam, obviously ready to erupt. They just pretended it wasn't there and wouldn't explode in fire and ash someday.

Mindy still hadn't dealt with her horror at her own behavior. So, okay, she had a better understanding of her mother now. That didn't erase the memory of how passionately, at fourteen, she'd hated and despised her for inviting a man into her bedroom when Dad had only been dead a few weeks. Dean had been gone longer— but not *that* much longer. A little over ten months now.

The weird part was, those ten months could have been two or three years. Mindy had trouble remembering who and what she was back when she'd first discovered she was pregnant. Maybe the fact that these ten months had been so eventful had something to do with it. If Dean hadn't died that night, she probably wouldn't have changed so much. She would still believe she was in love with him, and with the birth of Jessie she'd be convinced they were a perfect family. Quinn would still be Dean's difficult friend instead of her savior and a man of complexity and depth then unimagined by her.

At least, she *thought* her world would still be sunny and simple. But she wondered sometimes how Dean would have handled her need for bed rest. Would he have been willing to come home straight from work to wait on her, as Quinn had done? To give up fishing expeditions and eighteen holes of golf with his friends followed by drinks, because she needed him? Or would he have been solicitous when he was home, and full of excuses when he wasn't? He'd always been restless, wanting to eat out, have friends over, *go* somewhere.

She no longer knew whether she was being fair to Dean. She'd come to see him more clearly, she thought, than she had in only a year of marriage. Quinn and the Howies had all said things that made her think.

At the same time, since leaving Quinn's house Mindy had been able to recover some of her memories of the Dean she'd loved. With that huge grin and freckled face, he'd been one of those rare people everyone liked. He was kind, funny and an eternal optimist. She'd marveled then, considering his background, at his faith that everything would always come out well. Now she knew it for what it was: a major case of denial. But, oh, how nice it was to live with someone who was always upbeat!

She wanted to believe she would have stayed happy with Dean. That she wouldn't have looked up one day, met Quinn's eyes across the room, and realized that she'd fallen in love with her husband's best friend. But she couldn't imagine that happening; Quinn, too, had changed. All she had to do was recall the cold, critical man determined to do his duty by her after Dean's murder. She'd come close to hating him!

Mindy was starting to find peace in the knowledge that she'd never know how their lives would have turned out if only Dean had waited for the police that night instead of swaggering in to confront the intruders himself. Just because now she loved Quinn with a frightening intensity didn't mean she would have betrayed Dean had he lived. She was a different person. Quinn was a different person. And Dean was dead.

But she did hate knowing how quickly she had been willing to replace her husband. So, she was in love; did that make her any better than her mother, who had probably just been frightened of being alone?

As she went to order the pizza, she thought with profound depression that all of her attempts to reconcile her wedding vows with her deep, passionate feelings for Quinn were irrelevant, anyway. He obviously wasn't interested in her. Not that way. She should just be grateful that he plainly intended to continue to be a presence in Jessamine's life.

And surely, surely, these visits would get easier with time.

HE SHOULDN'T HAVE STAYED for dinner, Quinn thought during the lonely drive home. All he'd done was torture himself.

Quinn wasn't sure he should remain in Mindy's life at all, but some temptations were too great for a man to resist. Yeah, he was the closest thing Jessie had to a daddy, and he told himself she needed him. But he knew he was there as much to see her mommy.

Just to make sure she was all right, that she didn't need him. Maybe to give himself an early warning should she start to date someone. A wedding announcement without the chance to inoculate himself might kill him.

These few hours with her and Jessie, snatched a couple of times a week, were lifesaving if painful at the same time. Quinn could hardly bring himself to go home anymore. His house was worse than the morgue: dark and silent and empty. He'd really hoped that, as the weeks went by, he would find he was glad to regain his solitude.

Grind that hope under his heel. All he wanted was to have Mindy and Jessie back.

Except he knew that, too, was a lie. Because he wanted a hell of a lot more from Mindy than her cheerful presence as a roommate. He wanted promises and passion from her. He wanted her in his bed every night.

He wanted the illusion that she and Jessie were his to be reality.

And that made him feel like scum.

If there'd been one constant in his life, it had been Dean. Dean had never let him down. Quinn would have died before he let Dean down.

But here he was, wanting to step into Dean's shoes and have his wife and kid.

He tried like hell not to think about that kiss and what it might have meant. His worst fear was that Mindy had intended to peck him on the lips in gratitude. Friends kissed lightly.

But, God, he thought in anguish, there she'd been in his arms, her slim, supple body pressed to his, her mouth brushing his. Every dream come true. Desire had smashed into him with the force of a semi speeding on the freeway. He could taste her, and he needed more. He'd ground her up against him, shoved his tongue in her mouth, his erection against her belly. He-man ready to take what he wanted, the hell with scruples.

Until he'd felt…something. A ghost behind him. A hand tapping his shoulder. A voice threaded with amusement and anger saying, "Hey, buddy, she's mine, remember? Find your own woman."

He still wasn't sure he would have had the self-control to stop if he hadn't seen Mindy's face. Her mouth had looked swollen, her eyes huge and dilated and wet with tears. Revulsion at what he'd done had sent him staggering back, especially when he saw her fall across the coffee table in her haste to escape him.

At home tonight, he parked in the garage, stopped to look at the birdhouses she had in various stages of completion, and went on into the house, where he sank into his easy chair without turning on lights.

Was it possible to go on like this, half living? Maybe he should say to her, "I don't want to let you down, I don't want to let Jessie down, but I love you and if I can't have you I think we're all better severing this relationship now." Given a few months, a baby Jessie's age wouldn't remember him, wouldn't miss him.

But then he wouldn't even have this half life. He'd be left in the dark for good. Once upon a time, he might have been content to exist that way, but he wasn't anymore.

He made an animal sound of pain and continued to sit without moving for a long, long time.

REPLETE WITH THE LUNCH Nancy had put on the table, Quinn lifted his brows at George. "Like to walk down to the dock?"

"Wouldn't mind if I do."

After extracting a promise from Nancy that she would let them wash the dishes, they left her clearing the table. George pulled a heavy Irish-knit sweater over his head and Quinn shrugged on his leather jacket. They stepped out the back door to find that the day had remained chilly but fine, clouds scudding across a pale blue sky. Spring might actually be arriving. Quinn had spotted some crocuses about ready to open near the front porch.

The two men walked slowly down the long flight of

wooden steps toward the narrow inlet, Quinn keeping the pace slow.

"Watch that one," he said once. "Board's getting rotten."

He noticed the handrail, constructed of two-by-fours, was getting shaky, too. Seemed to him Dean had meant to get over here last summer and do some work. Quinn felt bad that it hadn't occurred to him to come in Dean's stead.

"Don't get as much done as I used to," George said regretfully. "I can replace that board, though. I'd hate to have these stairs rot away."

"Once spring comes, I'll come over and give you a hand," Quinn said. "I'm pretty well done with my house. Wouldn't want to forget how to saw a board."

George glanced at him, blue eyes faded but shrewd. "You wouldn't want to do that," he agreed. "I'd appreciate it, son."

Years ago, Quinn and Dean had helped their foster father build a bench along one side of the small floating dock. It, too, was gray and beginning to rot in places. Choosing their spot carefully, the two men sat, lifting their heads to smell the salty breeze.

"What's on your mind?" George said after a long pause.

Nice to know he was transparent, Quinn thought. Or maybe he only was to this man.

The question that came out of his mouth wasn't the one he'd intended to ask. Where the hell it came from, he had no idea. "Did you and Nancy ever think about adopting Dean and me?"

"Sure we did. But it was pretty clear neither of you

would have it. Dean would have felt he was abandoning faith in his mother, and you'd have thought we were trying to hog-tie and brand you. You didn't want to be claimed."

Quinn shook his head. "I must have been crazy."

"Just scared." George laid a hand gnarled with arthritis on Quinn's for a brief moment. "I'm glad to see you're not running so scared anymore."

Quinn gave a grunt that could be interpreted as a laugh, by a charitable man. "I'm not so sure about that."

George studied him. "What do you mean?"

"I've been seeing Mindy and Jessamine."

"Dean's little girl. Of course you are."

Voice thick, Quinn confessed, "I'm in love with Mindy."

The gnarled hand patted his knee. "I know you are."

Quinn turned his head to stare at his foster father. "You know?"

"The way you looked at her… Nancy and I could tell."

"Damn," he breathed.

"Oh, I don't think Mindy noticed, if that's what worries you." George sounded quietly amused. "It's outsiders looking in who see that kind of thing."

Quinn swore. Bracing his elbows on his thighs, he let his head fall. "She's Dean's wife."

"She's Dean's widow," the older man corrected.

"Does it matter?" Quinn asked, with near violence.

"Sure it matters. He's gone, Quinn. You can't bring him back. None of us can. You and Mindy and Jessie, you have to go on with your lives. Have you got yourself convinced Dean would mind if you and Mindy fell in love now?"

"I thought…" His throat closed. God, this sounded stupid. "I felt him."

"Ghosts are mostly the voices of our conscience. That's my suspicion, anyway."

Quinn hunched his shoulders.

"Do you want to know what I think?"

This grunt was closer to a real laugh. "You haven't noticed I dragged you down here for a talk?"

George chuckled, deep and satisfied. "I noticed."

"Yeah, I want to know what you think."

"Well, then, here it is. I think Dean would be cheering you on. There was nothing in life he wanted more than for you to like Mindy. Maybe even to love her, in a way."

"That's…different."

"But he's gone, so everything is different."

Quinn scrubbed a hand over his face. Was it that simple?

"Who would he want raising his daughter? Some man he didn't know? Or you?"

This part he could buy. "I love her like she's mine." He paused, examining his powerful emotions for the little girl with her blue eyes, milk-pale skin and huge toothless smile. "But maybe because she's Dean's, too. I see him in her sometimes. That smile, as if she is absolutely, one hundred percent sure the whole world will love her."

"Mostly, the world did love him."

They sat silent for a moment, both remembering.

"For what it's worth," George said finally, "nothing would make Nancy and me happier than to see the two of you married."

"I don't know how Mindy feels."

"Sometimes, you just have to step off the cliff and ask." George slapped his back. "Now, what say we go clean that kitchen?"

Quinn did help. Then he kissed Nancy's cheek, accepted a handshake from George, and walked out to his car. He stood there for a long moment, his hand on the open door, gazing back at the house.

How many hours had he and Dean spent shooting hoops there in the driveway? The ball thudding against the backboard must have driven Nancy crazy, but she never said a word. There were the hours out in the small boat on the inlet, too, when they pretended to fish. Sitting in the boat, rocking on gentle waves, they'd used a pocketknife to cut their fingers and rub them together to share their blood.

"So we'll really be brothers," Dean had said, his face crinkled earnestly. "Then when my mom comes, I can ask her to take you, too."

Quinn hadn't believed in Dean's mother; he'd never been able to believe in his own. But by then he understood that Dean needed this faith, as inexplicable in its own way as the pastor's at church, so he kept silent. He'd gone along with the whole "blood brother" thing even though he was too old for it, too, because it seemed to matter to Dean.

He glanced down to see that he was rubbing his thumb against the pad of the forefinger he'd cut open that day. When he looked carefully, he could still see a faint white scar. The blade had sliced more deeply than he'd intended. He was pretty sure he'd washed Dean's blood away with his own when they went back to the house, that none of it had actually run through his veins even briefly, but their intentions had been heartfelt. Face it, he thought: it had mattered to him, too.

Shaking his head, he got in the car. For just an instant, before he slammed the door, he thought he heard the thud of a ball hitting the backboard and a faraway, laughing taunt.

NOTHING LIKE BEING PUNCHED in the nose to earn early dismissal. Ice pack pressed to the bridge of his nose at red lights, Quinn drove home.

He knew what he was going to look like tomorrow. He'd taken an elbow to the nose during the high-school state basketball play-offs his senior year. He'd bled what felt like a quart and woken up the next morning to grotesque swelling and two spectacular shiners. His nose had been a little crooked ever since.

Anticipation was half the fun. Damn, he hurt.

Double damn, he thought, turning onto his street. He'd forgotten Mindy would be here. He didn't want her to see him like this. Maybe, if he parked in the driveway and scuttled in the front door, she wouldn't know he was home at all until she went to leave and saw his car.

No such luck. She emerged from the side door before he could slam his.

"Quinn! I thought you were the UPS…" Her mouth made an O. "You're hurt!"

"Nothing serious. Just didn't duck fast enough."

"Oh, no!" She hurried forward, expression distressed. "Is your nose broken?"

"No, it just feels like it is." He tried to smile. "Listen, don't let me bother you. My ice pack and I are going to commune."

"You won't choke on blood or anything, will you?" she asked doubtfully.

Touched by her worry, he said, "No, I think I've lost all the blood I'm going to lose. Now, breathing may be a challenge."

"Oh, Quinn!" she said again, laying her hand on his arm.

He stiffened.

She snatched her hand back. "I'm sorry. I…"

"You don't have anything to be sorry about." He stepped a little closer to the edge of that cliff by taking her hand in his. "Thank you for worrying."

She seemed to relax. "I think I owe you some worry. Can I come up and check on you later, before I go home?"

"If you bring Jessie with you."

"Okay." Her smile blossomed. "You look awful, you know."

He found himself grinning back at her even though it hurt like hell to do so. "Thanks."

Upstairs he took the painkiller they'd given him at the hospital, then lay down on the couch instead of his bed, the ice burning his face. He could just barely hear the whine of the saw, and a little later a baby crying.

Somewhere in there, he drifted off, waking when he heard the front door open and close.

"Quinn?"

"Here," he croaked. "In the living room."

Mindy circled the couch and laid Jessie on his chest, then sat on the coffee table. She had a raccoon look, with a fine wood powder clinging to her face everywhere her safe goggles hadn't covered.

He laughed. "You're almost as cute as I am today."

She pressed her hands to her cheeks. "Oh, I forget how awful I look!"

"Personally, I'm afraid to see myself in the mirror."

Head tilted to one side, she inspected his face. "Um…you might want to avoid that mirror for a few days."

"Thanks." He lifted Jessie, whose eyes widened at the sight of him. Then her mouth opened, and she let out a wail.

With a groan he sat up and handed her back to her mother. "I scared her."

"No, she's just hungry. Um…" She nodded toward the easy chair. "Do you mind?"

"Help yourself." He stood, stretched and staggered to the john, where he winced at the sight of himself. Not good, he decided, turning his head to see himself from both sides. The bruising on his nose was already creeping under the eyes.

Once, he would have lingered in the bathroom until he'd thought she was done nursing. Now, he went straight back to the living room. Panic at his sexual response aside, he loved the sight of mother and child so close.

Mindy glanced up in surprise when he eased himself down on the couch near her. She self-consciously tugged her shirt down a little to shield Jessie's head and her breast.

Quinn put the ice pack back over the bridge of his nose even though it was barely chilly any more.

"She's asleep," Mindy murmured. "I should get her home to her crib."

"Don't go."

"What did you say?"

His throat felt raw. "Please don't go."

She eyed him warily. "Okay. I guess I can put her on the floor."

"I'll go dump clothes out of a drawer." He stood. "Just a minute."

He set the empty bottom drawer from his dresser in Mindy's old room and padded it with a top sheet folded over a cushy throw. Mindy appeared in the doorway with Jessie. "That looks cozy." She laid her down on her back, then pulled a flap of the sheet over her.

Both stood looking down at the little girl, who had popped her thumb in her mouth when her mother had set her down. Frowning in her half sleep, she sucked fiercely for a moment before the thumb began to sag from her rosebud mouth.

They tiptoed out.

"Do you feel awful?" Mindy asked, when they returned to the living room.

Seeing the anxiety in her eyes, he realized she thought he wanted her to stay because he was afraid to be alone. "Not as bad as I look. The painkiller helped."

"Oh." She bit her lip.

He sat on one end of the couch again. After the briefest hesitation, she chose the other end. Déjà vu.

"I went over to the Howies the other day. Had lunch."

Her face brightened, probably with relief at the innocuous subject. "How are they?"

"Good." The same as they were a month ago. "Being there made me think about Dean. Remember some good times."

"I've been doing that, too."

"He was a good guy." Saying that, he felt something ease inside. He wasn't having to shoulder the hundred-pound pack loaded with conflicting emotions.

Her smile was tinged with sadness but not grief. "He was, wasn't he? I'm glad I have some videos of him being goofy for Jessamine to see someday."

"I've been wanting to talk to you."

"Really?" She didn't remind him that he'd been by her place four days ago. They didn't yet have to watch what they said in front of a two-and-a-half-month-old baby.

Damn, how did you start something like this? He'd never been slick.

Worse, he realized that not since his mother died had

he said to anyone, "I love you." Even then, it had had a quality of desperation. *Mommy, I love you. Don't go.*

He set down the ice pack and wiped his palms on his thighs. "I've missed you. Both of you."

"Even getting woken up every two hours all night long?" she teased.

Deadly serious, he said, "Even that."

At his tone, her smile faded. After a moment, she said in a small voice, "I've missed you, too."

God, this was hard. His timing probably sucked, too. His whole face throbbed. He didn't exactly look like any woman's dream. Oh, hell, face it, he *wasn't* any woman's dream. He was too screwed up emotionally.

He almost chickened out then. What if her eyes widened with alarm and she had to gently let him down? The damn kiss had been bad enough; words couldn't be forgotten. He had everything to lose.

And everything to gain.

Quinn gritted his teeth. "We've never talked about this, but, uh, the way I kissed you…"

"I kissed *you!*"

His brows drew together. "Sure, but I'm the one who took it further than you meant."

As if she hadn't heard him, she exclaimed, "I felt like such a slut!"

Whoa. He'd missed something here. "A slut?"

"Have I ever told you that two or three weeks after my dad died, I came out to the kitchen in the morning to find a strange man half-dressed and pouring a cup of coffee? He'd spent the night with my mother."

Enlightenment. "And you thought kissing me put you in the same category."

She turned her head away, her hair now long enough to swing down to veil her profile. "Yes!"

"I'm not a stranger."

"No." She drew an audible breath. "I think…that almost made it worse. You were Dean's friend. I knew all along you weren't being so nice for my sake." She cast him an embarrassed glance. "I mean, of course you were, but it was also for Dean. Because he would have done the same if you'd died and left a pregnant wife."

There she went again, and this time it pissed him off.

"I love you," he said.

An appalling silence developed. Mindy slowly lifted her head and turned to stare at him, lips parted. Finally, when he was ready to crack, she whispered, "You… love me?"

He muttered an obscenity. "Is that so improbable?"

"I…" Her voice died.

Crap. He rubbed his palms on his thighs again. "I'm not telling you this to put you on the spot. I thought you needed to know why…" His shoulders jerked. "Why I act the way I do sometimes."

"You love me."

"I said it, didn't I?"

"As in, *in* love with me?" She was dotting her *i*s, crossing her *t*s. "Not just…like a sister?"

"Did I kiss you like you were my sister?"

"No-o." She was silent for a moment. "I thought…I tempted you. And…you're a man."

Yeah. He was. Which did not mean he ached for every pretty woman who happened his way.

"Listen," he said, starting to rise. "We can forget about this. I wanted to be honest. That's all."

"Wait!" She started to untangle her legs.

He hesitated, then sat back down. His chest felt like it was being crushed. Forget his broken nose; it was nothing in comparison.

Her chin was up, her cheeks touched with pink. "Are you asking me out? Or suggesting Jessie and I move back in with you?"

That damn metaphorical cliff edge was crumbling beneath his weight. He closed his eyes for an instant and stepped off into a sickening free fall.

"If I thought there was a chance in hell you'd say yes, I'd ask you to marry me."

Her eyes filled with tears. "Oh, Quinn," she whispered.

The jagged rocks below rushed at him.

"I love you so much." Her tears overflowed at the same moment she launched herself at him.

His arms opened automatically to receive her.

She flung hers around his neck. "I love you, I love you, I love you!" Rivulets tracked the sawdust on her cheeks. "I can't believe... I never thought..." She gulped even as her smile glowed as brilliant as the most glorious of sunrises over the Cascade Mountains.

He felt as if he'd had a bungee cord attached. The ground suddenly stopped coming at him. Instead, he was hurtling toward the sky.

Head spinning, he asked, "You love me?"

"Yes!" How she could cry and laugh at the same time, he had no idea. "I think I've been in love with you since the moment you walked into that espresso shop. Except..." she bit her lip and her glow dimmed "...it's more complicated than that. I've felt so guilty. I think there was always something. I could never make myself feel *comfortable* with you."

He wrapped a hand around her chin and lifted it so he could see her face. "Ditto. I'm just glad I didn't understand then why I was avoiding you."

"Oh! Me, too."

He sucked in a breath. "Can I kiss you?"

She sniffed. "I must look awful! Oh, and you must hurt!"

He said something that was probably profane and bent his head. This time, her lips met his gladly. The kiss was different. Tentative. Tender. A brush of mouths, a nip. He gently suckled her lower lip. She did the same to his. They kept pausing to draw back and look into each other's eyes, as if confirmation were needed.

You love me?

I love you.

She was the one to murmur, "Do you think Dean..."

As sure as he'd ever be, Quinn said, "We were the two people he cared most about. Jessie would have been the third. I can't believe he wouldn't be glad that we were together and happy."

After only the tiniest of pauses, she nodded. "Me, too."

He kissed her again. This one deepened, became urgent and hungry. He wanted her like he'd never wanted anything or anyone in his life.

They both heard the cry at the same moment and stiffened.

"Damn," he muttered.

She gave a husky laugh and rubbed her cheek against his before sitting up. She gripped his hand. "Quinn?"

He cupped her face, the pad of his thumb moving over her lips. "Yeah?"

"Um…I'm wondering. I want you. I guess you noticed."

His body was painfully hard. He'd been hoping like hell she did. Thinking she couldn't kiss like that if she didn't. He waited.

She took a deep breath, face serious, tone apprehensive. "But I'm wondering if we can wait. It probably sounds stupid, but I'd feel better if it had been a year."

So she knew she wasn't like her mother. He almost groaned.

"We can wait." It might kill him, but he could do it. "Maybe we'd both feel better."

Relief and regret in equal measure flooded her face. "Oh, Quinn, I love you so much. I didn't know I could be so happy." She grabbed his hand and jumped up. "Let's go tell Jessie!"

He let her pull him along. He felt stunned. Incredible. He hadn't hit the top of the bounce yet.

She was his. Jessie was his.

I love you wasn't that hard to say, after all. Maybe trusting in forever would come, too.

SEVEN WEEKS LATER, on the anniversary of Dean's death, they took flowers to his grave. Jessie, carried by Quinn in the sling, looked solemnly around at the bronze plaques embedded in the grass.

Quinn didn't know whether Mindy silently asked for Dean's blessing. He guessed he did, even though he didn't expect an answer.

A month after that, they got married in a small ceremony in a white-steepled church a mile from Quinn's house, George, Nancy and Mindy's mother all smiling and crying in the front pew. A fair number of Seattle's finest filled the rest of the church.

That night, the little girl he loved like his own asleep in her crib down the hall, his wife in his arms, Quinn felt whole for the first time in his life.

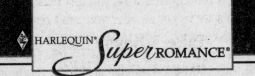

If you enjoyed what you just read,
then we've got an offer you can't resist!

Take 2 bestselling love stories FREE!

Plus get a FREE surprise gift!

Clip this page and mail it to Harlequin Reader Service®

IN U.S.A.
3010 Walden Ave.
P.O. Box 1867
Buffalo, N.Y. 14240-1867

IN CANADA
P.O. Box 609
Fort Erie, Ontario
L2A 5X3

YES! Please send me 2 free Harlequin Superromance® novels and my free surprise gift. After receiving them, if I don't wish to receive anymore, I can return the shipping statement marked cancel. If I don't cancel, I will receive 6 brand-new novels every month, before they're available in stores. In the U.S.A., bill me at the bargain price of $4.69 plus 25¢ shipping and handling per book and applicable sales tax, if any*. In Canada, bill me at the bargain price of $5.24 plus 25¢ shipping and handling per book and applicable taxes**. That's the complete price, and a savings of at least 10% off the cover prices—what a great deal! I understand that accepting the 2 free books and gift places me under no obligation ever to buy any books. I can always return a shipment and cancel at any time. Even if I never buy another book from Harlequin, the 2 free books and gift are mine to keep forever.

135 HDN DZ7W
336 HDN DZ7X

Name	(PLEASE PRINT)	
Address	Apt.#	
City	State/Prov.	Zip/Postal Code

Not valid to current Harlequin Superromance® subscribers.

Want to try two free books from another series?
Call 1-800-873-8635 or visit www.morefreebooks.com.

* Terms and prices subject to change without notice. Sales tax applicable in N.Y.
** Canadian residents will be charged applicable provincial taxes and GST.
All orders subject to approval. Offer limited to one per household.
® are registered trademarks owned and used by the trademark owner and or its licensee.

SUP04R   ©2004 Harlequin Enterprises Limited

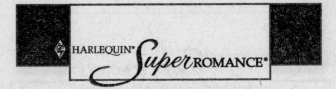

COMING NEXT MONTH

#1278 STRANGER IN TOWN • Brenda Novak
A Dundee, Idaho, book
Hannah Russell almost killed Gabe Holbrook in a car accident. Gabe's been in a
wheelchair ever since, his athletic career ended. He's a recluse, living in a cabin some
distance from Dundee, and Hannah can't get over her guilt. But one of her sons is on
the high school football team and when Gabe—reluctantly—becomes the coach, she
finds herself facing him again....

#1279 HIS REAL FATHER • Debra Salonen
Twins
Lisa never had trouble telling the Kelly brothers apart. Even though they were twins,
they were nothing alike. Joe was quiet, and Patrick the life of the party. Each was
important to her. But only one was the father of her son.

#1280 A FAMILY FOR DANIEL • Anna DeStefano
You, Me & the Kids
Josh White is trying to care for his late sister's son, but Daniel's hurting so much
nothing seems to reach him. The only person the boy responds to is Amy Loar,
Josh's childhood friend. Amy has her own problems,but she does her best to help.
Then Daniel's father shows up and threatens to sue for custody, and the two old
friends have to figure out how to make a family for Daniel.

#1281 HIS CASE, HER CHILD • Linda Style
Cold Cases: L.A.
He's a by-the-book detective determined to find his niece's missing child. She's
a youth advocate equally determined to protect an abandoned boy in her charge.
Together, Rico Santini and Macy Capshaw form an uneasy alliance to investigate the
child's past, and in the process they unearth a black-market adoption ring at a shelter
for unwed mothers. The same shelter where years earlier Macy had given birth to a
stillborn son. At least, that's what she was told....

#1282 THE DAUGHTER'S RETURN • Rebecca Winters
Lost & Found
Maggie McFarland's little sister was kidnapped twenty-six years ago, but Maggie has
never given up hope of finding Kathryn. Now Jake Halsey has a new lead for her, and
it looks as if she's finally closing in on the truth. The trouble is, it doesn't look as if
Jake has told her the truth about *himself.*

#1283 PREGNANT PROTECTOR • Anne Marie Duquette
9 Months Later
The stick said positive. She was pregnant. Lara Nelson couldn't believe it. How had
she, a normally levelheaded cop, let this happen—especially since the soon-to-be
father was the man she was sworn to protect?